THE MOUNTAIN FORTRESS

Escape to the Outback

John J. Horn

Published by
Grace & Truth Books
815 Exchange Ave. Ste. 101
Conway, AR 72032
www.graceandtruthbooks.com

Cover Design and Photography by Daniel R. Prislovsky

ISBN: 978-1-960297-17-4

Printed in the United States of America

To my niblings.

Being your uncle is one of my favorite things in the world.

Contents

Characters from Previous Stories in the Men of Grit Series

Lawrence Stoning

A perfect day for Lawrence would be reading history in a snug armchair next to his mahogany writing desk. He hasn't had many perfect days since he reluctantly became a bodyguard's bodyguard in Peru, and then stumbled into an Ancient Roman civilization in Greenland. At least his adventures led him to Pacarina, the love of his life, and his wife.

Chester Stoning

With little more than looks in common with his twin, Chester yearns for adventure and has done an impressive job finding it. A brief stint in the British Legion turned into searching for Incan gold in Peru, followed by a search-and-rescue mission to Greenland where Chester met Colonel Nobody and became a member of the famed Squad One.

Pacarina Stoning (née Garnica)

Spanish-born, Pacarina matches Lawrence for smarts and Chester for vivacity. She grew to love Lawrence amid the wilds of Peru and matured that love in Greenland as his wife, where she and Lawrence adopted an abandoned Roman baby.

Otho Stoning

The orphaned baby Lawrence and Pacarina adopted in Vallis Deorum.

Colonel Nobody

As a mysterious young English colonel in Siberia, Nobody led the 42nd Regiment of Mounted Infantry, a singular British fighting force which used new technology and nontraditional tactics to confound their Cossack enemies. After leaving the army he was falsely accused of being a pirate and penetrated the heart of Greenland to prove his innocence.

Lady Liana Halmond

Colonel Nobody's betrothed wife, Liana grew up in England as an orphaned ward of the King. She followed her betrothed across frozen steppes, coconut-scented beaches, and Nordic mountains.

Squad One

The most elite squad in the most elite unit in the British Army in Siberia. Its members are fiercely loyal to Colonel Nobody and Lieutenant-Colonel Burke, and they have followed their colonel across the world, losing beloved members along the way. Lawrence and Chester were made honorary members.

Patrick O'Malley

A flame-haired giant of an Irishman with a kind heart and disdain for all things French.

Jacques Lefebvre

A Frenchman who cooks much, speaks more, and somehow maintains a close friendship with O'Malley.

Thomas Bronner

The last recruit to join Squad One before it left the British army. His brother is Colonel Nobody's nemesis, Lord Banastre Bronner.

Richard Dilworth

Once the owner of a dry goods store in Massachusetts, Dilworth fell upon hard times and joined the British army.

Petr Kamenev

A taciturn Russian who provides Squad One some much needed stability.

Chronology

Chapter 1

Lawrence

"I told you I could have worn a sword," Chester whispered.

I tried to speak between my teeth without disturbing my smile.

"Colonel Nobody was an officer. He can wear a sword at his wedding."

"I was an officer too," Chester said.

I eyed the crowd watching us to see if anyone noticed that Chester was talking. Groomsmen are not supposed to talk while standing alongside the groom. There simply being two groomsmen instead of one was odd enough.

The rector cleared his throat and opened the Book of Common Prayer. "Dearly beloved friends, we are gathered together here in the sight of God . . ."

In the sight of God, and hundreds of people. I don't know how many people fit into St. James's Church, Piccadilly, but the building was fuller than I have seen a church be in a long time. Everybody who was anybody, plus many bodies who weren't anybody, were here to see Nobody marry.

The rector continued. "Which holy estate Christ adorned and beautified with his presence . . ."

Colonel Nobody and his betrothed, Liana, wanted a quiet wedding, but if there's one thing the Boy Colonel can't do, it's get married in London without drawing a crowd. Everyone from counselors like that scamp Banastre Bronner's father, the elder Lord Bronner, to Society ladies like young Lady Maria, to the workmen gawking from the galleries, was here.

"But," the rector said, "reverently, discreetly, advisedly, soberly, and in the fear of God . . ."

I smiled across at my wife, Pacarina, one of Liana's two bridesmaids. She tilted her head. That is her way of telling me to be less stiff. I elongated my smile and rolled back my shoulders. Occupying a platform in front of a crowd is Chester's idea of a fun day, not mine.

Between Pacarina and Liana stood Elyssa, Liana's maid and friend. The half-light filtering through the ceiling-height glass windows behind us struck a sharp contrast between Liana's bright bridal gown and Elyssa's black dress. Let the Society girls whisper (which the gaggle around Maria were doing). Liana was insistent that Elyssa be her bridesmaid.

Chester stood where Edmund would have stood, were he here. I wondered if anyone in the crowd watching today was there when they wrongfully hung Edmund for being a pirate.

"I say," Chester muttered, "even Jacques gets to wear a sword. At least you can't keep me from wearing swords when I get to Australia."

Answering Chester would continue the conversation, so I said nothing. Of course Jacques wore a sword, as did the rest of Squad One, sitting in the front row on the right side of the church. Each man wore full military uniform, though Jacques was the only one to have a white flower poked through his buttonhole. He also happened to be holding Otho, my adopted son. I asked my mother to hold him, but she doesn't like to be reminded that she is old enough to be a grandmother.

I turned my attention back to the rector.

"Therefore," he said, "if any man can shew any just cause, why they may not lawfully be joined together, let him now speak, or else hereafter forever hold his peace."

The rector paused, as customary. I sucked a breath and prayed my little boy would not pick this moment to wail.

The rector's lips parted as he prepared to give the charge to Nobody and Liana, but they froze without making noise. I whipped my head to see what he was staring at.

A man in a floor-length brown coat stepped from behind the pillar closest to the church doors on the left side.

"I have a reason," the man said, his words curled by a thick Russian accent. His arm rose. "Dead men can't marry."

There was a tremendous noise, a burst of black smoke from the end of the man's hand, and a pistol-bullet shrieked past Nobody's head.

Shrieks from the congregation echoed it as two bearded men leaped from the pews into the aisle and ran towards us, short swords in their hands.

Chester turned to me, the light of battle in his eyes. "I told you we should have worn swords!"

He pulled a knife long enough to be called a sword from his sash and another from his boot.

"A Stoning!" Chester yelled, and he rushed to meet the attack.

Men leaped from the galleries, their boots thudding on the stone floor.

Colonel Nobody pulled Liana behind him and drew his sword with his left arm. He crouched into his fighting stance, legs taut and ready to strike.

I snapped my brain into action. I hadn't held a weapon in anger since we fought the Romans in Vallis Deorum, but I had family to protect.

I spun to find Jacques. Chester forward-rolled down the aisle and leaped up into the charging men, sending them flying into the pews.

Squad One—O'Malley, Dilworth, Petr, and Thomas Bronner—formed a line in front of us across the center aisle. The only man missing was Jacques, and he had my child.

"Lawrence!" Pacarina called. "I have him."

Jacques ducked into line with his comrades. Pacarina cradled Otho to her bosom.

One of the gallery-jumpers was the first to reach us. He raised his sword. I crossed my arms into an X to cover my face and prepared for the blow.

Colonel Nobody brushed past me, kicked the sword from the man's hand and jammed a boot into his solar plexus. The attacker crumpled.

Someone shouted in Russian. The other attackers stopped, the closest barely a sword's length from us.

Both sides stood, staring. The man who fired the pistol wasn't there. One of the men locked eyes with me. His eyes were steady, cold. I think I expected to see rage, though I didn't have any idea why he wanted to kill us, but he was as calm as the clerk who took my pence that morning at my favorite book store. Gray framed his beard and salted the long wave of hair swept across his forehead.

There were four men, two of which, the man Nobody decked and a man Chester cut down in the aisle, were on the floor.

The gray-haired man barked another word. They grabbed their hurt comrades, turned, and ran from the church.

I blinked. It felt like an hour, but it couldn't have been more than thirty seconds since the first shot. The tunnel vision that comes during battle faded.

Chester walked up the aisle towards us, grinning and sliding a bloody knife through his folded handkerchief.

"I say, if I knew weddings were this exciting I would have gone to more." He winked at me.

Boots pounded the pavement in the vestibule and another bearded man burst into the church. He leveled a pistol at Chester.

Chester dived into the pews and the bullet ripped past him—towards us. Elyssa gasped and collapsed backwards.

The voice that belonged to the gray-haired Russian rose outside the church and the man who shot Elyssa flashed us bared teeth and ran away.

"Doctor!" Colonel Nobody yelled. "We need a doctor!"

Half the people in the church escaped through the doors. Of the rest, the few carrying weapons had drawn them and watched the doors and windows for another attack.

"I'm a doctor," someone said. A middle-aged man in a black coat knelt over Elyssa. "I need a table."

Colonel Nobody snapped his fingers. "We need to get out of here. Rector Ward?"

The rector shook himself. "M-my rectory." He pointed to a door in the church wall about thirty feet from us.

Police rattles clack-clacked towards the church.

Anyone in the gallery above could shoot us at any moment.

"Move," Nobody said.

We made it through the passage in the side wall to the rectory. Chester and Dilworth swept a clutter of papers and inkpots from a table and lowered Elyssa onto the wood. Her face was the color of flour.

After hour-long minutes, the doctor looked up and wiped his forehead. "I've stopped the blood for now, but I need time and space to properly examine her."

Colonel Nobody had his ear to the closed door between the rectory and the passageway to the church.

"They might come back," Nobody said. "We have to leave now."

"Moving isn't safe," the doctor said.

"Staying isn't safe," Nobody said. "Will moving kill her?"

The doctor grimaced. "I don't know. She has lost much blood."

"If we stay here, she'll die, and so will the rest of us. We have to risk it."

Petr strode into the room from the front of the rectory. "Covered wagon outside."

Colonel Nobody said something in Russian. Petr shook his head.

"All right," Nobody said, "we're taking the wagon to a place I know. Pray they don't see us leave."

Chapter 2

I rubbed circular patterns into the knotted nerves in Pacarina's shoulders as she sat, cradling our sleeping baby.

The room could have fit four of my bookcases across one wall and the same across the other, meaning it was twelve feet by twelve feet. Not that the exact measurements are important, but the overall effect when you have nine people in such a room is decidedly cozy.

Chester paced the three feet of floor available to him.

"This whole thing looks straight as a corkscrew to me," Chester said. "Two questions. Who attacked us, and why? Sure, weddings can be boring, but that doesn't give people the right to execute the groom."

We were on the top floor of a three-story house five minutes' ride from St. James's Church. I don't know why Nobody happened to be renting a random house here, but he tends to do odd things like that. Learning about him is like onion-peeling—there's always another layer, and some of them come off with tears.

Jacques flicked his mustache. "Zhe attack does not make sense. Zhe ruffians, zhey look like zhey know how to fight, but zhe attack, it vas terribly planned. And zhen zhey stopped vhen zhey had barely begun."

"And shooting women," Chester said. "It's not sporting. Poor Elyssa."

I cleared my throat. "I think the most important question is, are they going to attack us again?"

Colonel Nobody nodded. "We have to assume so. They weren't robbing us, it was organized and intentional, though like Jacques said, not planned well. I don't think attacking us then really was the plan. But if they meant to attack us at some time—they will be back."

Chester raised his hand. "I vote we be gone when they come back. But seriously, is there anybody who would want you dead?"

Colonel Nobody smiled. "Would you like the list alphabetical or categorical?"

"Ha. Rather, do any of the random gents who want you dead happen to have the pull to hire a parcel of assassins to make it happen?"

"That does significantly narrow the list. There is one possibility that's very concerning, but I don't see how it's possible. Not that many." He held up his hand before Chester could ask a question. "It has to do with my past. As you know, that's not open for discussion."

Liana, still wearing her wedding dress, spoke. "What about our voyage to Australia? I can't leave Elyssa."

"I don't know," Nobody said. "Finding Edmund's brother is much less important than keeping you safe."

Chester chewed his bottom lip. He hadn't talked of anything besides this trip to Australia since Nobody first told us he had reason to believe that Edmund had an older brother, and that brother was in Australia. For my part, I thought a trip with Colonel Nobody might teach him some good things. Although him being on a separate continent without me along to rein in his more reckless ideas might not turn out well.

Colonel Nobody plucked a leather satchel from the mantel and pulled out four metal strips.

"They may be watching this house. No one leaves until we have a plan."

He strapped two of the steel strips to his shins, under his trousers, and tied the other two to his forearms, beneath his sleeves. Chester nodded approvingly. He and Nobody had devised some kind of odd—fighting style, I suppose you could call it—that involved a great deal of moving. According to Chester, it was based on 'speed, movement, and dexterity.' Chester used it because he would rather somersault into a fight than approach like a rational human being. Colonel Nobody used it because his right arm never fully recovered from General Tremont's bullet and the subsequent poor setting.

"Do you think my brother is behind this?" Thomas Bronner asked.

Nobody shrugged. "Banastre would certainly be glad of anything that stopped me marrying Liana, but I think an attack in broad daylight in the middle of half of London Society is a little beyond him."

"Don't underestimate him," Thomas said. "I should know. His grudges go deep, and he's working on something. I've heard rumors at court. And you, Chester, you would know about the rumors. I saw you and Lady Maria talking about it at the ball last Wednesday."

Bright red spots bloomed on Chester's cheeks. "You mean you saw her talking to me. It wasn't mutual. That girl is as persistent as flies on rotten beefsteak."

Colonel Nobody straightened. The steel plates were hidden from view, but if he kicked or struck someone, that someone would have a significant surprise—and a broken body part.

"My first step is to break the rule I just made. I received word a few days ago that a boy who knew Edmund and his brother would be in the city today. I know where he'll be today, but he may be gone by tomorrow. If he has more recent information we'll want to know it before we're on a ship for the other side of the world. I'll also learn if we are being watched, and that will inform our plans."

Colonel Nobody nodded at me.

"Lawrence, I'd like you to come."

Chester cocked an eyebrow. "No offense, but I'm an awful lot handier in a street fight than brother Law."

"You are," Nobody said, "but I don't want to be in a street fight, and Lawrence is much more likely to keep me out of one than you."

Jacques tweezered the flower from his buttonhole with two fingers, set it on the mantel, and dusted his hands.

"Vhile zhe colonel is avay, I vill see vhat revolting foods are in zhe cupboards and use my culinary magic to prepare us a meal fit for Frenchmen."

"Don't ye forgit the murphies," O'Malley said.

"And definitely forget that Béchamel sauce," Chester said. He waved at Nobody. "Don't worry, I'll make sure the Frenchman doesn't ruin dinner too badly."

We checked on Elyssa on the ground floor. The doctor had replaced Chester's sash with a proper bandage, and sat reading a book by her bed. He raised a finger to his lips.

"Now that I have the bullet out, she should mend. She'll need a great deal of rest and quiet. Another fingernail to the left and it would have hit an artery and bled her out in a few minutes."

Colonel Nobody nodded and watched the slight rising and falling of the sheet over her chest that showed she was breathing. How much of his quest to find Edmund's brother was personal, and how much was him wanting to give Elyssa closure?

I wrapped myself in the cloak he handed me and waited while he peered through the window-blinds next to the front door.

Dilworth, the Yankee, took the pipe from between his lips.

"I've been watching ever since we came here, sir, as you ordered, and I've seen neither hide nor hair of anyone watching us."

Our house was at the corner of two streets. The dust-encrusted glass panes showed the usual traffic of pedestrians, a few carriages, and cabs.

"Hmm," Nobody said. "Either they're not watching us, or they're very good."

He took something from beneath his cloak and handed it to me. My fingers brushed the cool handle of a dueling pistol, and I flinched.

I coughed. "Remember, I'm more dangerous with one of these to you than I am to anyone in front of you."

"I think that was true, once," Nobody said. "Now, I think you're better at adventures than you like to admit."

"I don't want adventures. I want a quiet life with my books and Pacarina and Otho."

"Here's our ride," Nobody said.

He threw open the door and dashed into the street. I followed, tripped on the doorstep, and almost fell on the pistol I still held in my hand. Somehow, I got into the cab Nobody spotted and we raced away, impelled by the handful of coins Nobody thrust into the driver's hand.

I leaned into the darkness of the cab's rear wall and watched London grind past me. I've never much liked the city, but it never felt foreboding. Until now.

"Is it really wise to do this right now?" I asked.

Colonel Nobody pushed his hat brim above his eyes. "It's poor timing. I know. But you know how hard I've worked to find out what happened to James Burke. Ed didn't talk much about his older brother, just that he disappeared when they were street urchins in London."

Colonel Nobody shook his head.

"Remember, this is my wedding day, I should be married right now. And I felt it was important enough to do this on my wedding day. I'm told most brides wouldn't appreciate that, but Liana is an angel. She told me I should go."

"Yes, we're both blessed with gems for wives. But in fairness, that was before people were trying to kill you." I locked eyes with him and tried to make my gaze piercing. "I know Edmund was incredibly special to you. I wish I had met him. But I think I know you well enough to say that you can't blame yourself for his death, or seek some kind of replacement for him by finding his brother."

Colonel Nobody nodded. "I know. I saw what misplaced guilt did to Matthew. I know Ed made his own choice, and there is no way in the world I could replace Ed, and I will never try. But I feel a duty to find his brother and at least tell him what happened to Ed. And if I can learn anything more about where Ed came from—all the better."

"What if Edmund's brother is dead?"

"Hopefully we'll find out today."

Chapter 3
Lawrence

London needs to be scrubbed.

Societies for moral reform are excellent, but how can you expect to reform people's morals while letting them live in conditions a pig would find palatial?

We picked our way through heaps of stinking rags, broken chairs, glass shards, and worse. Well, I picked my way. Colonel Nobody just marched a straight line through it all. He did have boots.

The alley twisted between paint-peeling walls, the end behind us leading into the quiet street in which we left the cab, and the other end threading into a sort of courtyard. A few feet inside the yard, a boy slouched against a jumble of splintered barrels.

His skin was pale and stretched tight over his cheekbones. He unslouched when he saw us.

"About time."

"Did you know Edmund Burke?" Nobody asked.

"Course I did. That's why I'm here." He scowled at us. "Let's get this over with. I'm a busy man."

"Edmund Burke was my best friend."

The boy squinted. "I didn't know that. Ed was a brick, and anybody he made friend is worth talkin' to."

Colonel Nobody scanned the walls surrounding us. "Is there anywhere a bit more private?"

"Uh . . ." the boy rubbed his palms up and down his blotchy pant-legs. "They just kicked old Jones out for missing rent. No one'll mind us borrowing the rafters." He led us to a door in the far wall.

Colonel Nobody followed without hesitation. I lingered in the door-way, not just because the room smelled like sweet dead fish, but because I wasn't sure if I should stay outside and watch for anyone following us. The alley was empty. If someone was lurking past the corner at either end they could trap us in this stinking room.

Nobody spoke from the gloom. "Lawrence, what would you do if you saw someone watching us?"

I chewed my lip. So, he knew what I was thinking. I don't like being predictable.

"I would come tell you," I said.

"Then save yourself time and come in now."

I stuck my head through the doorway. Rubbish littered the room's corners. The only furniture was a three-legged table with a couple of old hatchet-scars. The table's fourth leg was probably in one of those piles. The door on the other side of the table was closed.

"I was Edmund's colonel," Nobody said, "and I want to find his brother to tell him what happened to Edmund."

The boy blinked. "You're Colonel Nobody, eh? Guess I should have figured. Funny, you don't look as grumpy as your newspaper pictures."

Colonel Nobody grunted.

"Anyways, if you're Colonel Nobody, good for you. You was always a credit to us boys. Assumin' you're a boy, which is what they always calls you."

I scanned the yard one last time and entered the room. The doorway would be a dangerous place to be if Nobody had occasion to use his due-ling pistols, so I stepped to my left and halted near the pile of rubble in that corner.

"Do you know where James Burke is?" Nobody asked.

"Jamie, you mean. He were named James but we always called him

Jamie, being born Scottish and all. Don't know why he weren't named Jamie, but then neither did he. I was a little runt those days, but I kept up with the best of 'em. Jamie was a decent chap, didn't cause much trouble. More selfish then Ed, but weren't we all. Ed was special."

Colonel Nobody swallowed. "That he was."

"Jamie was the older brother, but Ed had to watch out for himself. Good thing, too, else he might have not made it when Jamie left."

"Where did Jamie go?"

"Jamie got hard up for food, see? Don't we all some days." The boy eyed his thin belly. "Cold day in winter, folks mostly huggin' their fires and sippin' their brandy, and Jamie says he's had enough. Pinches a loaf from a baker. Weren't it his luck a copper was talking to a lady friend next stall over, and before you can say Guy Fawkes, he nabs Jamie with the goods."

The boy snapped his fingers.

"Judge bangs him up, and off he goes to Van Diemen's land."

Colonel Nobody looked at me. "I was afraid of that. There aren't many ways for a poor boy to end up in Australia." He turned back to the boy. "Do you know what penal colony they sent him to?"

"I don't even know the fever didn't get him on the way."

Our colonies in Australia are full of men and women transported from England for crimes they would pay for with hard labor. Convicts rarely return from Australia even after their sentences end.

Colonel Nobody rubbed his eyebrow like a man with a headache behind his eyes.

"Look," the boy said, "I didn't know it was you."

Colonel Nobody stared at him. "What do you mean?"

"They said they just wanted to talk." His eyes shifted to the door behind him. "I'm sorry."

Colonel Nobody reached for his pistol. The door flung open and a man pressed a pistol to the back of Noble's head.

"Don't move," the man said. His accent was Russian. A brown cloak brushed the tops of his boots. He was the man who fired the first shot at Nobody in church and then disappeared.

I barely thought to reach for my own pistol before hands grabbed me from behind and clamped my arms to my sides.

The urchin raised his hands and pressed back against the wall. "You said you just wanted to talk to a bloke, you didn't say nothing about guns."

"That's right," the Russian said. "No one needs to be hurt."

Another man stepped from behind the Russian and tossed a coin at the boy. That totaled four men, including the two holding me.

The boy caught the coin with his left hand, flashed us an apologetic grimace, and slipped out.

"Well?" Colonel Nobody said. "You have us. What do you want?"

"I had hoped we could meet more friendly," the bearded man said. He motioned to his companion, who brought three chairs from the other room and arranged two on my side of the table, with their backs facing the door to the courtyard.

"Please, sit."

Colonel Nobody did so. His face was rigid but showed no fear. How was he so calm? Of course, I forced my face muscles to be rigid as well, but I knew it wasn't cold enough to shiver as much as I was. I sat.

"Have we fought before?" Colonel Nobody asked.

"My name is Bogdan. I am a child of Mother Russia."

Bogdan sat on the other side of the table and glanced over my shoulder. His men must be behind us.

"I want you to save your country."

Colonel Nobody's face did not change. "Does England need to be saved?"

"England is not your country."

Something flickered in Nobody's eye. "Explain."

Bogdan leaned back in his chair and folded his arms.

"I know who you are, Colonel *Nobody*."

A muscle in Nobody's right cheek twitched. "I am Colonel Nobody. I make no secret of that."

Bogdan leaned forward. "I know who you truly are. Behind the name. Behind the secrets. I know who your father was."

Colonel Nobody swallowed. "That is impossible. Everyone who knew my secret then is dead."

"Then your violent friend does not know?"

"No," Nobody said.

Violent? How am I violent? I almost asked, but now did not seem the best time to interrupt.

"Then," Bogdan said, "I will tell him." He spoke to me, but looked at Nobody.

"He is not English. His mother was English, but his father was Russian. And not just any Russian."

Next to me, I sensed Nobody tensing. The man was speaking truth.

"No, not just any Russian. A most important Russian. *The* most important Russian." Bogdan's tone changed. He stopped sounding superior. Now he was nothing but serious, and he no longer pretended to talk to me.

"You are the son of Tsar Alexander, who did *not* die without an heir. Your uncle Nicholas is a usurper, and you are the rightful ruler of Russia. I am here to bring you back to your country."

Colonel Nobody took a deep breath.

I could hardly breathe. Colonel Nobody was the blood heir of the Tsar? Impossible. Absolutely impossible.

Colonel Nobody spoke as if each word he said surprised even himself. "That is a secret which should be dead. How do you know?"

"I'm one of the fighters who kidnapped your father and faked his death. He was a kindly man. I knew your mother, too. I was very sorry when they died in truth on the journey to Moscow."

Colonel Nobody shuddered. "How many people know who I am?"

"Enough. We are ready for your return. With you at our head, we will overthrow the tyrant and restore freedom to Mother Russia. And the other powers, they will recognize you as the true Tsar, because you are. It is your right. And duty."

Bogdan sprang from his chair and bowed to the ground. I glanced over my shoulder. The three men behind us were doing the same.

I couldn't be silent any longer.

"I don't understand," I said. "If you want Colonel Nobody to go lead a rebellion, why did you try to kill him today?"

Bogdan laughed. "Me, kill him? My duty is to protect him."

"You tried to shoot him."

"Bah. If I wanted him dead, he would be dead. I fired to warn him."

I turned to Nobody. He does not lose composure. When he laughs, he does so in moderation. When he speaks in anger, it's a controlled, purposeful anger. I don't know what he does when he shows fear, because I've never seen him do it, but his face at this moment was the closest I've seen to consternation. He was not in control.

"I don't understand," I said. "After you fired, your men attacked us. Your men shot one of us."

Bogdan's thick eyebrows narrowed. "You think I would be so stupid as to attack you in a church, in front of hundreds? No. They were not my men. I warned you. I—what is your English phrase—I forced their hand. They thought it was a signal. They attacked when they were not supposed to. There were more of them, waiting outside, they were going to attack you on your way to the wedding breakfast. They would have killed you."

"Who is *they*?" I asked.

Bogdan stared at me, appraising me.

"He knows." Bogdan tilted his chin at Nobody. "Ask your colonel."

Colonel Nobody blinked and shook his head, involuntary, like a tic. Red crept back into his cheeks.

"Yes," Bogdan said. "He knows. Who else would want you dead? Who would come so strong to London, to do it under the nose of the English queen? Hmm?"

Colonel Nobody leaned forward. Bogdan's right hand flinched towards his pistol, but Nobody ignored it.

"How would they know?" Nobody demanded.

"How do they know everything they know?" Bogdan said.

That was enough for me. "Look, stop it, both of you. I probably shouldn't talk this way to someone with a loaded pistol two feet from me, but I don't care. Stop talking in riddles and tell me what is going on."

Colonel Nobody squeezed his forehead. If he wore glasses he would have taken them off and rubbed his eyes, it was that sort of motion.

"I'm sorry, Lawrence. This was never supposed to happen. I spent my life guarding my secret so this would never happen." He leaned back. "There is only one force who would want me dead so badly they would, and could, do what happened today. I just couldn't believe they knew."

"Who?"

He said a Russian word that sounded suitably barbaric, but which I could not translate, as Russian is not one of the languages I have learned yet.

"It translates literally to English as one word. Assassins. But really, it should be The Assassins. Because there are none others like them." Nobody shrugged. "They have existed for as long as the Tsars, probably longer. Loosely aligned with whoever is in power, but a power of its own. Not the Nizari sect. Maybe better." He grinned without humor.

"And they want to kill you . . ."

"Because I could claim the throne from their Tsar, Nicholas, and any threat to him is a threat to them." He stood. "I thank you for your warning, Bogdan. I couldn't imagine it truly was the Assassins, not until I knew others knew my secret. Now it's my duty to get as far away from my friends as possible."

"That won't help this one," Bogdan said. He turned to me. "You have made yourself a mark almost as high as your colonel."

"What are you talking about?" I asked.

"You killed one of them."

"I . . . oh. I'm not the one who killed him. I'm a twin."

Bogdan shrugged. "They will not take chances. They will kill you both. Probably your wife as well. The man your brother killed had a brother. It was he who came back and shot at your brother, when he found out what happened."

I blinked. Did Chester just get me into a blood feud with an ancient order of assassins?

Bogdan rose. "Tsar, they are all here. Sixteen Assassins. Well, now fourteen, but still far more than needed to put you all in graves. There is one way for you and your friends to survive. Come to Russia. Surround yourself with true men, true Russians, *your* people. Help us throw off the tyrant and the Assassins will become bound to you. It is your destiny. Come to Russia." He held out his hand.

Colonel Nobody gazed at the hand. It wasn't a particularly special hand, just a little too fat and quite dirty, but people in stories always look at hands.

"I have done my duty," he said. "I made no promise to Russia. I owe her nothing. I don't want power, and even if I did, that's not truly why you're here. You want me to help you and your friends gain power. I know you. You're Russia's curse, you've happened again and again, and will continue to do so, even when all of us are in the grave. Go back to Russia and fight your war without me."

He turned to leave. The three men behind us blocked the door, but Bogdan called them off.

"Tsar," he said. "You will change your mind, and you will do your duty. Until you do so I will remain and protect you as best I can."

Colonel Nobody gave a bark of a laugh and pushed through the men into the rainstorm. I plunged after him.

Chapter 4
Lawrence

"You look better today, Law."

I opened my eyes to a glare of sunshine. Pacarina was awake and standing by the window. I blinked a few times to clear the rheum from my eyes and the memory of present events pushed back into my brain.

"Did you sleep well?" Pacarina asked.

I groaned. "Two blankets and a pillow do not a bed make."

I sat up and inched my fingers down my backbone. When I wake up in my four-poster bed in Herefordshire my frame is stretched out, the tallest it will be for the day, and the rest of my waking hours cause a gradual tightening as gravity takes its toll on my body. Today I felt as if gravity had been hard at work all night.

Pacarina smiled. "You're getting soft in your old age."

"How is he?"

She handed Otho to me. The little rascal did his favorite trick, pretending to be shy and snuggling his face into my waistcoat.

"Law," Pacarina said, "can you imagine if—if that bullet had hit—" she stopped smiling.

The thought of again being childless twisted my innards. We rescued Otho from Vallis Deorum, where his mother abandoned him to death. He rescued us from childlessness and brought us a joy I can't translate into words.

"Praise God it didn't," I said. I clenched my fist at the thought of someone hurting my family.

Pacarina patted my cheek, a signal that we needed to pull ourselves together and face the day's dangers.

We were still in Nobody's rented house. Curtains divided the second-story room in half. Our half had the wall with the window pointing at the house next to us, while the other half had the window looking over the street. Some of Squad One were sleeping there. Well, technically, Chester and I are honorary members of Squad One, but I don't really think of myself as one of them. They have so much more history with Colonel Nobody than us. The gold ring on my pinkie with the fiery 'S1' encrusted in gemstone blue didn't measure against years of battles, hardship, and dead friends. But if this current adventure went anywhere—maybe I would come to feel more worthy of the ring.

I threw on the clothes Nobody lent me last night and then we were ready to meet the others, as there were no new clothes in the house for Pacarina to change into.

Everyone else was gathered downstairs. As we came down, brewing coffee and tea captured my olfactory senses.

"Thank me!" Chester called out. "Our Froggy friend was trying to sneak us breakfast with only coffee, no tea, but I caught him at it and made the tea myself."

Colonel Nobody nodded at us and motioned to sit near him. Liana, O'Malley, Petr, Dilworth, and Thomas Bronner sat at the table. Jacques and Chester alternated between hovering over the fire and scurrying to the table with plates of steaming food.

Colonel Nobody continued his conversation. "Petr, what are the chances they leave us alone if we stay alive long enough?"

"There is no chance," Petr said. His thick Russian accent reminded me of Bogdan. "Assassins will never leave their mission. We die, or they die."

Why was Nobody asking Petr this question? Perhaps Petr, being Russian, had some special knowledge of these assassins.

"Speaking of the assassins," I said, "how would you capitalize the word?

Is the 'a' capitalized, referring to a specific group, or lower case, a general noun?"

Chester snorted. "Law, who cares how you spell the word? The word means we're playing hide and seek with a bunch of professional killers. It's like asking your pallbearer how to spell 'death.'"

"I know how to spell the word, Chester. I asked how to capitalize it. I believe things should be done decently and in order, and when I update my diary, I want to capitalize the word correctly."

Chester stalked to a mirror and shrugged at it. That's his non-subtle way of saying he has no idea how we're not only related, but twins.

"Capital 'A,'" Nobody said. "That's how I always wrote it in my reports."

I sipped the tea and the discomfort in my back faded as the warm fluid progressed through my internal passageways. Chester did deserve thanks for the tea.

"Noble," Liana said, "I think you owe it to them. An explanation."

Colonel Nobody cupped his mug of coffee in his hands and stared into its depths.

"I should say so," Chester said. He ambled back and propped his right boot on a chair. "Russian Assassins hunting you down in London? This is better than *Swiss Family Robinson*. I wager even Law has raised his nose out of a book far enough to be curious, eh, Law?"

I shrugged. "I already know."

Chester blinked. "You—" he turned to Nobody. "All right, colonel of mine, you had better not tell me brother Law can keep a secret closer than Chester Stoning. Explain thyself!"

Colonel Nobody sighed. "I've kept this secret my entire life. It's not easy finding out that half the world seems to know it."

With that, Colonel Nobody explained who he was and why the Assassins were here.

No one said anything for several moments.

Chester was the first to speak. "You mean to say I've been teaching

Free Fighting to a Russian Tsar?" He grinned. "That's fantastic!"

Petr stood, his face grave, and bowed before Nobody.

Colonel Nobody grabbed Petr's arm and pulled him up. "No, my friend. Don't bow to me, we are brothers."

"Hmm," Chester said, "you sure you don't want to be Tsar? Seems like an awful lot of fun."

Colonel Nobody shook his head. "I can't think of a job I would like less. If the Assassins understood that, they could go back about their business without giving me another thought. But they'll never believe I will pass the opportunity for a try at the throne."

"What if," I said, "we were able to convince them of that?"

Colonel Nobody shook his head. Petr did the same. I was not convinced, but I held my tongue. They knew the Assassins better than me. But, if an opportunity to negotiate presented itself . . . I give logic more credit than most.

"So," Chester said, "do we go hunt them down in the streets, or fortify this place and prepare for siege warfare?"

"We need to leave London," Colonel Nobody said. "The Assassins have operated here for centuries. I'm sure they have friends, safe places, even weapons caches. And in London an army of Russians could melt into the streets with no one the wiser. We need to go somewhere they have no network. Somewhere they'll stand out from the crowd."

"That," Chester said, "is the guidebook description of Australia. It's perfect. Russians will stand out like icicles in a bakery, you get to find Edmund's brother and cry on his shoulder. We kill two birds with one stone—or, rather, we kill a bunch of Russian birds."

Colonel Nobody nodded.

I agreed. "That seems logical. Pacarina and I can stay and nurse Elyssa."

"About that." Colonel Nobody tipped his cup to his lips and knocked back the last of his coffee. "You need to come with us."

I held up my hands. "We already had this discussion. I don't do the adventure thing. That twin is over there." I pointed at Chester.

"And I agreed with you. Before your twin killed an Assassin—an actual brother, no less. You know what Bogdan said. You and Pacarina are probably marks, and that means the safest place you can be is with the rest of us."

I practically felt Chester's excitement. "Wey-ho!" he said. "This is glorious! This is going to be like the old times! I feel a little sorry for the Russian bloke I decked, but this is what I call a silver lining."

I snorted. "I don't call making Pacarina a mark for Assassins a silver lining."

"Oh," Chester said. "You're serious. I suppose that's fair—sorry about that. But seriously, an adventure isn't the same without you grumbling in the background and Pacarina prodding you along."

I shook my head. The old times? As in, Pacarina being kidnapped by a Roman dictator? Or being stretched on a rack by a crazy archeologist and her brother-in-law? Every 'old time' we've been through had Pacarina in mortal danger. And now I have a son. How can I take them to a land on the other end of the world full of convicts, outlaws, and Aborigines?

"Law," Chester said, "don't be a wet blanket. You know you have a better chance with us than by yourself here. Live together die together, eh?"

I scraped my teeth against each other. The thing that hurt was that he was right. I couldn't protect Pacarina and Otho by myself. I had to go with them.

I cocked an eyebrow at Pacarina.

"I'll do whatever you think best, Law. But I think they're right. Otho is already an experienced little voyager, he'll be fine."

I sighed. "Promise me one thing, Chester. No lost settlements of Ancient Carthaginians."

Chester laughed.

So, it was settled. A few years ago, I was a normal young Englishman reading books in my father's country estate. Now I was a slightly less young Englishman with a Spanish wife and a crazy twin brother, preparing to follow a Russian Tsar and his bodyguard to Australia. Just wonderful.

A groan from the next room underscored a wrinkle in our plan.

"What about Elyssa?" I asked.

Colonel Nobody nodded. He had not forgotten her.

"May I speak, sir?" Dilworth asked. He and Petr were recently returned from America, and if his Yankee accent had tempered at all during his long absence from his native country, his recent visit brought it all back.

"There's a street in the East End populated by Yankees. They're good people, and if we sneak the lady there, I think I can keep her safe. No Russian is welcome in that part of the city, and anyhow, these Assassins will be busy following you."

Colonel Nobody stroked Liana's hand and frowned at his empty cup. It had to be a hard decision for him. Protecting Elyssa was a sort of a sacred bond, Edmund's dying request, and trusting her to other people would not be an easy decision. Then again, in many ways, the farther he was from her, the safer she was.

Tap, tap.

Jacques and O'Malley drew pistols and jumped to the windows on either side of the door. Colonel Nobody pushed Liana behind him and stood tensed, the steel on his forearms tight against his sleeves. Petr and Thomas Bronner leveled rifles at the door. I put myself between Pacarina and the outward facing wall, and Chester crouched and put his ear against the door.

Tap, tap.

I have little experience with assassins, but I doubt they usually knock.

Chester held his forefinger to his lip and reached his left hand up for the door handle. The person or persons knocked again, louder this time. Chester flung the door open and Jacques and O'Malley swiveled to his side, pistols pointing at the intruder.

An enormous hat covered by white- and blue-dyed peacock feathers stared at us. For a moment I thought it was Chester, but Chester still crouched in the doorway like an arthritic monkey. The pair of red lips below the hat parted, a terrible scream assaulted our eardrums, and the woman fainted into Chester's arms.

Chester staggered back on his haunches. I waited for some terrible attack to burst through the door, but nothing came. A quite normal-looking coach with a rather bored-looking coachman waited outside. The fellow seemed accustomed to seeing ladies faint into strange doorways.

Chester tried to back away, holding the woman's upper half off the floor, but scrunching his nose as if she had not bathed for a week. "Law, it's *her*. You've got to take her away before she wakes up."

A spark of understanding warmed the back of my brain. I coughed. "You're the chivalrous one, remember, Chester? Or so you always say. She does look like a damsel in distress to me."

"I don't want *this* damsel in distress," Chester said, "I want a big hairy Russian I can sink my knife into."

The female groaned. Her hat dropped away from her fluttering eyes and I recognized Lady Maria.

"Wh-what happened," she faltered.

"Nothing," Chester said. "Nothing at all. Here—" he grabbed Jacques' arm and shifted the young lady's weight onto him. It took him half a second to sprint to the farthest end of the room, behind Liana and Pacarina, where he pretended to become engrossed in whittling a stick.

O'Malley closed the door. Petr and Thomas Bronner lowered their rifles and I stepped forward to bow.

"What a pleasure to see you, Lady Maria. To what can we ascribe this honor?"

Maria removed herself from Jacques' supporting arm and dusted her skirts.

"I'm so sorry," she said. "It was such a shock to see weapons pointed at me."

I wanted to say 'get used to it around here,' but my inner diplomat quashed the idea.

Colonel Nobody stepped to my side looking less than diplomatic.

"How did you know we were here?" he demanded.

"Oh, I know I should have sent my card," Maria said, "but I was so concerned to know if my dear friends were unhurt."

She inclined her head towards Liana and Pacarina, which was helpful, as without that indication I would have had no idea what 'dear friends' she was talking about. The only one of us she ever showed interest in was Chester.

"How did you know we were here?" Nobody asked again. His face was tight.

"Oh, I was talking with Lord Bronner about the dreadful thing at church," she put her hands over her heart, "and he suggested I visit you to see how you were. I was afraid it would seem irregular, but Lord Bronner is the epitome of consciousness, and if he thought it was a good idea, of course it must be, and besides, not *everyone* has to be regular *all* of the time."

Chester whittled harder and pretended to not have noticed her looking at him as she said this.

"How did you know we were *here*?" Nobody repeated.

"What? Oh, la, didn't I say? Silly me, I do run on so sometimes. Well, I had such a shock in the church, that I was sitting near the rectory to recover, and I saw one of your men taking a carriage into the side yard, and I wanted to be sure you would be all right, so I told my man to follow you."

She preened like the peacock slaughtered to pretty her hat.

"Which Lord Bronner?" Nobody's voice was hoarse.

"The handsome one, of course, Lord Banastre Bronner."

"You told him where we are?"

"Yes, I told you, he suggested I come check on you."

Colonel Nobody groaned.

She dangled her gloves by their cuffs. "Did I do something inappropriate?"

Colonel Nobody took a deep breath. "Thank you for your visit, and your concern. We are as well as can be expected, given the circumstances. You need—" he stepped closer "—to tell absolutely no one where we are. Is that clear?"

"Oh, la, a secret? I love secrets!"

"And unlike the ones you're used to hearing, this secret gets told to no one. Our lives are at stake. Do you understand?"

She gulped. "Why, yes, yes, of course. I will be as quiet as the grave. Oh, dear, was that a pun? I am sorry."

Colonel Nobody gave that kind of forced smile that says 'I'm being polite, but it's time to go.' That's when I thought of something.

"Colonel," I said, "I think I know how to get Elyssa to the East End." I tilted my head at Maria.

"Hmm." Colonel Nobody looked at Liana.

The two of them excused themselves to go into the next room. They shut the door. The rest of us did all the things you do when you're pretending you're not in awkward silence, until the door finally reopened and they returned. Liana's eyes were red, and Nobody scratched at his suspiciously.

"Lady Maria," Nobody said, "would you be willing to take my friend, Elyssa, in your carriage? She has been wounded and we need to get her to the East End."

"Oh, what an adventure! But . . . wounded? Is she . . . does she . . ." Maria put her hand to her middle. "I'm afraid I have a delicate stomach."

"And she has a bullet in her stomach."

"Oh . . . yes."

"My betrothed wife will be going with you."

Well, that was unexpected. And yet, logical. I couldn't see Liana leaving her friend with a bullet in her stomach to strangers' care. And with Nobody, Chester, and me going to Australia, the farther she was from us the safer she would probably be. Still, I remember the day I married Pacarina, and the thought not only of the wedding being interrupted, but of having to leave her immediately, made me shiver.

Twenty minutes later, Elyssa was on her way to the East End, with the doctor to keep her stable on the journey, Liana to nurse her back to health, and Dilworth and Thomas Bronner to keep her safe among the Yankees.

Chapter 5

Lawrence

The next morning, we gathered around breakfast to plan the remaining details for our voyage.

"Here's what concerns me," I said. "You didn't charter the ship in secret. If the Assassins knew about your wedding and were all ready to attack after it, I assume they've been following you—us—for a while. That's probably why Bogdan went to all the trouble of intercepting the boy and setting a trap instead of approaching you himself. He was afraid they would see him."

"And," Nobody said, "you're afraid the Assassins will be waiting for us on the docks."

"Seems reasonable."

Nobody nodded. "I'm counting on them thinking we're thinking that way. Sometimes the best plan is the one that's too obvious."

"And if they've stowed away already on the ship?"

"We're going to charter a new ship. I'll dangle enough gold in front of the captain's eyes to buy passage to the heart of the Arctic, if we wanted."

"Someone is coming," O'Malley called from upstairs. His shock of red hair poked past the corner at the stairs-top. "Carriage. Looks like that Lady Maria again."

Colonel Nobody growled. Chester spun to the other side of the room and settled into the corner behind Pacarina.

Tap, tap.

Colonel Nobody threw the door open.

The peacock hat and everything below it swept into the room. Maria was—panting?

"I'm so sorry," Maria said. She pushed something at Nobody. It was a newspaper. "I promise you I didn't tell anyone, not a soul."

Colonel Nobody flipped the paper, glanced at it, and shoved it towards me.

The headline read: *Update on Tragedy at St. James'. Colonel Nobody and Wedding Party Fled to*—and it named our neighborhood.

Colonel Nobody clenched his fists. "Did you tell anyone about Elyssa?"

"No, no, not a soul. I didn't tell anyone where I went yesterday, I promise, you must believe me! No one knew I was coming here, except of course Lord Bronner, who I told you suggested I visit you, but I did not tell him where you were."

Colonel Nobody grabbed his sword-belt from the back of his chair and buckled it around his waist. "Bronner made this happen."

"At least," I said, "it doesn't say exactly where we are."

Colonel Nobody snorted. "No need. They know where to look—and now Lady Maria has run like a homing pigeon straight to us."

There were shouts outside, then a whoosh of oxygen sucked into something, then the window to the left of the door shattered and a plank speared the room. People screamed outside but the roaring of flames rose to block their voices.

There was another crash into the side wall, and another into the opposite wall. Black smoke plumed into the room.

Maria stared at us. Either she was the greatest actress ever to grace the stage or she had no idea what was going on. The latter was far more likely. The Assassins followed her and found us, and they were not wasting time.

"We have to get out!" I shouted over the din to Nobody.

"They're waiting to kill us as we come out," he shouted back. "Upstairs, now! Lawrence, take your wife. Chester, take Maria."

Chester looked at him in consternation. "Er—O'Malley's taller, I think he would do a better job."

"You get her up those stairs," Nobody shouted.

Maria looked at Chester wild-eyed and held out her arms. Chester snorted.

"I'm not carrying you. Run!"

There was little smoke yet on the second floor. The instant the last man was up the stairs we slammed the door shut and stuffed strips from the curtains into the gaps around it.

Chester spoke. "I hope this isn't your long-term plan."

Colonel Nobody held up his hand. "I've seen this trick before. They're waiting to shoot us as we leave."

"Excellent. How did you survive it?"

Colonel Nobody gave him a tight smile. "I've always been the one on the outside."

We had two minutes at most to leave the house before the floor beneath us collapsed and plopped us into a baker's fever dream.

"I've got it!" Chester said. "I've always wanted to firewalk. Let's try it!"

I shook my head. "You can't firewalk through a burning building, Chester. Firewalking is done on burning coals, which are very poor conductors of heat."

Colonel Nobody ran to the partition where Pacarina and I slept and kicked the wall. Instead of breaking his foot, as I expected, the wall-panel fell back and revealed a set of stairs leading downwards.

"You just happen to have a secret passage in your house?" Chester said.

"I rent the house because of the passage. The previous owner welcomed nighttime visitors who didn't use the front door. O'Malley, give them something to shoot at."

"Aye, Colonel." The tall Irishman wrapped my blankets around the back of a chair and thrust the chair through the glass window. Three bullets ripped through the blankets and thudded in the top of the window frame. Judging by the trajectory, the men who fired the shots stood in the street below.

I scooped Otho from Pacarina's arms so she could keep her dress from tripping her as she climbed down. We stepped into the gloom, her breath hot on my neck. I hunched my body over Otho's.

"Beware ambitious neighbors," Colonel Nobody said. "This passageway was built to withstand the weight of two floors. The fellow whose house we're about to walk under decided to add two more. Part of the roof has collapsed, and the rest is ready to follow. Don't touch anything."

"Do you hear zhat, O'Malley?" Jacques whispered. "If you hit our roof vihz your head and crumble us all into dust, I vill never forgive you."

The Irishman growled. "No doubt ye're well familiar wi' sich places as this. It's jist sich the spot I'd expect a Frog tae call home."

As we forged deeper into the cool night of the passageway, the flames above seemed a world away. Only a very, very faint whisper reminded me of the inferno. If the Assassins were in the open, as they must have been to be able to fire those three shots through the window, then they had little time remaining before the police arrived. Yes, they could kill police, but that was not a long-term strategy. They would probably wait to kill us until they were certain we burned to death inside, then they would vanish into the underworld.

"We're here," Nobody whispered.

I sensed, rather than saw, a mass blocking the left half of the passageway and spilling into the right side. It must be debris from the collapse. Any motion could bring the rafters down on our heads.

"Single file," Nobody whispered.

"Ah," Chester said, "I'm happy to test it."

It was too dark to see, but Chester's tone told me Maria was with him. She was probably holding his hand. I suppose I can understand why an impressionable girl might become infatuated with Chester, even if he did have the same face as me. But Maria? Not exactly sister-in-law material. I mentally squeezed Pacarina's hand and thanked God for the blessing of such a wife.

"I'll lead," Nobody said.

Bits of gravel crunched beneath his boots as he inched through the narrow passage. A board in the roof creaked. Colonel Nobody froze. No more creaking. He took another step, then another, and he was through.

"The women next," he whispered.

The first person through the passage braved the greatest danger, because none of us knew if the roof would hold. Now that we knew it would, the next people through were safest. Each person increased the likelihood of a mistake, resulting in a collapse. Pacarina went first, then Maria.

Then it happened.

Crack. Something gave way in the roof. Fine dust thickened the air. A terrible creaking crescendoed towards the ultimate crash which would block the passageway and separate us from them.

"Everyone through now!" Chester said.

He slammed into the small of my back and rammed me through the passage. The atmosphere filled with arms and legs as Jacques, O'Malley, and Petr followed on our heels and we all devolved into a sprawling heap as the roof just behind us collapsed with a roar and filled the air with clouds of dust.

I shielded Otho with my chest and struggled to my feet.

A shaft of light skewered the end of the passageway and Nobody pointed up, through a trap door, to the world above.

I stumbled into the light. Otho wailed, his baby arms raising poofs from the inch-thick layer of plaster dust on his blanket.

"I know, little fellow," I whispered to him. "I feel the same way."

Chapter 6

Lawrence

Two weeks later, I ducked under a door frame and stepped into the ship's cabin.

Whiz-thunk.

"Ouch!"

I blinked at the blade buried in the cabin wall a foot from my nose, then swiveled to look at Chester.

Chester sucked the knuckles of his right hand and scowled at me.

"Chester, what are you doing?"

The knuckles in his mouth turned whatever he tried to say into a garble more unintelligible than the Mayamuran language.

"Fingers out, please?" I said.

Chester thrust his fist at me. Blood streamed from two or three of the knuckles.

"I'm sucking my knuckles," Chester repeated. He growled and thrust them back into his mouth. Dribbles of blood dotted the beginnings of a beard.

I drew my handkerchief from my breast pocket and made him let me wrap the white cotton around his bleeding hand.

"I think I need to elevate it," Chester said.

"Your hand?"

"No, this." Chester slapped something on his right wrist. A leather gauntlet gripped his forearm, and, bound by leather straps to the gauntlet, was a metal contraption with three slots pointing over Chester's hand. The middle slot was empty, but the two outside spaces held blades.

I let go of his arm rather abruptly.

"What are you doing, Chester?"

He unstrapped the gauntlet and flung it upon the thin worktable that folded from the cabin wall. A swell in the ocean beneath us tilted that side of the cabin up until the table leveled with my chest. A litter of screws and springs slid to the edge, where a lip caught them before they could waterfall to the cabin floor.

"Inventing," Chester said. He smiled at his own annoyance. "Anything to get a break from Maria, eh?"

I leaned against the wall and watched him tinker with the contraption.

We were on our way to Australia. After escaping from Nobody's rented house via the unstable passageway we dashed to the docks and chartered another ship. A healthy payment convinced the captain to expedite his affairs and we sailed confident that no one on board would try to kill us.

Maria, of course, was the problem. She knew where Elyssa and the others were, and the Assassins obviously knew about her since they followed her to us. Petr said that when they got their hands on her, she wouldn't last a minute before she spilled the entirety of her life story and where our friends were. Who knew that she would be thrilled when Nobody offered to take her with us. Apparently, she had an uncle living in Australia, and said she could live with him.

Chester tapped the metal thing on his gauntlet with a hammer.

"Jammed again. It won't be handy if it decides to do this when it's the last thing between me and a Russian's knife."

"You're seriously contemplating strapping that to your forearm and launching knives at people?"

"Just people trying to kill me. The problem is, I can't seem to get it right. It's too low, so I add some metal strips to raise it, then it jams, so I hammer the slots larger, and then the blades wobble out."

I sighed. "If you're going to risk all our lives with this contraption, I'd better have a look. Let me see the sketch."

Chester raised an eyebrow. "Sketch?"

"You have planned this, of course? Drawn a diagram, calculated the angles, adjusted the tension in the springs based on Hooke's law?" I waited for him to respond, but the eyebrow did not lower. "Chester?"

He coughed. "As a matter of fact . . . you know I never wasted much time on mathematics."

I shook my head. "Chester, you can't invent a killing machine without considering the mathematical realities involved."

"Speaking of killing machines!" Chester brightened and ushered me to the other end of the tiny cabin. "What do you think of this?"

He tapped a long, thin pine box.

"I think that building coffins, while productive, is slightly morbid."

Chester laughed. "This is not a coffin. This is where I cut you in half. Look." He inserted a saw into a slit through the middle of the coffin and let it fall to the bottom. "Remember ages ago when I said I was going to be Chester the Great? I think I'll take that as my stage name."

As usual, Chester was not making a great deal of sense. I told him as much.

Chester grinned. "I wormed the secret for this thing out of two of the sailors. They had a show in a circus until a misunderstanding between them and the government pointed them towards sea-life." Chester slapped the coffin. "This box is going to make you and me famous. Let's work a trade. You promise me you'll help me do this performance when we get to Australia, and I'll let you help me sketch my Death Gauntlet."

"That's a rather one-sided trade, Chester."

Chester shrugged.

I poked through the scraps of wood and metal littering our cabin.

"What's that?" I pointed to another box, larger than the saw-in-half-coffin.

Chester's nose was stuck two inches from the folding desk as he fiddled with his Death Gauntlet.

"Disappearing Box," he grunted. "I had those two sailors build it for me. Brought it up this morning."

I rapped the lid. The box didn't sound hollow. I tried lifting the lid until I realized the front of the box unhooks and drops to the ground. The inside was padded with sail cloth.

It wasn't impressive. Doubtless there was some hidden trick to it, but encouraging Chester's illusion act was not my plan, so I closed it without any questions.

Thud.

I turned back to the closed box. I was eighty-five percent positive that something heavy dropped inside. Chester remained focused on his Death Gauntlet. No doubt he was laughing in his boots. He had some trick planned for me with this box.

I don't particularly enjoy Chester's tricks, but when you're on a long sea-voyage, any break to the monotony can be worth it, so I decided to let him have his fun. I unlatched the box again and let the front fall.

A man stared back at me.

I leaped backwards and it felt like my internal organs leaped upwards into the base of my throat. I can't lie, I screamed. A bearded man in a long brown coat should not be lying in a box in my cabin, staring at me.

Chester growled. "Law, what are you fooling with—wa-hey!" He swung his Death Gauntleted hand towards the man and almost broke my jaw with it in the process.

"What are you doing in my Disappearing Box?" Chester yelled.

I grasped my chest while my organs slid back to their proper places. "More importantly," I said, "what are you doing on this ship, Bogdan?"

Chester frowned at me. "Bog-what?"

"This is the man who warned us about the Assassins."

Bogdan planted his elbow on the bottom of the box and rested the side of his head on his open palm.

"Please stop pointing that at me," Bogdan said. "It's very unstable."

Chester looked at his right arm, then dropped it and raised his left, holding a pistol.

"Happier?"

Bogdan yawned. "I will be happier when you let me out of this thing. I did not realize last night when I went to sleep that this box was destined for your cabin this morning."

"You'll get out when you tell us what on earth you're doing here."

Bogdan shrugged. "I believe they call it 'stowing away.'"

I reached over and lowered Chester's arm. "He's had opportunity to kill us before, and didn't. I don't think he's going to kill us now."

Chester looked doubtful, but I think part of it had to do with being furious that somebody scared him with one of his own illusion tricks.

I took charge. "Go gather everyone, and make sure Maria isn't near the railing. I don't want her falling overboard when she faints."

Someone had been able to stow away on our ship. That was frightening. We thought we got away from the house without anyone following us, and it was straight from there to the ship and sailing the next day without a soul going back on land.

As Bogdan explained it to us under a gray-clouded sky on deck, he had been following some of the Assassins when they found Maria's trail and landed at our front door. He couldn't hang around close to the house, because the Assassins would have spotted and gutted him, so he holed up several streets away, between us and the river, and saw us after we exited the tunnel. It was simple after that to stalk us to the dock, swim to the ship that night, and stow away in the hold.

The real question was, why?

That's what Nobody asked.

"You know why already," Bogdan said. "I am here to convince you to come to Mother Russia."

"You don't understand me," Nobody said. He eyed the foreboding sky. "When I make a decision, it's exactly that. A decision. This is not a debate, and I don't need convincing."

"You don't understand me," Bogdan said. "I accomplish my missions." He bowed. "And my mission is to help you see your duty and return to save your Mother Russia."

"Duty?" Nobody gestured at the rest of us, standing and sitting around the main mast. "You see these friends of mine? You know why they're all running for their lives? Because of me. My duty is keeping them alive. I don't owe your Mother Russia anything."

Bogdan rubbed his beard. It was short, maybe an inch thick, and black as the edges of the clouds above.

"I think you are a good man." Bogdan unhooked a leather pouch from his belt. It smelled of herbs. He lifted a necklace strung with what looked like white beads. "Do you know what these are?"

Colonel Nobody shook his head.

"My mother's teeth."

Bogdan coiled it on his palm and held it out towards Nobody.

"I picked them from the street after a soldier struck her for being in the way. The mothers and the daughters of Russia cry to you to save them. Think of the good you could do as Tsar."

Colonel Nobody looked away from the teeth. "I'm sorry for any pain your family has gone through, Bogdan. But creating a civil war is not the way to fix it."

"A wound is burned to staunch the blood. It is pain, but it saves the life."

Colonel Nobody was silent. Wetness touching the backs of my hands was the first sign of rain, but in a few moments, fat raindrops pounded us and splashed off the deck.

Bogdan gestured at the rest of us. "Each of you will become wealthy and famous with the close friendship and favor of the Tsar."

"Russian," O'Malley said, "ye've heard the Colonel answer. Leave it be."

Bogdan threw up his hands and walked away. I assigned myself the task of watching him for the rest of the voyage. He did not look the type of man who gives anything up, and he had already risked much to get where he was now.

Chapter 7
Lawrence

That was the first of several storms on our voyage. The only good thing about a storm at sea is that it breaks the monotony. No matter how much you like people, spending months within a thousand square feet of each other is wearing. The only exception to that being Pacarina. I could, and hope to, spend the rest of my life next to her and never tire of her. And Otho, of course. Although the little rascal had quite the pair of lungs.

We were all delighted when the crow's nest sighted the Sydney Heads. The Heads guard the passage, which I estimate is about a mile wide, into Sydney Harbor. It was around noon on a Friday, with a cloudless sky overhead, so we didn't need the warning from the lighthouse glaring at us on the South Head.

As we sailed deeper I expected to see the town on the left shore at any moment, but we kept sailing on and on without sight of it. Even though I read Sydney Harbor was massive, I didn't appreciate it until I was there in the flesh.

Sydney has the most beautiful harbor I have ever seen or am likely to see. You could anchor all the navies of the world in that harbor and not be crowded.

"Any first wishes?" Colonel Nobody asked.

I turned to look at him. All of us were here on deck, leaning against the bulwarks and watching this strange new land materialize.

"What's the first thing you want to do on land?" Nobody asked.

Chester grunted. "First thing I'm doing is a complete re-outfit. Rifle, pistols, swords, knives, hatchet, and I've got to learn those native boomerang things."

"And I," Maria said, "absolutely must find new dresses."

No doubt both of the women would make dress-buying a priority. Pacarina did valiant work transforming some cloth that was part of the cargo into clothing, but it didn't look like the height of fashion. Not that I knew what the fashion in Sydney was, these days. Word was that the Aborigines didn't have much use for clothes at all.

I signaled Nobody to join Pacarina and me.

"Colonel, is there any chance the Assassins are already here?"

"Possible, but unlikely. They'll find us, because that's what they do. How long it will take them, I don't know."

The warm sun on my face made me more cheerful than I knew I should be. The convicts, ex-convicts, Aborigines, strange beasts, and unfamiliarity of the Australian continent before us were plenty to feed my brain cells, but that we should come here to escape a greater danger gave perspective to our situation.

Pacarina sighed. "I half-hoped it would look like Spain."

"Just think what it must look like to convicts," I said.

I find our government's policy of deporting criminals to Australia rather odd. There must be a more efficient way to deal with crime than to ship the criminals to the other side of the world. When father was in his philosophic stage he thought the idea of segregating criminals to a separate geography was brilliant. And yes, it is convenient to get them out of the way, but it hardly seems like a balanced punishment. It would be fascinating to watch the theory working in real life.

Chester tapping me on the shoulder brought me back to the present.

"This is the first time we'll go somewhere and not look like twins." Chester tugged his beard, which he had grown into an impressive bush.

I nodded. "Yes, and the first time I won't be blamed for your antics."

"Come along, you know you've been copying me your whole life. In a week you'll be growing a beard to match."

"No, Chester."

Chester shrugged and winked at Pacarina. "Give it time."

"No, Chester! I will not be growing a beard. What do you not understand about the word 'no?'"

"Your 'no' is more of a 'not yet.'" Chester nodded at Colonel Nobody. "When the colonel says 'no,' he means 'no.'" Chester coughed in Bogdan's direction. "But when you say 'no,' you mean you're not ready yet."

I turned to Pacarina for support.

She grinned. "When it comes to you saying 'no' to Chester, Chester is about right."

I threw up my arms. The whole world was out to discount my word.

I turned to the Frenchman. "What about you, Jacques? What is the first thing you want to do on land?"

Jacques cleared his throat. "Zhe first zhing zhat I shall request to do after setting feet once more upon zhe blessed ground is to find a fresh lamb, roast it, and eat zhe beast whole."

"Aye," O'Malley said, "that's jist like ye. Think more of yer own stomach than sharing wi' yer friends."

Chester nodded. "You're not cooking me my first bite of lamb on Australian soil, Mr. Jack Frog. I'll suffer through your French sauces in the future, but for my maiden voyage I'm cooking the beast myself."

I laughed. "You should have a contest."

I clapped my mouth shut as I exhaled the last word. I forget they take my jokes seriously. And that was how I found myself sitting in a public house listening to Jacques and Chester insult each other as they roasted sheep.

The public house across from the wharf was our rendezvous after an afternoon of visiting the tailor, seamstress, and blacksmith. The sun was down by six o'clock in the evening, and the chill air made the fire welcome. Australia's early summer feels like England's early winter.

We weren't the only people in the public house, but our presence was felt. A group of deadly-looking military men, two pretty women, a bush-faced man in a sash, and me, were a peculiar sight even in this peculiar land. Add to that Chester and Jacques cajoling the owner of the public house to allow them to have a cooking contest, and we immediately became the center of attention.

"You have already lost," Jacques said to Chester. "You do not *roast* a lamb. You English zhink you can zhrow anyzhing in front of a fire and it vill of a course become a dish. Zhat is not how you treat zhe tenderness of a lamb."

"That's ridiculous," Chester said. "Lambs have been roasted since the days of good King Alfred playing hide-and-seek in a swamp."

Jacques made one of those French grunting sounds as he cut slits in his hunk of meat. The French communicate disgust better than any other country I've encountered.

"Your lamb vill be dry, charred, and flaky."

Chester snorted. "Says the chap *marinating* his meat. Your chop is going to be so tender it falls into mush. As if braising is better than roasting."

Jacques stuffed garlic slices into the slits in the meat. A pot of Béchamel sauce simmered at low heat in the corner of the fireplace. Too tender or not, it smelled amazing after months of ship food.

"My lamb," Jacques said, "vill have the tenderness of angels playing harps in your mouhz."

Chester blinked. "You do realize how flighty that sounds?"

Jacques waved his knife. "It is a metaphor."

"No, that's not a metaphor. A metaphor is—Law, what's a metaphor?"

"A metaphor," I said, "is a figure of speech in which a word or phrase literally denoting one kind of object or idea is used in place of another to suggest a likeness or analogy between them."

Chester and Jacques both blinked at me.

"That's what you get for memorizing the dictionary," Chester said.

"Anyway . . ."

I turned away from their banter and reentered the conversation at our table.

"Maria," Pacarina said, "are you all right?"

Maria sat statuesque next to Pacarina on the bench, her back straight enough to delight a Sergeant Major. I think she was trying to minimize the number of square inches of her dress in contact with the bench.

"It's just a little . . . strange," Maria said. "I've never been in a place like—this."

True, Society's ballrooms and parlors were a distant scene from a tavern that smelled like fish and the sweat dripping down the sailors' exposed chests.

Pacarina laughed as she bounced Otho on her knee. "If you were staying with us you would become used to such places. Colonel Nobody says he feels more comfortable here, but really I think Chester is the one to blame."

I took the cue. "Yes, this is all natural to Chester." I nodded at him slapping the innkeeper's back as he watched his lamb roast. "This really is his world."

Maria snagged a fan from her left sleeve. "I suppose it is because he is a man of the world." The fan wagged like the tail of a lap dog trying to make friends with a hound. "There is always a place for exploration, and, understanding a part of the world, even if it is—less than ideal."

"Certainly, and I think that's how Chester feels about High Society. He would much rather grab the world with both hands and work through muck and sweat to accomplish his goal."

Words like 'muck' and 'sweat' were evil to Maria. The best way to break her of her obsession with Chester was to pound it through her thick brain that Chester liked all sorts of things she found repulsive. Now, granted, he could hold his own in High Society—he wasn't like me, who dislikes both High Society as well as muck and sweat—but he and Maria are about as compatible as beef pudding and sour milk.

"The world," Maria said, "is very full of different people. I think it's good breeding in a man to embrace many experiences."

Pacarina grinned at me. I was trying to turn Maria away, not convince her that Chester being on back-slapping terms with sailors was a sign of his breadth of character.

An exclamation from the fireplace dragged my attention back to our amateur chefs.

"I must attend to nature's necessities," Jacques announced. "If any of you *boeufs* lay a finger upon my lamb, I vill braise *you*!"

Colonel Nobody shifted closer to me on our bench. "Do you think he would make a good leader?"

"Jacques?" I asked.

Colonel Nobody smiled. "No, not Jacques. He makes an excellent soldier, but he'd have a mutiny on his hands before three hours. I mean Chester."

I paused. "He has the kind of force of personality that men follow."

"And?"

I smiled. "I would be concerned about where he would lead them. His ideas can be a bit harebrained."

"Sometimes it takes a harebrained idea to survive. Like me being an English colonel. And sometimes, such an idea gets you killed." Colonel Nobody sipped his drink. "Chester is very good at tactics, but he doesn't have your natural bent towards strategy. It wouldn't hurt if you could teach him a few things about thinking before acting."

My cheeks warmed. The day the Boy Colonel compliments your thinking is a day to remember.

Colonel Nobody waved the innkeeper over to us. "The Lady here is looking for her uncle. His name is . . ." Nobody gestured to Maria.

Maria colored. "His name is, I think it is, Donovan Deveroux."

The innkeeper's eyebrows raised the wrinkle lines on his forehead. Then, he laughed. "That's a good one. Had me believing you there for a minute, you did."

Maria's fan stopped. "What do you mean?"

"You said Donovan, my lady. You're pulling my leg."

Colonel Nobody leaned forward. "Explain."

The innkeeper looked back and forth between Maria and Nobody. "Are you fresh off the boat? Everyone knows Donovan." He pointed at a poster tacked to a beam.

Chester dived from his fire long enough to rip the poster off and scan it.

"I say, your uncle is an outlaw!" He looked at Maria with what I would almost call admiration. "Belay that—apparently he's in charge of a lovely little group of them."

The color left Maria's cheeks. "An outlaw? I . . . didn't know."

"How well did you know your uncle?" Colonel Nobody asked.

"Not very well. I—I'm sorry, I never met him."

"What do you know about him?"

She looked down. "He was my father's youngest brother. They called him the black sheep of the family. And he went to Australia."

We waited for her to say more, but that was all. Colonel Nobody looked at me.

"It seems he kept himself busy once he arrived."

"I'm—sorry," Maria said. "I thought he would be here. I wanted very much to come with you. I—will figure something out."

Pacarina laid her hand on Maria's. "Don't worry. We'll take care of you."

I could have reminded them of Assassins and running for our lives and other delightful such things that rather competed with us taking care of her, but I refrained.

"Ahem."

I looked up. Jacques and Chester stood before our table. Each held a plate of lamb.

"Zhis," Jacques said, "is purely a formality, but ve need someone to taste and judge zhe results of our endeavors."

Pacarina patted Maria's hand. "I'm sure Maria will be the perfect judge."

She smiled a little at that, and the chefs delivered their plates and provided Maria with a fork. She held it up, turning it so the firelight gleamed off the tines and root. Apparently, her belief that all parts of culture should be embraced didn't extend to eating with a dirty fork. Once she was satisfied it was clean, she slipped it into a piece of Chester's roast and lifted the chunk to her lips.

"Divine," she announced. "Absolutely divine."

Chester winked and dusted his shoulder.

Maria lifted a piece of Jacques' meat into her mouth. Her eyes bulged, and she did the most unladylike thing I've seen her do—she spit it out.

"It's—awful!" she gasped.

Jacques' eyes bulged further than hers'. "I protest against zhe bias of zhe judge." He grabbed the fork and scooped a bite into his own mouth.

The Battle of Waterloo played across his face for about ten seconds, but at last, the French retreated. He disposed of the lamb in his handkerchief and wheeled around to Chester.

"Vhat—did—you—*do*!"

Chester shook his head. "I didn't touch your food."

Jacques pointed a finger in his face. "You—" he turned, inch by inch, like a snake coiling to strike. He pointed at O'Malley.

"Irishman, vhat did you do?"

O'Malley's face burst into a grin from the tip of his chin to the roots of his flaming red hair.

"It's called a joke, Jack Frog. I thought as it could use a touch of extra salt . . ." He mimicked dumping salt into a pot.

"A—*joke*!" Jacques pronounced the word like 'choke,' which is what it looked like he wanted to do to O'Malley. "You should be hung, and drawn, and quartered, and burned, and ground, and baked, and frozen, and—" He either ran out of creative ways to end O'Malley's life or became too angry to keep speaking English.

Jacques straightened and tugged the corners of his tunic like I imagine

Napoleon did when he surrendered. He spun on his heel and marched out of the public house. His braised lamb whispered steam like the debris of a battlefield in the Frenchman's wake.

If I were uninitiated to the ways of Squad One I would assume he was out plotting how to murder O'Malley. As it was, Jacques and O'Malley spend their lives in friendly war. Jacques would revenge himself. The key is to not be caught in the crossfire.

Chapter 8

Lawrence

The next day found Nobody and me standing in front of Government House, home to Governor Sir George Gipps. I counted four or five different levels to the roof, and as many styles in the exterior walls. According to what I've read, governors have been adding on to the house since the original six-room home that was Sydney's first real building. Hammers clanked from where a new Government House was being built several hundred feet to the South East.

"How did you get an interview with the governor?" I asked.

Nobody smiled. "The name 'Boy Colonel' comes in handy sometimes."

A servant answered the governor's door and led us into the drawing room. Most servants were convicts, current or ex. I wondered what crime brought this man so far from his native land.

A high-backed leather chair and an oak desk occupied one side of the room. Across from these were a pair of windows, half hidden by drapes, and between them stood two more leather chairs with low, round backs.

Nobody spoke low. "Governor Sir George Gipps served with my friend Colonel Campbell in the Peninsular War. He's a good soldier, but of the breed that doesn't look kindly upon irregularities. Like a boy commanding a regiment. Tread carefully."

I nodded. In this place, thousands of miles from British courts and the British sovereign, the governor's word was law.

"Colonel Nobody. Mr. Stoning."

Governor Sir George Gipps stood in a doorway to the right of his desk. He had a firm mouth, a Roman nose, steady eyes, and a high forehead. Groomed strips of hair grew on both sides of his face, reaching below his ears, then curving towards his mouth.

We bowed one-quarter. The lower Nobody bows, the stiffer he looks, but he managed this one decently.

"May I offer you a drink?" the governor asked.

We declined.

"You won't mind if I have one." Gipps said it as a fact, not a question.

The sunlight sparkled the brandy into light and dark shades of brown as the liquid tinkled from the decanter into the governor's glass.

Gipps sighed as he set down the empty glass.

"What brings the 'Boy Colonel' to New South Wales?" he asked.

"A rather unpleasant situation," Nobody said, "which I want to explain, so you will understand some things that may happen in the future."

Governor Gipps motioned us to the two chairs and seated his own thin frame behind his desk. He nodded for Nobody to continue.

"Some men are trying to kill me. I have reason to believe they are going to follow me here. My plan is to kill them before they kill me, and I wanted to be sure you understood the situation so that, if I'm able to kill them, I'll have as little trouble with the law as possible."

Governor Gipps cocked an eyebrow. "Are you asking for protection?"

Nobody smiled. "No offense to your men, but they're not able to protect me from the men following me."

"I see. And, why are they following you?"

"Suffice it to say that they feel they have a very good reason, and it's not due to any misdeeds on my part."

Gipps poured himself another bottom of whiskey. "Australia is a very long way to follow a man. Perhaps you are, shall we say, overestimating your danger?"

Nobody's left ramus mandibular twitched through his cheek-skin.

"Trust me, Governor, I know how to accurately assess the danger of a situation."

"Hmm." Gipps fingered his glass. "What indications do you have that someone is trying to kill you?"

I coughed. "Trying to shoot, stab, and burn us to death."

"Ah." The governor creaked back in his chair. "Colonel Nobody, I'll be frank. I'm dealing with a colony full of squatters who think I'm trying to steal their land by enforcing fair laws. I have convicts to keep in hand, robbers to bring to justice, I have to keep us from killing the Aborigines, and keep the Aborigines from killing us. I don't have time to deal with your personal troubles. Your group is already causing enough of a disturbance."

"What do you mean by that?"

Gipps' lip twitched. "If you don't know what I mean, you had better get a tighter grip on your men."

Colonel Nobody paused. "I don't wish to cause you any additional trouble, and I apologize if there is any. I felt it my duty to explain to you what may happen."

"I will see that justice is done, for whoever is in the right."

Gipps pulled a stack of papers across the desk towards him. I gathered my legs to stand up, but Nobody wasn't taking the hint.

"I had one other reason for coming," Nobody said. "I'm looking for a man, the brother of an old comrade of mine. His name is James or Jamie Burke."

Gipps looked up from the papers.

"James Burke. Yes, I know of the convict. Why are you looking for him?"

"I'd like to tell him how his brother died."

"I see." Gipps looked at both of us. He opened, then closed his mouth. He repeated this three times. At last, he cleared his throat.

"How familiar are you with Australia?" Gipps asked.

"Mr. Stoning knows more than I."

I blinked. Yes, of course, I had a rudimentary understanding of the topography, geography, and linguistic makeup of the continent, but I wasn't prepared to be quizzed. I never liked quizzes. I always tried to convince my tutor to let me stick with essays.

"Then," Gipps said, "you must be aware that a small but aggressive percentage of our people live—shall we say, outside the law?"

"Outlaws, you mean?" I asked.

"Bushrangers, we call them. They live in the back-country and steal cattle, horses, and so on. A despicable lot of ex-convicts, escaped convicts, a few Aborigines, young rascals . . . they are a thorn in our flesh."

Colonel Nobody nodded. "This has to do with James Burke?"

"He's one of them."

I let my breath out. Really? Is every single person we're looking for in Australia an outlaw? Well, I suppose yes, as there are only two people we are looking for.

I shook my head. "Why?"

"He escaped from the work gangs."

A slight web of creases deepened on Nobody's forehead. They showed when he was particularly tired, angry, or sad. In this case I think it was the third. It must cut to think of Edmund's brother being a robber and maybe even a murderer.

"I'm very sorry to hear that," Nobody said. "How do I find him?"

"If I knew where to find the outlaws, you would find them back in the work gangs."

"Tell me what direction to go and I'll leave Sydney."

Gipps pinched his glass between his thumb and first finger. "I'm a fair man, Colonel. Nearly driven to distraction by the people here, but fair. I won't let my perspective on your—peculiar military career affect my judgement of you, but I ask that you and your unconventional ways don't make my life more challenging than it is. I will see the law enforced without respect of persons."

"I respect that," Nobody said. "I'm not asking for any preferential treatment. You're in charge here, surely you know in what areas the outlaws are most likely to operate, where we might be able to find someone in contact with them. I don't want to help them. I simply want to do my duty by a dead friend."

Gipps sighed and plunked his glass back on the desk. "He's with the biggest lot of them. Donovan's gang. Go there—" he pointed to a spot on the map hanging from the wall behind him. "A suspicious number of their lads have ended up with Donovan's rapscallions."

Colonel Nobody touched his hand to his forehead and I glimpsed an inch of the steel strip beneath his sleeve. "Thank-you, Governor."

As we walked away from the governor's house, I found myself lengthening my stride to match Nobody's.

"What do we do now?" I asked.

"We go looking for outlaws. And keep a weather eye for Assassins."

I smiled through my teeth. "Jolly."

We were approaching the wharf when we spotted something which brought us both to a standstill.

A man strolled towards us. He wore black trousers, a black cloak, and a slouchy leather hat. Two bandoliers crisscrossed his chest. A saber hung from his right hip. A rifle was slung over his left shoulder, the butt of which dangled next to the butts of two pistols tucked into a waist-sash beneath the bandoliers. Two sword-hilts rose over his shoulders, and a knife-hilt peeked from each of his knee-height black boots. He held a wicked-looking curved stick that must be a boomerang.

A red sash wrapped around his head, pierced with two eye-holes.

Colonel Nobody snapped into a defensive posture. "Here already?"

I grunted. "I wish. That, Colonel, is what I grew up with."

The man waved at us. "There you are. I thought you would come this way."

I tried to smile through my clenched teeth. "Chester, everyone on this entire street is staring at you."

Chester cocked his head. "Really? I need to make these eye-holes bigger. Can't see much."

"Take off the mask, Chester."

"Hardly. This adds to the mystique, Law—and you should appreciate me using a fancy word like that."

Colonel Nobody cleared his throat. The creases on his forehead softened, and his lips twitched the way they do when he tries to not smile. He does that a lot around Chester.

"I don't think the ladies will think highly of the mask," Nobody said.

"Oh, Pacarina won't mind. I say!" I knew Chester's eyes were widening beneath the mask. "Do you think this would keep Maria away?"

I glared at Nobody. If Chester thought wearing a mask could lessen Maria's interest in him, he would wear that mask until newspapers stopped printing lies.

"Chester, I think she would love that mask."

"Nice try, Law."

"Not to mention that if you keep wearing that you're going to end up in jail."

"There's no law against being prepared."

I sighed. "In this case, there should be."

Chester tossed the boomerang from hand to hand. "I'm not going to be caught napping next time these coves show up. I'd rather you be embarrassed than dead."

A gaggle of children on the street giggled and pointed at us. I sighed. Hello, Australia.

Chapter 9
Lawrence

"We're all here?" Nobody asked.

We all were here, in a private room at the public house.

"As soon as we're stocked up we're leaving for the back-country. Petr, any chance the Assassins will cause trouble in Sydney if we're not here?"

Petr shook his head. "Unlikely."

Chester raised his hand. "May I ask a question which may be out of order, but I really want to ask anyway?"

Colonel Nobody smiled. "Can I stop you?"

"You keep saying Petr is the best man, or to ask Petr what he thinks, or the like. What I want to know is, what does Petr know that we don't?"

Colonel Nobody looked at the Russian. "A valid question. Petr has no obligation to answer it. I leave the choice to his discretion."

Petr examined Chester like a scholar scouring a bookshelf for the right volume.

"You saved my colonel. You, I trust. You also." He tilted his head at me and Pacarina. "Her, I do not trust." He looked at Maria.

Red dots spotted her cheeks. "Me? What have I done?"

Colonel Nobody raised a hand. "Petr means no offense, Maria. But we have not lived as long as we have by trusting lightly. I'm glad to offer you my protection, and I feel partly responsible for the danger you share with us, as it would not exist if I did not exist, but frankly, you have not done anything to earn our trust."

Maria's lush lashes fluttered. "You mean you want me to leave just when you're going to share exciting, dark secrets? It's like reading *Rob Roy* and just when you're about to learn who the mysterious man in the Hall is, someone comes and throws the book in the fire."

She turned pleading eyes on Chester, probably because he was certain to have read the book and would understand her literary allusion.

No one spoke.

"Very well." She left the room.

Petr rested his hands on his knees. His hands were meaty, solid as a paperweight when clenched in a fist, but not fatty. They bore old scars and stains of burnt gunpowder and oil.

"You ask why I know about the Assassins. It is because I was an Assassin."

I blinked. Chester opened his mouth, but O'Malley quieted him.

"Let the laddy talk. Ye won't hear this many words from him fer a long year tae come."

Petr continued. "When the Colonel was not a colonel, and Colonel Hayes led the 42nd, I was sent to be a spy in the English army. I pretend to be a traitor, that the Cossacks kill my family, that I want to kill Cossacks."

Petr's eyes did not change expression. He spoke as if describing yesterday's lunch. With less passion than Jacques would describe yesterday's lunch.

"At first I was not trusted. I fight good. I must make the English trust me, so I fight good for them. I save lives. I am trusted. I learn secrets, and send them to my brother Assassins. Colonel Nobody, he befriends me. He becomes my friend. He learns Russian from me."

Colonel Nobody and Petr's comrades in Squad One all watched the floor, their faces grave. They knew the story, and respected Petr's secret—and the trust he was extending to us.

"I spend years with the English. I learn them, I learn they are men like me, not monsters, not men to hate. But still I steal their secrets, because it is my duty. Then an order comes."

Petr folded his hands. "Colonel Hayes, and the Lieutenant-Colonel

Nobody, they have become dangerous. They are too good. I am told to kill them, and come back to the Assassins. The end of my mission. I am torn. I want to kill, and I do not want to kill. I have my duty, my brothers I cannot betray, but also my new English brothers, my friend, my leader."

Petr looked at Nobody. I think the patch of wet in Petr's eye was a tear.

Chester coughed. "I'm guessing you didn't kill Colonel Nobody?"

"I could not. I did not. I betrayed my training, my people. I am the only Assassin to fail his mission."

Chester blew out a deep breath. "I think I know now why you know the most about these jolly Assassins."

"I know how they fight. I know how they think."

"And knowing that, you honestly think they'll find us here?"

Petr's lips curled in what, for Petr, was a smile. "I did not fail my mission because I could not find my quarry."

I blinked as the news percolated through my brain. This was proof that the Assassins could change. They weren't just bloodthirsty ninjas. Petr changed. If we could just figure out how to talk with them before they killed us, we could figure something out.

Colonel Nobody lifted a hand. He was staring at the door. "Yes," he said, rising, "any Assassin would feel especially revenged to put a knife in Petr."

He flung open the door.

Bogdan knelt, his ear where the keyhole had been. He straightened his back and nodded at us.

"You were spying on us?" Nobody said.

"Yes."

"You have a death wish?"

Bogdan smiled. "I am not threatening you. You will not kill an innocent man."

Colonel Nobody clenched his teeth. "Get out of here."

Bogdan bowed. "When you are Tsar, you will thank me."

Chapter 10

Lawrence

"You *boeuf*, you do not know how to hurl zhe zhing."

"Aye, as if ye do!"

Jacques tossed his head. "I am confident zhat I could do better zhan your ridiculous display of incompetence."

The sun hung hot and heavy over the Australian back-country. We rested in a clump of trees five days' ride from Sydney. Miles of knee-high grass circled us, the blades swishing in layers of brown and gold as the breeze rippled through them.

Jacques and O'Malley stood at the edge of the plain. O'Malley clutched a boomerang and eyed the pile of spares by his right boot.

"It's yer jabbering as is distracting me," O'Malley said. He held the curved stick behind his back, his wrist brushing his neck, waiting for a gust.

I couldn't see his face from where I sat next to Pacarina, but I guessed he had one eye closed in concentration. Jacques twirled his moustache.

O'Malley threw his arm forward and released the boomerang dead ahead. It swished across the plain, knifed into the grass and kicked a spurt of dirt into the air about one-hundred yards from our grove. An impressive throw, except he wanted the weapon to fly back to him.

"You see!" Jacques threw up his hands. "And you vonder vhy zhe Irish still live in mud huts! Vhat, vill you tell me zhat you vere aiming for zhat novhere zhat you hit?"

O'Malley thrust his boot into the pile of boomerangs and kicked one up at Jacques.

"Arrah, Jack Frog, ye try it."

Jacques caught the stick and swept it low over the ground, like a top hat, as he bowed to us.

"In zhe rare occasion zhat zhe French do not invent somezhing, zhey vatch zhe expert, learn, and become zhe expert." He clasped the boomerang to his chest and gave Chester a quick, three-quarter bow. "I have learned. Now, I demonstrate."

Jacques stepped sideways from the throwing sticks and tested the ground with his boot until he found a satisfactory spot. He planted his feet, squared his hips, and raised the boomerang. He pointed the stick at a forty-five-degree angle from his body, stood rock still—a dramatic pause, I think—and threw.

The boomerang landed a foot from O'Malley's.

Jacques gazed after it for a moment, turned, and stalked away, looking like a cat emerging from an unexpected bath.

Chester burst into a laugh. "Sorry, fellows, I couldn't resist. You've got the style right, but you're throwing the wrong thing."

He lay propped against a tree trunk with his hat slouched over his eyes. That hat, I should mention, is the same hat he introduced along with his assassin getup in Sydney. Kangaroo leather, very strong, very light, and popular for whips. Chester pushed his hat up, rose, and pulled a boomerang from his sash.

"These things aren't all made the same. Yours are straighter. I think they're supposed to kill what they hit, or break a wing, that sort of thing. This chap here is a decoy boomerang. The Australian version of the hounds flushing a fox."

He walked to the edge of the trees and flicked the stick into the wind. It flew right about fifteen yards then curved left, gaining elevation as it flew, semi-circled, and dropped back to Chester. He clapped the stick between his hands and shoved it back into his sash.

I don't know how Chester learned to throw a boomerang perfectly in five days. Chester does things like that. I think he received my share of the brain that controls muscle movement.

Something in the grass moved. I sat up. Not far from where Jacques and O'Malley's non-returning boomerangs landed, two pointed ears poked above the grass. They quivered a moment, like antennae scouting the landscape, then a brownish red body burst from the grass.

My first kangaroo.

He ran towards the sun, in the direction we were traveling, with an uncanny gait unlike I have ever seen before.

The kangaroo's stubby arms hung close to his chest, perpendicular with the ground except at the wrist where the arm bent ninety degrees so that the animal's front paws pointed at his back legs. They were shaped like big L's. The back legs were long and powerful and propelled the kangaroo in great leaps. The beast was jumping, not running. Its three-foot tail scraped the ground before each leap, then bounced high as the animal launched forward.

"Do you think we scared it?" Chester asked.

I shook my head. "He would have run as soon as the first boomerang fell. Something else startled him."

Those of us sitting stood and we all checked our weapons. Even I had a pistol and a sword. Not my wardrobe accessories of choice, but I would be prepared to protect my family when the Russians came again.

For a moment I thought there was more movement in the grass from which the kangaroo sprang, but it may have just been the wind. A slight gust swept the grass like fingers through long hair.

"I don't think we're alone," Nobody said.

"More kangaroos?" Maria asked. With no uncle to leave her with in Sydney, we had to bring her along.

"Aborigines, more likely."

The wind stopped, and so did the rustling in the grass. If men were there, they knew how to not be seen. The colonists were technically at peace with the Aborigines, some of whom worked on farms or tended flocks for the white men, but the relationship was tense. There were rumors in town of murders and reprisals.

I can't think of many reasons why I would want to finish my life on the end of a spear, but being there because some drunken ex-convict happened to have killed the spear-thruster's brother was one of the worst.

We waited, but nothing happened. Maybe no one was there. Or, someone who did not want to be seen was watching this strange caravan of white men.

We ended our rest, remounted our horses, and resumed our journey.

Chapter 11

Lawrence

"Law, you've got to!"

I shook my head. "Why would I make a fool of myself in front of an entire village?"

"Let's ask Pacarina," Chester said.

We were at the settlement Governor Gipps directed us to. There were some tense moments when we started asking how to contact the outlaws, and if Pacarina and Maria were not with us, I don't think we would have made progress, but having women made us look less like some kind of mercenary squad. A few well-placed "gifts" eventually convinced a chap to disappear into the backcountry promising to do "what he could do" to find Donovan's gang.

That's when Chester convinced Nobody that we should do something to prove we were friendly and harmless. His logic was sound, sadly, as there was little chance that Edmund's brother would agree to meet with us if he thought it might be a trap. That's when we found out that Chester's idea of demonstrating that we were likable people was to cut me in half.

"You know it's a good plan," Chester said to Pacarina.

She grinned. "I'd like to see it."

"No," I said. "There are many reasons why your idea is ludicrous. Firstly, getting into your box looks extremely uncomfortable."

"I'm glad you said 'firstly,' because that means you know it's not a good enough reason by itself."

"Secondly, I don't like the idea of pretending to do magic."

Chester waved this away. "Oh, I'm not calling it magic. It's illusion. I'm just going to make it look like I cut you in half."

"Thirdly, I don't want to risk you being disappointed if the illusion doesn't work."

Chester snorted. "Do you think I lugged my table and box out here for firewood?"

I opened my mouth, but Chester cut me off.

"I suppose you're going to say that nextly, you'll look ridiculous out there. Relax, Law. It's good for your humility. Isn't that right, Sister?"

Pacarina patted my shoulder. "You know you want to do it, Law."

I knew distinctly that I did not want to do it.

Chester stepped closer and lowered his voice. "Law, please, this is my thing. Everyone knows your things, you're smart, and you come up with the best ideas. I want to be more than just the chap who's first into the breach."

I checked his face, looking for the smile to show that this was all some joke. He wasn't smiling.

"All right," I said. "I didn't realize it meant so much to you."

He exhaled and flashed a grin. "You're the best brother I have, Law."

A huge bonfire lit a cleared space near the colonists' homes. Foot-thick logs leaned against each other in a ring above and inside the dancing flames. The circle of light was bright enough to show O'Malley's red hair, while the surrounding darkness was blacker by contrast.

Chester's table stood just far enough from the fire that he could stand behind it, facing the audience, and not be singed.

Chester led with a disappearing coin act, where he pretended to pull coins from his kangaroo hat. The hat was big enough to hold rabbits, had there been any rabbits in Australia. Kangaroo babies might have worked.

The second act was knife-juggling. Chester faced us holding three knives in his right hand. The knives were ten inches long, about half of which was hilt. The blades curved like small-scale sabers.

Chester flipped one knife in the air. It twirled above his head, catching and reflecting light-beams from the fire. As it reached its peak, Chester tossed the second knife, then the third, and the weapons sliced the air in a never-ending cycle. The children howled with delight.

Faster than I can write it Chester reached into his right boot and added a fourth knife to the mix.

The children screamed. I clapped. How could I resist? Chester looked calmer risking momentary amputation to his fingers than Jacques looks eating breakfast. The Assassins might think twice about hunting us down if they could watch this.

Chester caught the knives and bowed to the cheers of all assembled. I wondered what would top that—oh, no. I was supposed to.

"Now, ladies and gentlemen," Chester said, "I'd like to finish this little demonstration with a special treat for you. I've just shown you how to master blades. Now I will show you a blade master a man."

He snapped his fingers at me.

"Join me in welcoming to this, the first performance of Chester the Great, my brother at arms, Lawrence the Luminary."

I wanted to hail a passing kangaroo and hop back to Sydney. What could I do? I gave my word. Now I had to do it. 'Lawrence the Luminary,' indeed.

I kept my back to the audience so I wouldn't have to see them watching me. Chester swept the blanket off the table to reveal the coffin. With the fire in the background and the coffin in the foreground, it was a compromise between burial and cremation.

Chester chattered to the crowd while I climbed into the box. I lay on my back, scooted my legs into the compartment in the table, and rested my neck nape on the curve in the box's edge. I had to round my shoulders and squeeze them into my body to fit. That meant my arms couldn't quite rest on my chest, so I was stuck with them pointing at the other end of the box, held by my body tension about three inches from my chest.

Chester dropped a wooden collar over my neck and something like half a pair of stocks over my feet. Right about then, when I couldn't move, I remembered Chester had not explained what he was going to do.

"You do have a plan?" I whispered. "You know what you're doing?"

"Don't worry," Chester said. "Theoretically, you'll be just fine."

Chester winked and lowered the lid. I was trapped, with only my head and feet in the open air.

It took three seconds for my nose to start itching. Another three seconds reminded me of the experimentation I've done with muscle elasticity and how painful it quickly becomes to keep my arms tensed in the same position for even a minute.

Chester began his speech.

"Here, ladies and gentlemen, you see before you a box. You have seen my assistant climb into the box. You see how narrow and small the box is. What is the purpose of the box, you ask? An excellent question. Why would my assistant climb into the box? Is he so dedicated to the amusement of the masses that he would risk life and limb for the honor of contributing to this night's spectacle?"

I could have given him a mouthful.

"Yes, that's right, what you're about to witness is a feat of nearly unparalleled amazement. You will question your senses. You will question reality. You may even question my sanity."

I snorted. "There's no question about that."

Chester raised his voice. "Prepare!"

He stepped behind the coffin. The crowd gasped. He must have picked up the saw.

"Scream when I wink," Chester whispered.

"I'm not screaming," I whispered back.

Chester frowned. He inserted the saw in the slot in the middle of the coffin and rasped away.

The fire now felt much closer than it appeared when I sat in the audience. Sweat beaded on my forehead, cheeks, the nape of my neck, and everywhere else on my head pores exist. It streamed to my earlobes, and dripped.

I saw Chester's head and the upper half of his torso, but I couldn't see what he was doing with the box. I swiveled my head to watch the audience and get some sense of what was happening. Faces showed incredulity and what I think was horror. Otho stared unblinking at Uncle Chester. I locked my eyes on Pacarina's face, knowing if I was in real trouble, she would be the first to stop Chester. Her eyes widened. Oh, no. She trusts Chester, and for that matter so do I, but—

Pain bit into the left side of my neck and I yelled by reflex.

The crowd yelled back. Half of them were on their feet.

"What was that?" I snapped at Chester.

"That was an excellent yell, Law. Next time I tell you to yell when I wink, watch and do it."

The rascal had pinched my neck to make me yell. I'm not a violent man, but I confess at that moment I felt very much like shattering a few small inkwells on Chester's skull.

Chester did something to the box, and the crowd cheered. I think he put me back together. Not that I was apart, of course, but apparently it looked like I had been split in two. Now I was supposed to leap from the box and dance a waltz to show my wholeness, which would be interesting since my legs were numb and my arms ached with shooting pains.

I was ready for Chester to pull the collarish thing off my neck when something happened.

The light changed. Not like the moon bursting through clouds, but like a small red sun flaming behind my head. I did not need to see it to know that fire, unbidden fire, was somewhere behind me. Not to mention everyone was screaming "fire" and rushing away from me, towards the houses.

"Duty calls!" Chester said, and took off after them.

"Get me out of this!" I called.

I pursed my lips. I'm no stranger to feeling useless, it's just I never had that thought in a coffin before. Come to think of it, our own planned bonfire was becoming much too warm for comfort. And I couldn't get away from it. That made me think of people who can't stand small spaces, which made me consider how small my space was, which led to a certain itching across every inch of my body and an intense desire to move.

"What do we do?" someone said.

I almost shouted with delight. I say 'almost' because the someone was Maria. Anyone else would have merited a shout. I gave her a cough.

"Could you please release the thing on my neck?" I said, trying to keep my voice calm.

"There's so much fire," Maria said. "Wherever could it have come from? Do you think someone left a bed warmer open on a bed?"

This was not the time to mention that bed warmers wouldn't be a common article in the colonists' sparsely-furnished huts. This was the time to mention that I was getting quite warm, and request to be removed from the fire. I mentioned it.

"What is that?" Maria said, pointing where the audience was seated a few moments before.

I tried to stay calm. "Kindly get me out of this thing and I'll do my best to tell you."

Crack.

That was a pistol shot.

Laughing men on horses trampled into the glade.

My first thought was Russians, but the men spoke English. Rather, they spoke the Australian-English dialect that passes for English. It became clear what was happening. These were outlaws, who robbed the houses while we were here watching illusions, torched the houses for a diversion, and were now riding back to their lair.

Maria screamed and collapsed as if she had been shot. She hadn't, of course. I've never once seen Pacarina or Liana faint, but watching Maria has schooled me in the fine art.

The outlaws heard the scream and pistols swung towards me.

"It's a fainted sheila," one of them said. "What do we do?"

"An' what's with the grinning corpse in the coffin?" another said.

I was not grinning, I was grimacing from joint pain.

"Should we shoot 'em?" the first man asked.

Another man wheeled his horse toward me. "See the sheila's clothes? Aristocrat, that. Leave the servant and take her for ransom."

There was a sound somewhere between a panther screaming and a sad seal clearing its throat. Chester charged into the glade with pistols waving. He ended his war-cry with "A Stoning!" and ran at the closest horseman.

One of the outlaws dropped his rifle-muzzle from his arm-crook and pointed it at Chester's chest.

"No!" I shouted.

From the darkness behind Chester a lone horseman spurred into view. He twirled something and flung it at Chester's head.

My brother fell.

Chapter 12
Chester

Talk about a headache.

Oh, right, I should say this is Chester writing. Law wasn't along for this part, and anyway he has no color to his writing, so I grabbed a pen to do it justice.

I was aiming for one of the ruffians' jugulars when something hit me in the back of the head.

I woke up feeling like the back of my head sprouted a crop of eggs and the chicks were pecking to daylight through my skull. I've never been drunk, but I'd bet ten guineas my head felt like a boozer's on Sunday morning.

So here I was, strapped flour-sack style on a horse, looking under the beast's belly and between my ankles on the other side. A skinny horse. I could care less about looking dignified, but being a flour sack is a bit too much.

"Hello," I said. "I can ride. Cut me loose."

Somebody moved his horse beside me.

"You look like the kind of fellow safer tied up," he said, with more than a touch of Scots brogue.

"If your little party here doesn't feel strong enough to keep one man from cutting your throats, I recommend a heart-to-heart talk with your recruiters."

The Scot laughed. "Fair."

"Scot," a bloke behind us called. "Let him up if he'll quiet his lady friend."

"Say what?" I said.

Then I heard her voice. *Oi vey*, the French say. Or maybe it's the Jews. Anyway, it's a lovely little phrase that means unmitigated disaster, and that's exactly how I felt. How many hours have I listened to that voice? I tried once to get Law to do some of his mathematical magic and figure it out.

"Maria," I said, "what are you doing here?"

"Oh, you're awake! I've been so worried, oh so incredibly worried, why, these people told me that you rushed to rescue me! You were like Ivanhoe saving Lady Rowena!"

"I didn't know you were there. Where were you?"

"The shock was simply too much for me. I fainted."

Should have known.

The Scot and another rascal cut me off the horse and tied my legs to the stirrups, so I rode right side up.

The moon didn't give enough light to see much more than three or four horses ahead. From the saddle-clanking in front and behind, I'd estimate there were twenty men in the group, plus me and Maria. My first plan, of course, was to pick a good time, maybe crossing a river or something, and ride out of there. Having Maria totally changed things. I couldn't leave her, and I certainly couldn't count on her having the wits to dash behind me if I took off.

It sure would be handy to have Law's brain-gears grinding out a plan.

The best plan I came up with was to wait until we got to wherever we were going so I could prepare Maria for escaping, and hopefully she wouldn't get us killed.

Best as I could tell by moonlight, the Scot was somewhere around my age, clean cut, with a rifle, and three boomerangs tucked into his waistband.

"Why am I here?" I asked.

"Partly because of imbeciles," he said, raising his voice. Someone behind us grunted. "We heard there were strangers in our part of the country. We were supposed to scout, not set fires and kidnap, but *somebody* hasn't learned to think ahead."

"You'll see," a man behind us said. "The boss's gold teeth will do a jig when he sees the loot we pinched."

The Scot looked back at me. "You're partly to blame, too. The boys were going to grab the girl for ransom, then out you come screaming like a banshee. I knocked you out, and some of the boys had the brilliant idea that you were worth more as a recruit or a ransom than a body on the ground, so here you are."

I grunted. "Boomerang, eh? Nice throw. I suppose I should thank you for only partially cracking my skull."

A white gash in the fellow's face might be a smile.

"You don't seem very concerned about being kidnapped."

I shrugged. "Not my first time. Try getting yourself kidnapped by Mayamuras and you'll find out what 'concerned' means."

"Who are you?"

"A tourist." I grinned back.

We rode for hours.

I must have been looking around us for landmarks a bit too sharply, as they decided to plop a sack over my head. Why they had an empty manure sack, I've no idea. There was such a ruckus behind me I'm sure they did the same for Maria, which was silly. She'd probably lose herself in her own rooms. Maybe they wanted some stout cotton between her mouth and the world.

A few more hours and several mountains later, we reached their lair. They cut me off my horse, marched me out of the cold night air, and jerked the sack off my head. Fire glare attacked my eyes.

I blinked the spots away in time to see them unveil Maria. She looked like a cat who accidently chomped a fistful of pepper flakes. I may or may not have experimented with that.

The rascals blocked me from the fireplace, so I stomped some circulation into my legs. That, and tried not to trip over Maria. The girl stuck closer than a limpet on salty rocks.

We'd walked through enough mooing, and baaing, and neighing on the way to the door to tell me we were in some kind of farmyard teeming with stolen animals.

An old woman paused from shooing the fellows away from her pot on the fire to look me over.

"You joining them?" she asked.

"Kidnappee. Can I bother you for a taste of what's in that pot? Smells amazing."

She grinned and ladled me a bowl of mutton stew. Always compliment the cook, is my motto. Unless it's Jacques. His head is big enough as it is.

The stew and a cup of billy tea chased the cold from my bones.

The cabin was largish, big enough to fit all twenty or so of the fellows, with space besides. The only door was in the front of the house, except a bit of a hatch that might open into a cellar. There were two windows big enough to fit through.

Most of the chaps settled around a rough table in the middle of the room. Three or four girls, late teens or early twenties, gave Maria the evil eye. They were pretty enough, but looked fiercer than a trapped fox guarding her whelps.

Maria tried to squeeze even closer to me. I don't know why the bushrangers' girls thought Maria was here, but they obviously weren't voting in her favor.

The Scot nodded at me. "Word of advice, laddy. Don't try escaping. If thirst don't drive you mad, the snakes'll get you, or the spiders, or the bees, or the Aborigines. We've even got ticks that kill." He leaned back in his chair and folded his arms behind his head. "Australia isn't friendly country."

Maria shivered.

Snakes and spiders don't scare me, but if they scared her enough to keep her from escaping, we were stuck. Well . . . all right, there is something unnatural about spiders. The way they creepy-crawl around and wait in their devious little webs for innocent victims to suck the blood out of—ahem, the less spiders, the better.

I didn't need Law's brilliance to see that escaping on foot wasn't going to work. We needed the fastest two horses and a good head start, which is why we'd escape at night.

I folded my arms so I could palm the knife strapped beneath my shirt-sleeve between my left armpit and elbow. The bushrangers hardly searched me. Sure, they took my rifle, and pistols, and swords, and hatchets, and boomerangs, and a few knives, but I still had at least five blades hidden.

"Are you man and wife?" the Scot asked.

I jumped.

"No! Absolutely not. Me and her? No, not a bit of it, nothing like that, the wrong track entirely." I scooted away from Maria to make sure he got the message.

"Walking out together?"

I held up my hands. "This is a Viscountess. I was just a private gen-tleman trying to survive a few assassins when she came along and—well, that's a long story. No, we're not walking out or anything of the sort."

Maria huffed. Well, she shouldn't blame me for it, I wasn't the one who suggested we were walking out.

One of the other men at the table, a chap with chin-hair just long enough to need a razor and just short enough to not look good, spit tobacco juice at the fire.

"She's available, then?"

I looked at him. "Touch her and I'll cut your throat."

Half Beard was out of his chair faster than a frog on coals.

I hated to see him leave the comfort of his seat, so I gave him a rap on the nose that plopped him back down.

The bushranger sitting next to Half Beard drew a pistol. Pistols are dangerous. Not wanting him to hurt himself, I grabbed his wrist with my left hand and relieved him of the pistol with my right.

In five seconds I could be on a horse. No good. Zero head start. It would take twenty seconds to bundle Maria out the door.

I dropped the pistol on the table.

"You bushrangers say the government doesn't respect you. Well, respect me. Ransom us if you want, but no funny business with the girl."

Every man's hand was on his pistol or knife.

"A Viscountess," the Scot said. Ah, he wasn't holding a knife, he was lighting a pipe. "More ransom money."

I tried not to grimace. Why did I have to tell them she had a title? Law would have been smarter.

The Scot waved his pipe at the others. "Don't hurt them, boys. Whole skins are worth more."

Half Beard snarled. "You're soft."

"We don't all have murders on us. The more attention we draw the more likely we'll have Governor Gipps on us with an army of settlers. Do you want that?"

Enough of the others grunted to keep us alive for the time being. Half Beard would need watching. His type prefers revenge to money. Plus, I think he was jealous of my beard.

The Scot crooked his finger at the old cook. "The lady will sleep with you tonight." He eyed me. "What's your name?"

"Chester Stoning."

"Chester Stoning, you're going to the cellar. I have my eye on you."

Chapter 13
Lawrence

"Lawrence, we have to rescue them," Pacarina said.

Her face was grim enough to scare lions. I almost pitied any outlaw she caught hurting Chester.

"I know." I wiped sweat from my forehead with my sleeve. No doubt the soot on my sleeve smeared my face, but we were all so sooty from beating out the house-fires that it didn't matter. Sweet smoke clogged my nostrils.

I strode to the silly box that prevented me from doing anything to help my brother and kicked it into the bonfire's ashes.

"We're going after them *now*," I said.

"Hold on," Nobody said. "We have to prepare."

"We have to go after them this moment," I said. "Who knows what the villains will do to them—are doing to them right now?" I clenched my fist.

Colonel Nobody blocked my path, his nose inches from mine.

"Lawrence, look at me."

I saw something in the dirt. I tried to push past Nobody, but he grabbed my shoulders.

"Look at me."

I stared at him.

"Lawrence, remember what I said makes you different?"

"Strategy? This isn't a chessboard, this is my brother. I'm not going to lose him."

"No, thinking before you act. Leaders can't allow emotion to impact their decision-making. Rushing anywhere blindly will put all of us in danger."

I gritted my teeth. "Well I'm not the leader, so I don't have to worry about that."

Colonel Nobody dug his fingers into my shoulders. "But I am your leader, and I have to worry about you. Breathe, Lawrence. This is not you."

"So you're just going to leave him to his fate?"

"Not a bit of it. He's my friend, he's Squad One. We will go after him. But we have to have a plan."

I sucked a lungful of smoky air. My heartbeat pulsed in my neck. Colonel Nobody was right, this wasn't me. This was not how I should react. But the thought of losing Chester terrified me.

I drew myself up and nodded. Colonel Nobody undug his fingers from my shoulders.

Pacarina picked up the thing in the dirt and handed it to me. Chester's hat. I grabbed it, the leather cool against my hot hands.

"What do we need to do?" I asked.

"Replace our horses," Nobody said. "I'm told there is a farmer a day's walk from here who keeps a herd of mustangs. Jacques and O'Malley, be back here mid-day tomorrow with horses."

"Will they ransom them?" I asked.

Colonel Nobody nodded. "I don't know why else they would have taken them. We just need to find them before the Assassins find us."

I steepled my fingers. I had to channel every ounce of my anger and fear into thought. A hundred scenarios—well, more like twelve—scudded through my brain.

"What if they catch us following them and kill Chester and Maria?"

Jacques snorted. "Zhis vill not be zhe first time ve follow and rescue someone. Ve are a *corps*, a body of men bound by a single bond, an ideal, ve hold to each ohzer, zhe enemy of zhe one is zhe enemy of zhe all—"

"We'll rescue them," O'Malley finished.

Chapter 14
Chester

Next morning, I slipped my knives into better hiding spots, then pounded the cellar door until they let me out.

The cabin door was open, and people scurried in and out like fleas on a dog pack. Most had pitchforks, or shovels, or scythes. No one paid attention to me, or to Maria, sitting in the corner farthest from the door. I don't think she's used to people not paying her attention, and she didn't look like she knew what to do with herself.

The only calm-looking person was the old cook, who beat dough on the table.

"Is there a circus in town?" I asked.

She chuckled. "It's the hairy panic. Half of them are too young to have seen it before."

I batted down some hair clumps. "I'm no sage myself, plus I've never been to Australia before. What is 'hairy panic?'"

She pointed through the doorway.

Imagine huge mounds of snow as tall as a man's head. Then imagine that snow is tumbleweeds, huge floaty mounds of brown tumbleweeds, piled against the other buildings in the compound and flicking through the air like paper in a gust. I've never seen anything like it. The outlaws' little compound was literally full of tumbleweed.

"Maria, have you seen this?" I asked.

Maria was at my side in a moment. "This country is unnatural." She stood as close to me as a frog on a lily pad.

I shrugged. I would travel a long way to see this tumbleweed convention. Come to think of it, I did travel a long way. I went outside and grabbed an armful of the stuff. It was just clumps of scratchy brown grass. Nothing dangerous about that, but waking up to a yardful of the stuff is a bit unnerving. I guess that's why they call it 'hairy panic.'

Next time I saw Law I would have to ask him about it. He probably knows the whole history of the stuff, plus the Latin name, and the name of the namer, and who knows what else.

Half Beard saw me, plowed through a few feet of hairy panic, and poked his scythe at my chest.

"Get in the house, galah."

I don't know what 'galah' means but it sure didn't sound like 'friend of my heart,' or 'noble person,' or even 'brave knight.' I considered knocking him down. No, right about now Law would be tapping me on the shoulder and nodding me back in the house. He's always right. I raised my eyebrow at Half Beard as a warning I owed him a trouncing, then went back inside.

Honestly, this kidnapped business could be worse. I wasn't trussed up in a dungeon or anything. They didn't seem to mind me moving around the cabin or grabbing my share of bread and berries from the old cook.

I could have killed several of them before they got me. I suppose they figured I wouldn't be stupid enough to do it, and I guess they were right.

The bushrangers sat around the table and dug into their breakfast with curses at the hairy panic. Maria stayed at my elbow. To be honest, even the outlaws' own women stayed out of arm's reach from them this morning.

Law would have pegged each man by his face, saying this one was a brute, this one was just misguided, that one was a coward. I looked at their arms and legs to see which ones I should take out first when the fight started. Speaking of faces, though, there was a lot of variety. Half Beard took the least beautiful award. The Scot didn't look like a bad chap, which meant he might be the most dangerous. A bad man who looks it is predictable. A bad man with a soft voice will surprise you. And he seemed to be in charge.

I aimed for a pair of empty chairs at the table and Half Beard snapped his fingers.

"Your sheila stands."

"My what?" I said.

"Your woman." He waved his knife at Maria.

I was going to repeat that she was absolutely *not* my woman, but she looked so miserable and scared that I shrugged it off. Wasn't anything to gain from talking to the ruffian.

I held out the chair for Maria, then sat beside her.

Half Beard stuck his knife-point into the table next to my right hand. I knew he wasn't going to cut me, else I would never have let the blade come that close.

I rested my elbows on the table. "Look, you unhygienic robber, let's get on the same boat here. I'll let you live, but you steer clear of me and my sheila, who isn't my sheila, but it really doesn't matter what you think. I've killed better men than you on three continents. I can make it four."

I pushed Maria a slice of bread. "You all right?"

She shivered.

I shoveled blueberries into my mouth with my slice of bread.

"Any trouble last night after they locked me up?"

She shook her head.

I paused my purposely-ignore-them-so-they-think-I-don't-care-act to take a quick peek at the outlaws' reaction to my little speech. They were giving me and Maria plenty of space at the table.

I lowered my voice. "Maria, I've never seen you miss a chance to talk. What's wrong?"

She laughed, a little too long and a little too loud, like Mother laughs before she goes into hysterics because the maid spilled gravy on Mother's dress.

"How can you ask me what is wrong? These are ruffians. They can do anything to us they want. Anything."

"Don't worry," I said. "They won't get ransom money if they hurt us."

"Who's going to ransom me?" Maria said. Red tinged her eyelids. "Do you really think they'll wait for a ship to get to England, then all the way back here?"

"Probably not, but who said anything about going to England for ransom money?"

"I don't know anyone in Australia who would ransom me."

I raised my eyebrows. "Why of course, Law and Nobody will do it, if it comes to that."

"Why would they? They don't care about me. You only brought me with you because you were afraid I was going to tell them where Elyssa was. You don't care about me, you don't trust me."

She put her face in her hands.

I chewed another blueberry.

I never want to be captured with a girl, but if it has to happen, couldn't it be Pacarina? She has a real head on her shoulders.

"Look, Maria, I can't say we exactly hang on your every word, or that I haven't at times considered asking Pacarina to gag you, or that I have confidence in your—" this probably wasn't the best approach.

"What I mean to say is, trust doesn't happen in a day. You have to earn it. Whether we trust you or not, we're not going to let anybody hurt you. Law and Nobody will absolutely ransom you if they have to."

I pulled her hands away from her face and leaned close to whisper.

"I'm going to get you out of here. You have my word as a gentleman. Better yet, as a Stoning. I need you to trust me and be brave, because if you don't, you're going to get us both killed. Understood?"

She sniffed and nodded.

I'm sure our little tête-à-tête didn't help convince the bushrangers there was nothing between me and her, but what can a fellow do?

Chapter 15
Lawrence

"Snake."

I jumped away from the campfire.

Jacques dangled something towards me. "I took off zhe vile creature's head. Vhat kind of snake you call zhis?"

I gulped and made myself look at the creature. Jacques held its tail at head-level and the snake's body reached the ground. The body was dark brown, with no color markings and a pattern like form-fitting scale armor.

"*Pseudonaja textilis*," I said. "It's often called a common brown snake."

"Common brown snake? Zhat does not sound dangerous. Is it poisonous?"

"Well." I tried to smile. "'Poisonous' means you have to eat it to be affected. So, no, it's not 'poisonous.' But it is one of the most venomous land snakes in the world."

"So, ve can eat it?" Jacques asked.

O'Malley snorted. "The French have nivir found a disgusting beast as they didn't want tae eat."

We camped in foothills where the outlaws' trail led us. We would not have ridden twenty yards from the settlement if finding the trail was my job, but Squad One applied years of experience tracking Cossacks on Siberian steppes and so far, they were confident we were taking the right path. Until now. The trail led out of the parched grass which cracked under hooves into a rocky stretch which left not a clue. That's why we camped on the other side of the rock, with hopes of re-finding the trail when light came again.

O'Malley tossed me another strip of kangaroo meat from the rack over the fire. "Tae bad Saint Patty nivir made it tae this island. That's the third snake as I've seen today, an' no mistake."

"I think the weather is changing," Nobody said. "I can feel it in my bones."

I grinned. "You sound like an old man, Nobody."

He laughed. "Have somebody break your shoulder with a bullet and don't let it heal right, and you'll feel a bit older yourself."

It was good to hear him joke about his shoulder. I know he went through a dark time, especially in Greenland, and even now he rarely mentioned it.

I attended to my kangaroo meat. The first couple times we ate the hopping beasts we cooked the meat too long and dried it out. This time Jacques halved the fire time and it was tender and juicy like a good cut of exotic beef.

If Nobody was right, and rain was coming, I wondered what the water would do to the terrain. I laid back under the half-shelter Pacarina and I shared and gazed at the canvas above me.

The endless parade of new sights and sounds helped distract my mind from the reason we were here, but I always came back to it, like now. The Assassins.

Were they already in Australia? They might be slinking through Sydney's streets this very moment.

"Do you know," I said to Pacarina, "I almost feel like an old campaigner myself. Spain, Peru, Greenland, Australia. There are generals who can't count that many campaigns."

Pacarina propped her chin on her arm and smiled at me in the firelight. "Don't forget surviving a London Society season."

I groaned. "Survived, but scarred."

It was a joy to just lie there, the fire toasting my feet, the shelter-canvass blocking the wind, Pacarina at my side. Poor Chester. And Maria. I doubted they were this comfortable.

"Who is there?" Jacques called.

I scrambled from the shelter. Outlaws? Assassins?

A form emerged from the dark. An Aborigine.

The man's bare chest was thatched with thick gray hair, the same color as his scraggly beard. He held a spear in his right hand, the spear-head pointing at the sky, which hopefully meant he didn't plan to bury it in any of our chests. He was a duller black than an African, with white chalk in smears from head to toe.

We were all on our feet. Nobody and Squad One fingered their pistols, but no one drew. How many more Aborigines scrutinized us from the gloom?

The man dropped his spear-butt to earth and leaned on the pole. He stared at Nobody.

"Hello," Nobody said.

The Aborigine stared.

Colonel Nobody removed his hand from his pistol. "Do you speak English?"

"You need guide." The Aborigine's words were thick, but discernable. His eyes showed no emotion.

"Why do you say that?"

"I follow you many days."

Jacques muttered something. Was he the thing I saw moving in the grass when we camped and threw boomerangs?

"I will pay you," Nobody said, "to track the men who burned the houses."

The Aborigine nodded. "Leave tonight. Not safe here."

"Why?" Colonel Nobody asked.

"Hunting grounds."

Colonel Nobody snapped his fingers. Jacques and O'Malley kicked dirt onto the fire and grabbed their bedrolls.

"Noble?" I said. "What's going on?"

"It sounds like we're in a tribe's hunting grounds. Probably not this fellow's tribe." He tightened the leather straps that held his wrist-plates in place. "They won't take kindly to us being here."

"But, I thought the land was at peace?"

Colonel Nobody snorted. "Take it from a man who grew up among a dozen people groups in Siberia. 'Peace' and 'war' have loose definitions. This fellow is a Godsend. If he gets us to the outlaws, we'll make him a rich man."

The Aborigine pointed at Pacarina. "No baby."

Pacarina tightened her hold on Otho.

"What do you mean?" I asked.

"No take baby. Make noise. They find us." He dragged his finger across his throat.

I looked at Nobody to know what to do.

He held a pistol towards me, grip first. "You'll want this."

I gulped. "I'm not sure this is a wise idea."

Nobody locked eyes with me. "He knows the country better than we do. Stay hidden and safe and we'll come back to you as soon as we get Chester."

If the Aborigine could get us to the outlaws, that was our best chance. The weak part of the plan was me, Lawrence Stoning, hiding under some Australian bush with a pistol in my hand trying to keep my family alive. It does seem the goal of most of the people in my life is to put me in situations where I have to do or be prepared to do something excessively physical. If we survived this adventure, I deserved to spend at least two years in no more danger than being hit by a falling book.

I waved a sad farewell to the fire and cozy shelter and shouldered my pack.

Chapter 16
Chester

"Chester!"

"Hmm?"

My pile of tumbleweed rustled. I shaded my face with my sleeve and popped one eye open to see why Maria disturbed my nap.

She crested my tumbleweed heap panting.

"You said you wanted to talk to me alone," she said.

I groaned. "Yes, I said I wanted to talk to you alone, which means discreetly, which means somewhere these ruffians won't notice, which means not on top of a pile of tumbleweed in the middle of the yard."

"Oh." She stood half-buried in the tumbleweed and stared at me.

"Well, it's too late now. Sit down."

"In this?"

I blinked. "Do you want me to get you a chair?"

"Would you?"

"No."

She lowered herself into the tumbleweed. "Why do you want to talk to me?"

"I wanted to plan an escape, but since one of the bushrangers is walking towards us, no doubt wondering what we're palavering about, let's talk about something else. Pick something, quick."

"All right, um, how about love?"

"Love?" I gave my head a shake to clear the cobwebs. "Is that really the first thing that comes to your mind to talk about?"

She blushed. "Well, it's what we talk about at Court."

"Do I look like a giggling debutante with gigot sleeves and enough fabric round my waist to sweep a ballroom?"

I'm normally a patient man—scratch that, I'm not patient, but I'm not normally so impatient—but Maria has a way of getting to me like a flea on a dog's spine.

I took a deep breath. "Sorry, that wasn't gentlemanly."

"What's not gentlemanly?" The Scot stood at the base of our pile and shaded his eyes.

"Long story," I said. "Pull up some tumbleweed."

The Scot grinned and made himself a little nest close to mine. My perch wasn't exactly a two-person affair, but Maria wasn't leaving, so I shrugged and made do as best I could.

"I say," I said, "does my being kidnapped prevent me from enjoying a nap in the sun?"

"Not at all. In fact, I feel a bit drowsy myself." The Scot lay back with his hands behind his head. "If I fall asleep, what's to stop you from slitting my throat?"

I shrugged. "My brother Law would say that statistically speaking, this would be one of the worst times to launch an escape."

"You don't strike me as a man who cares about statistics."

I grinned. "You have me there. I don't particularly want to cut your throat. You seem a decent chap, minus the fact you're holding me against my will, and you're hoping to bankrupt my friends, and you cracked my head with your boomerang."

"Yes, minus those things."

"Why are you with these fellows? You don't seem their type. Why go in for the life of robbing, pillaging, and plundering, eh?"

The Scot pursed his lips. "There is no type, here. We come for all reasons. Some run into trouble with the law, some tire of living as convict slaves, some want something more exciting than whistling sheep between fields."

"Your reason?"

"Maybe I like freedom."

Maria made a little gesture with her left hand. I think it was the kind of thing ladies do in ballrooms with their fans when they're telling you they want to talk to you.

"Sir," Maria said, "have you sent someone yet to collect a ransom for us?"

The Scot shook his head. "We're waiting for Donovan. He'll decide what to do with you." He sat up. He wasn't grinning any more. "Look, I like you two. Bringing you here wasn't my idea. We have to live, but I don't like hurting other people in the process, and plenty of the lads follow my line of thinking. That's not Donovan. Don't try anything flippant with him or you may get a bullet in your head. You may anyway."

I grabbed a handful of tumbleweed to chew. "I actually have a bit of experience with despots. He doesn't think he's Caesar, does he?"

"No, he's more the Genghis Khan type."

Maria rustled the tumbleweed. "Did you say . . . Donovan?"

I blinked. "Hold on—is this Donovan's gang?"

The Scot nodded.

"Then this is all a huge mistake." I pointed to Maria. "She's Donovan's niece. We were in that village because we were trying to find Donovan. Ever heard of the Boy Colonel?"

"Who hasn't?"

"He's trying to find one of you outlaws, name of Jamie Burke. Do you know him?"

The Scot shifted the blade of grass in his mouth. "Never heard the name," he said.

"Well, we'll see what Donovan says."

"I don't know how Donovan feels about family, but if you're expecting him to be soft on you—don't."

Chapter 17
Chester

Donovan came that night.

The fellow rode into camp on the prettiest stallion I've ever seen, dismounted near one of the other two buildings in the compound, and swaggered towards the main cabin as if he owned the continent.

He was barely taller than my rifle, with a devil-may-care mustachio that flared up on either side of his nose. He wore pistols in a thick leather band around his lower stomach. I rather liked his style.

The yard was so chock-full of tumbleweed that he disappeared in it a couple times on his way to the cabin. He looked like the kind of fellow who's always searching for something to be mad about and does a really good job finding it.

It wasn't night yet, but the clouds were dark enough to fool you. Lightning crinkled the sky far away, then came thunder, loud like a man-of-war unloading on a Frenchy, then rain pitter-pattered just as Donovan reached the cabin.

"Donovan!"

Everybody yelled his name and generally made him look like a conquering general in a Roman triumph.

I sat on a stool in the corner and folded my arms. I don't like people who think too much of themselves. Especially when they get to decide if I die or live.

With the extra men who came with Donovan crowded into the cabin, the air stunk of sweat, bad enough that I could commiserate with Maria, who had a handkerchief over her nose and a hand on her forehead. We were pretty nearly hidden in the corner, but there were enough gaps between arms and bodies to show Donovan grab a mug of ale and empty the thing into his mouth. He flicked his mustache as he plunked the mug back on the table.

"Good hunting?" he said, saying the last word loud and full like he was trying to be the hearty back-thumper type. Sounded more like a mocking bird with a sore throat.

The bushrangers upended a chest over the table and poured out a hoard of coins, bracelets, lockets, bank notes, rings, and other thing-buying paraphernalia. There's no way it all came from the last raid. Must be the haul of a number of raids.

Donovan scooped handfuls of the stuff and grinned at his men. One of his teeth was gold, not the kind that looks old and rotten, but fresh and wealthy. Good, the left side of his mouth was the best place to punch him.

"And who," Donovan said, "had the brilliant idea to bring them here?" He poked his finger at me and Maria.

The bushrangers did a Red Sea parting routine and created a nice, wide path between Donovan and me. They also stopped chattering. No one took credit for our capture.

I shrugged. "What if I told you I thought your boys were a sightseeing expedition and joined for laughs?"

Donovan's mustache twitched. "You ever hear of Huneric the Vandal? He cut people's tongues out. Maybe I should go Vandal for a minute, eh?"

I laughed. The fellow was a show-off. Law made fancy historical mentions like that because his brain is so full it comes out naturally. This fellow wanted to impress his minions.

"Speak up," Donovan said. "Who brought them here?"

Half Beard cleared his throat. "I thought as you'd be happy," he whined. "The sheila's a Viscountess with more money than a Duke."

"Have I ever told you to kidnap someone?" Donovan said.

"Well, no, but—"

"You know why not? Because people get touchy about their people. They don't like it when big bad wolves like us come stealing their people, and they start pulling strings and complaining to governors and putting out search parties and other nasty things. Savvy?"

Half Beard grumbled and tugged at the cap in his hands. The thunder up above was something fierce, plus rain pounded the roof.

"And another thing. Here's this Jackaroo watching everything you do, remembering your faces, plotting out our whole camp. You think he'd shrug and forget where and who we are if we ransomed him?"

"We blindfolded him," Half Beard said.

"I wouldn't trust you to blindfold a mole," Donovan said. "We're not ransoming them. Neither of them. Kill the Jackaroo. The sheila isn't bad-looking, so anybody as takes a fancy to her can marry her."

Maria moved the handkerchief away from her face. "Uncle Donovan?"

Donovan stared at her. "Say what?"

"Are you Donovan Deveroux? I'm your niece, Maria."

"Maria?" He swaggered toward us and clenched her chin, holding her face up, even though he was her height. I prepared to tackle him if he tried anything funny with her.

"You're Henry's girl? You have his face. What are you doing here?"

"I didn't know you were . . ." she motioned to the outlaws around us.

Donovan barked a laugh. "So Henry never mentioned I found the fun side of the law? Figures. Not much for a youngest son in our beautiful family to do. Do you know, they wanted me to be a minister?"

Donovan let her chin go and sighed. "It's just like Henry for one of his offspring to show up here and make trouble for me. Fine. I'll get you a Passage back to England, but your father had better repay me for my trouble." He jerked his head at me. "He a long lost nephew?"

"He's a friend," Maria said.

"Not my problem, then. Too mouthy to trust. You keep yourself quiet about what you see here, girl, if you know what's good for you."

Ah. So that was how it would be. I gritted my teeth. I'd always hoped that when my time came, someone like Law would be around to write about how I went berserk. Oh, well.

The way my arms were folded, no one could see that my thumbs and forefingers gripped sheathes beneath my sleeves. I was a flick and a shake away from having two knives in my hands. I would cut down the chaps between me and the left wall, run up the wall and jump off it into the crowd. From there, improvise. Free-fight.

Half Beard pointed a pistol at my head.

"Not in my house!" The old cook thrust her shaggy head through the bushrangers standing in front of the fireplace. "I ain't wiping blood off my floor. If you've got to kill the nice boy, kill him outside."

"Shut your mouth," Half Beard said. "I'm not going out in the rain when I can kill the Jackaroo comfortable inside."

"You do, and I'll poison you," the cook said.

I should be grateful to the old woman for fussing about them killing me, but somehow it would have felt nicer if it was for some other reason than her not wanting my corpse to dirty her floor.

Half Beard hesitated. I think the old lady really would poison the rascal.

"I ain't digging a grave in a blooming thunderstorm."

"Stop," Maria said. Everyone looked at her, me included. She trembled. "You can't kill him. He's my friend."

"Girl," Donovan said, "do you think I care? I'd put you in the ground if it weren't bad luck to kill family. Thank your stars we're not digging a grave for you."

Maria wavered, her head swiveling between me and Donovan. Then she dropped her handkerchief and put her arm through mine.

"If you kill him, you'll have to kill me too."

The Scot cleared his throat. "Why don't we throw them in the cellar until the sky clears? Give the girl time to think it through?"

Donovan waved. "Fine, get them out of here. I haven't had a decent dram in three days."

Chapter 18
Chester

The door slammed, and Maria and I were alone in the cellar.

Thunder cracked and groaned, and more rain puddles slammed the roof. Sometimes rain sounds like drummers banging on the roof, and tonight's drummers had fire in their veins.

The cellar was about large enough to lie in either direction. I knew because I tested it last night. Now, it could have been five miles wide for all I could see.

I folded my arms and talked in the general direction Maria must be.

"What are you thinking? He said he wouldn't kill you. You need to go back up there and apologize this instant."

"He can't kill you," Maria said.

"No, he can, and he's going to if I'm still here in the morning. This isn't *Ivanhoe*, this is real life."

"I know," Maria said. "I'm—I'm terrified. But I can't just stand by and watch them kill you. Is that who you think I am?"

I grabbed my beard with both hands. "To be brutally honest, yes. You think this is all some fairy tale of an adventure. You faint every other day."

"Do you think I *want* to faint? Do you think I like people laughing behind my back because they've seen me flop like wet newspaper? My body does it, I don't know what's wrong with me. My head goes all funny and then everything goes black."

I blinked into the dark. This was a Maria I never met before.

"I know I'm not like the rest of you," Maria said. "I don't know how to be. None of this is like—like how I grew up. Like Society. But I want to be like you. I don't want to be featherbrained. Yes, I've heard you call me that, and I know it's true. I want to be like Pacarina. If she were here, she would stand up for you, wouldn't she?"

I breathed a deep draught of musty air. "She would."

Maria didn't say anything more, but her breathing was loud enough to hear between the thunder booms.

I coughed. "I'm sorry. Maybe—maybe I've misjudged you." I shook my head, trying to get my scattered thoughts back. "Look, I'd like to delay my violent death by a few decades. That means I'm going to try to escape. You can come with me if you want, but we'll probably both get slaughtered."

"Don't leave me," Maria said. She grabbed my hands. "Please, don't leave me."

I grunted. "Right, then. I have a plan. A plan that requires the use of my hands . . ." I flexed my fingers to remind her to let go.

A spot of liquid wet my hand. Could be a leak in the cellar roof—so, two roofs—or it could be Maria crying. Not much of a choice there. I freed my hands and gave her an it's-all-right-we're-not-going-to-die pat.

My first task when locked up is always to find all exits, then figure out which is the weakest. I did that last night. Cellars are easy. Easy to identify the exits, I mean, since there's only one. Not easy to get out of.

It would take minutes of kicking and shoulder smashing to break the door and by that point I'd have half a dozen weapons ready to shoot me regardless of what the cook threatened. Hmm. How many is half a dozen? I always mix up my math. At any rate, enough bullets to make my heart a sieve.

The only other exit was through the walls. They were stone, but probably just loose stone facing to keep dirt from collapsing in. I could use the thunderstorm as cover and take a whack to find out.

I moved Maria to a corner where she wouldn't be impaled, took my longest knife, and scraped the wall until I found a crumbly spot between two stones. I jammed my knife into it. The knife broke through the mortar and lodged in dirt. Hurrah!

I went to work like a counter-miner going out from a castle to meet and destroy the fellows mining in. It took an hour to scrape enough stone from the wall for a person to squeeze through once I dug out the dirt. I built the stones and dirt into a platform until the hole was chest-high.

"Are you scared?" Maria asked.

Whenever someone asks you if you're scared, you know they are. Which I knew anyway since her teeth were clattering like a cold woodpecker on marble.

"Too busy to be scared," I said.

I had to keep talking to get her mind off fear.

"I really don't think I was born to be killed by some second-rate Australian land pirates. Ancient Romans would have made a good story, even Mayamuras add a bit of flavor to the retelling, but not robbers. Plus, I always wanted to die with Law. That's going to be complicated since he wants to die in bed with a book."

I shrugged.

"Maybe we can go to Japan after this. Getting disemboweled by a Samurai sounds pretty exciting. Now, I wouldn't be opposed to a non-deadly wound tonight, maybe a knife slash or a bullet in the arm or something. Colonel Nobody has a splendid old wound, and even Law has a little scar from that slash he got when we met Pacarina."

"I wouldn't like to see you get hurt," Maria said.

"Thanks." I stopped knifing the wall. I didn't want to say this, but had to. "Look, you know that I—I don't like—I mean, we're not—"

"I know," Maria said. "But we can be friends?"

I paused. "Honestly, yes, I think we can be friends. You have my word on that. Now let's get out of this place."

The last few inches of topsoil were sticky mud. It oozed between my fingers, dripped onto my face—scratch that, it sloshed and poured and dumped over my face, so by the time my hand broke through the ground, I was pure mud from head to waist.

I climbed down from my hole and wiped some of the mud from my lips.

"You ready?" I said.

Nothing.

"If you're nodding, I can't see," I said.

"I'm ready."

She sounded about as ready as Oxford is ready to make me a professor, but oh well. Nothing risked, nothing lost.

"I hope you like mud," I said.

I swam through the mud and heaved myself to the surface. I dug my boots into the muck, leaned over the hole, and hauled Maria up beside me.

If any poor souls had lookout duty they were hugging trees and cursing Donovan. I had to hope that was true because the lighting flashes may as well have been blinks of sunlight, they were that bright.

We were on the far side of the house, about thirty feet from a wooden fence that marked the end of the compound's clearing. Five seconds and we would be there.

That was before somebody plowed into my back and buried my face in mud. My body tingled. Finally, a chance to prove what I felt about the bushwhackers on one of their bodies.

I lay limp for a second to make the fellow think I was stunned, then jammed both elbows up into his ribs and heaved him off me.

"Oof."

I jumped into a fighting stance. Lightning cracked, and I almost saw the man before his legs swept mine from under me and landed me on my back. I might have blacked out if the ground had been hard where my head hit, but it was mud. I rolled over, grabbed my shirt collar, and ripped down so I could reach the knife in my sleeve.

The fellow leaped onto me and grabbed my throat. His body pinned my right arm to my chest, so I grabbed at his hands with my left hand and tried to stop him from crushing my windpipe. His fingers were deep in my skin, squeezing my air passages shut.

"*Boeuf*," he said.

I choked. I mean, obviously I was choking, but I also choked with surprise.

"Jacques?" I gurgled.

The hands froze. "Stoning Number Two?"

"Stop—strangling—me."

"Ah, yes."

The hands released and I took a few moments to pump air back in my lungs. I wonder if not having oxygen does damage to your brain. Must ask Law about that.

"You—zhat is to say, I did not recognize you. You look positively disgusting. I assumed you must be one of zhese robber barbarians."

"I'm muddy because I just dug out of a cellar in a thunderstorm, and I'll add that I don't remember seeing your helping hands at the top."

Jacques made that sound Frenchies make when they think something is good. Kind of like a happy hen saying 'oh-hoh!'

"You must admit zhat I beat you. A few seconds more and I vould have destroyed you."

"A temporary advantage, and very unsportsmanlike, by the way, kicking my legs out."

Maria's breath tickled the hair on the back of my neck. "Shouldn't we go?"

Sounded like something Law would say. Fact is, it really wasn't the best place and time to worry about keeping Jacques' towering self-importance under control.

"What's the plan?" I asked.

"It is good to see you as vell." Jacques harrumphed. "Zhe plan is zhat I vatch for lookouts here vhile zhe ohzers smoke zhe barbarians out."

"Hist," O'Malley whisper-shouted from the roof. "Are ye ready, ye crazy Frog?"

The plan instantly made sense. Clog the chimney and give the rascals a good smoking until they barrel out the door coughing and crying, and then the fun begins. Great plan, except I was already outside so now the last thing we wanted to do was scramble them out here.

Lightning lit the compound and showed me O'Malley and Nobody on the roof next to the chimney. They were stuffing something into it. Men inside shouted.

I shoved Maria's hand into Jacques's hands. "Take her to the horses."

I had to get on the roof fast to tell them I was already out. I can run up many walls and I thought about trying it here, but I couldn't build the speed I need while running through a swamp.

I ran round to the chimney-side and shimmied the chimney by gripping the crevices between the stones with my feet, knees, and hands. The rain scraped most of the mud from my face so Nobody and O'Malley recognized me by the light of a lightning bolt.

I shook Nobody's hand. "Thanks for coming for me."

"Looks like you had things under control."

I shrugged. "The thought of a bullet in the head is a great inspirer."

The cabin door creaked open and firelight washed a swath in front of the door. Boots squelched the mud as the bushwhackers ran out cursing and hacking. Colonel Nobody grabbed my arm and pointed to the back of the house. Jacques and Maria were mounted, leading three more saddled horses. Colonel Nobody thought of everything.

I jumped onto one of the beasts and waited for Nobody and O'Malley to climb down. The horse side-stepped away from the thunder-crashes. I yanked the reins to keep him from bolting.

"Please tell me we get to ride through the blackguards," I said.

"No other way out. Let's go."

O'Malley raised his hand. "Can we gallop, Colonel?"

Colonel Nobody laughed. "Yes, we can gallop. Forward!"

We dashed around the corner and cut through the outlaws, bowling them into the muck like wickets before a cricket ball. We were out of the compound and on the mountain path before they gathered enough wits to do anything, and it didn't really matter how many wits they had, since Jacques said he loosed all of their other horses into the storm.

Chapter 19
Lawrence

After the others left, I hunted for a place to hide. I found one in a tight little valley between two hills, where scraggly bushes half-hid a depression in the ground large enough to hold Pacarina, Otho, and me. I spread a piece of canvas over the bushes and covered it with more bushes I uprooted a few yards away.

The air smelled like rain. When it did rain I wanted something between us and the sky. We crawled into the little shelter and I must say I was rather proud of my accomplishment. It was cozy, blocked off from the wind and altogether rather nice. Snakes might also appreciate it . . . no, don't think about snakes.

Pacarina spread a blanket on the dirt and we folded our legs and sat Oriental-style beneath the canvas.

"This is cozy," Pacarina said.

"That's one word to describe it."

Pacarina chuckled. "You're too hard on yourself, Law. You're thinking right now that you're a bad husband because you've brought your wife into the middle of the Australian wilderness."

I coughed. "Well, Dear—"

"No. I don't want to hear it. I love this crazy life I have with you, and I wouldn't trade it for the world."

"I sometimes still think you married the wrong Stoning brother."

She giggled. "I see *quite* enough of Chester as a brother-in-law, thank-you very much."

"I wonder if our little Otho will take after his Uncle Chester." Otho was bundled into a heap of blanket between us. I tweaked the fabric away from his hand and eased my pinkie into his grasp. He grabbed it in his sleep. Pacarina frowned at me with fake—mostly fake—anger at the possibility of me waking him.

"How would you handle being separated from me like Nobody and Liana?" Pacarina asked.

I rubbed Otho's hand between my thumb and index finger. "About as well as you would do away from this little fellow."

She smiled down at him. "Sometimes I just can't believe this little miracle. He's our *child*, Law. I had almost stopped hoping."

"God is good."

"Sometimes I wonder if I love him too much." She grinned. "Then I see that little crinkle between his eyebrows, and I don't think it's possible. Oh, speaking of Nobody, have you given him any advice yet?"

"About?"

"Getting married."

I scratched my head. "Honestly, that thought never entered my brain. Why, have you advised Liana?"

"Reams and reams of advice. She's going to need it, too. Noble is a sweetheart, but he won't be an easy man to live with."

I choked a little. "'Sweetheart' isn't quite the word I'd use, but all right. You think he'll be harder to live with than me?"

She patted my shoulder. "I wouldn't try it for the world. He's been leading and killing men his whole life, however long that is. Never knew his parents, he's had friends die for him, others betray him. I know that shoulder of his not working really bothers him. Don't get me wrong, I think the world of him, but he gets in that mood sometimes where he thinks everyone is automatically going to do what he says. Which they do, generally. But still. Not an easy man to live with."

I nodded. "I can see that. Do you think Liana is up to the task?"

"If anyone is, she is. And he absolutely treasures her. I can't wait to see them finally married. I just hope he doesn't decide to put a bookcase in front of their window . . ."

I shook my head. "We already have a window in that room, and it saves steps to have the 17th-century poetry closer to the desk . . ." I paused. "All right, you win. If we get home in the next decade, we can leave the window bookcase-less."

As the hours passed, dusk came before its time. I pulled the canvas over the opening in the bushes and piled rocks on the edge inside our shelter to keep the wind from tearing it away.

The world was black long before night fell. Rain would be falling back home in Herefordshire, but here the storm was building its courage, preparing a mighty blast to balance the months or perhaps even years since the last rain.

"This is good," I said. "Based on what I know of native superstitions, the Aborigines will likely sequester themselves in some nook and pray to the gods of lightning until the storm passes. The outlaws will be under shelter, and that gives our party the perfect conditions to surprise them."

Or be hit by lightning. If anyone were to be struck, which was unlikely, it would be O'Malley.

The rain came in a torrent. One second the world was dry, the next, it was wet. I held both hands beneath the canvas, like Moses on the mountain, to keep it from sagging onto our heads, and the cold of the rain pooling on the canvas transferred through the material into my hands.

"Do you hear that?" Pacarina asked.

"I hear a very loud thunderstorm."

Ache built in my elbow-crooks. I grabbed Chester's kangaroo hat, put it on, and used my head as another prop. It was too dark for Pacarina to see that I was holding up the roof, which was all right, as that was my job, but I would have to ask her to relieve me soon.

"No, something else. I hear water."

I frowned. Pacarina wouldn't state something so obvious as that she could hear the rain. Maria might, but not Pacarina.

Pacarina gripped my shoulder. "I hear water rushing."

I heard it too. Roaring, spewing water close and coming closer. It sounded like a river, but there was no river here. I squeezed my eyes shut, thinking, thinking. What could it be? Wait . . . there was no river here when it was dry, but this downpour was changing the topography back to what it was when there was water. I looked at the ground between my feet.

"Oh, no."

I realized mentally what I had done one second before the physical reality crashed into us.

Water slammed me onto my back, then engulfed me and spun me away. I tried to grab Pacarina or Otho but the canvas wrapped round my limbs and head like a net. *Which way is up?* I kicked and punched at the canvas to free myself, to find air. My head and legs whirled round each other like a child's top. At any moment my skull could bash into a rock. Pain stabbed my right knee and I couldn't kick.

The urge to breathe fought the urge to keep water out of my mouth. I willed my mouth and nostrils to stay shut, to resist the core need to channel oxygen into my lungs.

My left fingers scraped the edge of the canvas. I tore down and floundered into the gap.

My head burst into the air and I gulped the gas of life. Something less dark than the water flashed past me on the left and I swam through the churn to solid land. I dug my fingers into the mud, then elbows, fighting against the flash flood's grip. I kicked my stiffened right leg onto the bank and hauled myself out.

My body wanted to lie there trembling and breathing until time ended, but I had to find Pacarina and Otho.

The foaming water gashed the night. Several dark bulks raced towards me through the flood. A bush, a tree, a chunk of dirt and sticks—there she was.

Pacarina was in the water twenty feet upstream and moving towards me fast.

"Lawrence!" she gurgled.

"Hold on!"

I dropped to my knees and elbows in the mud and dug my toes into the dirt like a sprinter coiling for a race.

Pacarina was a yard from the bank. I waited until her head came parallel with my position, then thrust myself into the water and grabbed for her. Her upper body slipped through my grasp, but I wrapped my arms around her waist and used her forward momentum to spin her towards the bank.

I locked my fingers over Pacarina's hip and pivoted with my legs, barely feeling my right knee, rolled onto my back, and dragged her from the water onto my chest. Pacarina lay still and soundless on me.

My limbs trembled with shock and lack of oxygen, but I forced myself onto my knees and leaned over her. I pressed my index and middle finger over the carotid artery in her neck.

"Breathe!" I yelled.

The rain, the crashing thunder, the roar of the water just behind us—I couldn't feel anything. I wiped away mud slick and pressed deeper, willing her heart to beat, her lungs to expand.

A pulse!

Pacarina's head jerked and water spewed from her mouth. She coughed.

I grabbed her shoulders. "Can you hear me?"

Sloppy coughs racked her body, then she relaxed, her head bending towards me.

A wail pierced the thunder-rolls. Otho wriggled out of her clutch and grabbed my shirt.

I grasped him with one hand and wrapped my other arm around my wife's shoulders, burying my face in her dripping hair. Thank God. They were safe.

"I'm all right," she wheezed.

I held her to me, trying to warm her freezing shoulders and neck.

"I should be shot," I said. "I should be hung and quartered. I should be written as an example of utmost stupidity for the lowest, dullest dunce in any logic class to understand exactly how low the human intellect can sink."

Pacarina half coughed, half laughed. "Law, you didn't cause the flood."

"No, but I did camp us in the middle of a dry stream bed on the cusp of a raging thunderstorm. Of course it was a nice depression in the country side. It's indented because that's where the water runs! How can I be so mentally void?"

She patted me. "You thought you were doing what was best."

"If I had thought at all I would have seen what any boy not yet out of his skirts could see."

"Law, stop it. It was an easy mistake to make. I know you would never do anything not meant to keep me safe."

I exhaled. I still had half a dictionary of insults to belabor myself with for my stupidity, but this was not the time.

"And," Pacarina said, "you pulled off a miracle worthy of Chester."

"What?"

"You're still wearing his hat."

"Yes, I—" I stopped. I heard something.

I thought at first that it was thunder, but the sound was too regular, and approached. I strained to hear over the torrent beside me. Hoof beats. Horsemen were riding towards us.

Chapter 20
Lawrence

My sword and pistol were miles downstream by now. I patted my dripping clothes, searching for a weapon. Maybe Chester hid a knife on me. No, no knife.

A lightning flash showed me a splintered tree on the bank. One of the river's unpredictable eddies must have thrown it ashore. I grabbed a branch about four inches in diameter and gripped it like I would a cricket bat. If the riders were outlaws, I would protect Pacarina and Otho as best I could.

Two horsemen rounded the corner. There was no time to hide, and even if there was, Otho's cries would have given us away.

I stepped between Pacarina and the horsemen and raised my hands.

The horsemen reined back their horses and grabbed rifles from saddle-holsters. One pranced his horse in a circle, looking on all sides as if expecting an ambush, while the other kept his gun trained on us.

Rain dripped from the rims of their wide-brimmed hats and splashed on full-length cloaks.

"It's him," one of them said. His accent was Russian.

I edged back against Pacarina, my banged knee twinging, trying to make myself look as unthreatening as possible. I was coated in mud, weaponless, with a woman and baby. What more could I do?

"Don't shoot," I said. "It's just us. My wife, my baby—we're not a threat to you."

The man who had pranced his horse urged the beast towards me. "You killed my brother," he said, snarling.

What was he talking about? A dead brother—this was the Assassins. This must be the man Bogdan mentioned, the one whose brother Chester killed. Of course he would be one of the first two Assassins who found us.

"I haven't killed any of you!" I said. "We want the same thing. We can negotiate. None of us wants to become Tsar."

"Egor," the second man said.

Egor turned in his saddle. "We kill them all," he said.

"First we find out where the others are." The first man, who talked like someone accustomed to others doing what he said, walked his horse up to me. "Where is Nobody?"

"This whole thing is a mistake," I said. "Colonel Nobody doesn't want to become Tsar. We can work this out without bloodshed."

"And yet, you know who he is." The Russian leaned towards me. His eyes were cold as balls of ice. "Who does he tell next? The English queen?"

"He didn't even tell me, it was one of you Russians that forced the whole issue. Call a truce, we can talk this through and come up with something each side is happy with."

The other man, Egor, stepped his horse to my right. I shifted, trying to stay between them and Pacarina and Otho.

"I will not be happy," Egor said, "until you have paid for my brother's blood."

"I didn't kill your brother. That was my twin."

Egor shrugged. "Brother for brother."

The Russian in charge looked like he was thinking, based on the little I could make out in the moonlight and rain.

"Where are the others?" he asked.

I explained about Chester.

"And when they come back?" he said. "If my men have not come by then, and you outnumber me, why should I trust that you will still want to talk?"

Ah, so the rest of the Assassins weren't with him. They must have split into groups to search for us. I suppose that made these two stumbling onto us more statistically probable.

"When they return," I said, "I promise you, if you are willing to talk, we will talk, and figure this out. We want the same thing. I know we'll agree, but if for some strange reason we don't, I promise you that we will let you go in peace. After that, if you attack us, we will defend ourselves, but we will have a truce for now."

"Let it be so."

Egor whirled on the other man and spat Russian words. The leader stared him into submission, but Egor looked at me over his shoulder with murder in his eyes.

"The baby is yours?" the leader said to me.

My breath caught. I nodded.

"What do you call him?"

"Otho." I pointed to my wife. "Pacarina. I am Lawrence Stoning."

"I am Vlad." The Russian swung down from his horse. "Words are easy to promise. I want to be sure."

I looked back at him, my arms aching from still being in the air, not understanding.

"Give your baby to Egor."

Pacarina gasped. I lowered my arms.

"Absolutely not."

"If you try to run, or your friends attack us, Egor will kill your baby. If you don't give him your baby now, we will kill all of you now."

I shivered. My shirt clung to my chest and back in wet blobs. My hair stuck to my forehead. Vlad didn't look angry, like Egor. He spoke like a man setting terms for a business transaction. And I think that's how he felt about it.

"Please," I said. "Take me, but don't hurt my boy."

Vlad laughed. "I already have you. All of you. You have my word you will get your boy back if you honor the truce."

I turned to look at Pacarina. She shook her head, her eyes dilated. I wrapped my arms around her shoulders, nestling Otho between us.

"We have to," I said. "I promise, I will not let anything happen to him. We'll talk, they will realize Noble isn't a threat, and they will leave." I squeezed her arms. "Trust me."

Chapter 21
Chester

We were getting close to where Nobody said Law and Pacarina stayed. I slapped my trousers to knock off more of the crusted mud that dried there after tunneling last night. The sun felt good when it was drying me off early this morning, but now I wouldn't mind it hopping behind some clouds. At least, until I could get back to Law and see if he still had my hat.

We pushed the horses hard in case the bushwhackers were chasing us. The plan was to meet up with Law and then keep riding inland as fast as we could.

"Smoke," Nobody said, pointing ahead of us.

I stood up in my stirrups. Sure enough, there were some wisps above the trees in front of us. This was about where they said Law was supposed to be waiting.

"Hmm," I said. "I thought Law was supposed to be hiding in case there are Aborigines around?"

I pushed to the front of our adventuring party, leaving Maria with Jacques and O'Malley. Perhaps we shouldn't have already parted with our Aborigine scout.

We rode on a sort of ledge, quite wide, that separated the hill above us from a twenty-foot drop-off below us. There was a stream at the bottom of the hill, and then another hill on the other side of the stream. Torn-up trees and bushes littered the stream's sides. Must have flooded with all this rain.

The ledge wrapped round to the other side of the hill. I rounded the bend first and saw the fire I expected, and Law and Pacarina as expected—wait—why were they lying on the ground? I pulled on the reins. Were those—ropes? They were tied up.

Something moved on the other side of the fire. Two men stood up. Men with thick beards and cloaks. Assassins.

I jammed my heels into my horse's flanks and charged. I grabbed the reins in my left hand, freeing my right hand to draw a pistol from my saddle-holster.

Law yelled something, but I was also yelling, so I couldn't really hear it. This must be a trap. Law and Pacarina tied up as bait, a few of the Russian rascals here on the ground and more in the hills ready to shoot me. Who cares, I would rescue my family or die trying.

One of the Assassins kicked a log in the fire, spraying sparks and ash-clouds. My horse balked at the flames and drew up, jolting my arm just as I shot into the ash. No one yelled so I must have missed. I could just make out through the dust and smoke that the two Assassins were running into the trees on the edge of the campsite.

"Stop!" Law yelled.

I jumped off my horse, wanting to run after the rascals, but getting Law and Pacarina out of here had to be first priority. And Otho—he must be with Pacarina.

I slid to Law's side—the more jerkily I moved, the harder it was to put a bullet into me—and whisked a knife from my boot.

"No, no, no!" Law yelled.

"Good to see you, too," I said, slicing the ropes on his hands, then feet.

"Otho!" Law screamed. He tore past me towards the trees where the Assassins went.

"Law!" I yelled. Why on earth would Law run unarmed after two Assassins? That's my style, not Law's. . .

A feeling I can't describe grabbed my gut. I looked at Pacarina, still tied. She tore at the ropes, specks of blood flying beneath her fingernails, her eyes dilated and burning into the woods Law was running into.

She didn't have Otho.

I spun, looking around the camp for any sign of the baby, or a pile of clothes that might cover him. Colonel Nobody and the others were off their horses, some with rifles trained on the hill above us, some watching the hill across from us.

I ran for the woods, dropping my pistol to grab another from my belt, but before I reached the edge of the trees there was a yell. Law.

I stopped. Blood surged into my head, made me dizzy, made me barely feel the pistol in my hand, only half-drawn from my belt. What had I done?

Law stepped from behind a tree, a bundle clasped to his chest. He charged past me, ignoring me, and knelt beside Pacarina. Everything happened so fast that she was still bound, but Law held the bundle to her chest. The bundle wailed.

That has to be the sweetest sound I've heard in my life. I thought I'd killed Otho. I mean not shot him, but the Assassins must have had him for some reason and dropped him in the woods when they ran. If they'd killed him—I held my head. I don't know what I would have done. Law and Pacarina would never have been able to look at me again.

I tried to shake the thoughts away and knelt to help cut Pacarina loose.

"What were you thinking?" Pacarina said. She gripped Otho so tightly I wondered how he had the breath to scream.

"I saw you tied up—"

"It was a truce!" Law said. "They were willing to talk. You could have gotten us all killed. If they had killed Otho—"

"I'm sorry," I said. "I had to make a quick decision—"

"You had to use your head." Lawrence stood and pressed nose-to-nose with me. "You have to think, Chester. You can't always charge in and kill people. You know what happens when you do that. You remember Peru."

I blinked. Law was talking about when I killed Pacarina's father's servant because I thought he was kidnapping her. Law never brings that up because he knows how badly I feel about that.

"I'm sorry, Law. . ."

Law stepped back and wiped his forehead with his sleeve. "Look." He sucked a breath. "I'm not myself right now. You can't know what it feels like to be a father and—" he shivered. "This was our chance to talk our way out of this death-warrant. You just destroyed that chance because the only thing you know to do when you see something that looks like danger is to attack it. That doesn't always work. I need you to grow up and see that."

Chapter 22
Lawrence

"It's kill or be killed," Chester said. "Law of the jungle."

I swatted an uncategorized species of fly.

"Chester, I don't dispute the jungle's laws, but if you look around you may notice that we are not in a jungle."

Chester shrugged. "It's a meta-thingy."

"A metaphor?"

"Right. Either we kill the Assassins, or the Assassins kill us. But since you want to visit the jungle, I can put together an expedition after we survive this adventure."

I raised my hand. The sun was less intense now that we were riding in the mountain's foothills.

"Chester, if God is merciful to us and grants us life through this crazy nightmare, we need to have a very serious conversation about the advisability of ever going farther than one mile from home again."

"Oh, sure, if you want to go somewhere else we can definitely talk about it. Africa would be good. I need to learn how to firewalk. Africa probably has firewalkers as thick as malaria."

Pacarina laughed. She urged her horse between ours. "You still need to learn a few things about what not to say when encouraging Law to travel."

I smiled. Sometimes, on beautiful days like this when the sun warmed the back of my head, and exotic smells wafted through my nostrils, and strange new animal sounds joined nature's orchestra, sometimes on days like this, I could understand what appealed to Chester. The adventure. The constant finding of new things, the occasional knowledge that no human feet have trod this ground for centuries, or ever. There is always something over the next horizon, and the adventurer must find out what it is.

It's the same feeling I have for books. With a new book between my fingers, I'm transported to a world of discovery, where each page may guide me to further depths of knowledge. Unless it's one of Chester's novels, in which case I call him to remove the contaminant from my library.

Nature was still fresh and wet. I felt part of a rebirth, a discarding of dust and a blooming of the true Australia. I tried to forget the fourteen Assassins following us.

"Halt," Colonel Nobody said. He twisted backward in his saddle astride a magnificent white beast which he said reminded him of his old horse in Siberia.

Colonel Nobody bent double and swung down from his horse. He snapped his fingers at us to do the same.

Naturally, I was the last off my horse, and by the time I was done, the others were leading their beasts to a grove fifty yards away. The hillcrest behind us blocked our view so whatever Nobody saw must be down in the valley on the other side of the crest. Assassins? I wet my lips. This place was too beautiful to die.

Squad One held the horses deep in the grove while Nobody, Chester, and I lay at the edge and studied the meadow.

"We're being followed," Nobody whispered. "I only saw one rider. Likely a scout."

"Are we going to kill him?"

"Capture."

I rested my chin on my thumbs and waited. The litter of leaves and grass was comfortable to lay on, but I found myself wondering what undiscovered species of spiders and death-striking insects might be sneaking towards my trouser legs. And snakes. Don't think about snakes.

A head and shoulders appeared over the crest, followed by the rest of the man's body and the horse he rode. He didn't seem particularly alert for a scout. His torso bounced a little with each step and he chewed a blade of grass. A rifle poked from a holster in his saddle.

Chester jabbed me below the ribs.

"I know him," he whispered. "Let me handle this." He waited until the rider was opposite us, then he stood and strolled from the trees. "Beautiful day."

The scout's head jerked up and his hand reached for his rifle butt, then stopped. He shifted the blade of grass to the other side of his mouth.

"You get around," he said. He had a touch of Scottish brogue.

Chester grinned. Rather, I assume he did, but I only saw his back from my place with the spiders and insects. It would be just like Chester to pick this time to have a long, leisurely conversation.

"Any particular reason you took your horse for a stroll in this part of the world?" Chester said.

"Looking for you. Donovan doesn't take kindly to his property running off. Not to mention rumors about strange fellows roaming the hills. It's put Donovan in quite a flap, it has."

"Well, you found us. What do you plan to do about it?"

The Scot shrugged. "That is the question, isn't it?" He jerked his head at the grove. "You might want to tell your friends in there that funnel-web spiders like burrowing around tree roots."

I jumped up and joined Chester. "Are you an Assassin?" I asked.

The Scot blinked. "Usually people ask if I'm an outlaw and I get to tell them 'bushranger' sounds more romantic, but . . . 'assassin?' That's quite the imagination you have."

Colonel Nobody was right behind me. "We don't mean you any harm. Leave us alone, and we'll let you be. The strange men you're talking about are Russian Assassins, and they're after us."

The scout leaned forward, resting the bottoms of his arms on his horse.

"You'd be Colonel Nobody, then. Your friend mentioned you. You have quite the reputation, even here."

"I'm flattered," Colonel Nobody said. He sounded about as flattered as a cook told his porridge wasn't burned too much. "Are you here to help us?"

"Why would I help you?"

"You didn't stumble into a trap. You intended to be here, however nonchalantly you're acting. And that Deringer you're holding in your left hand says you're ready for however we react."

I flinched.

The Scot smiled without losing the grass in his teeth and opened his left palm. A hand-sized pistol dropped into the grass.

"Sharp eyes, Colonel." He shaded his eyes with a cupped hand. "Truth is, Donovan and me are at loggerheads at the moment. That rascal Colin—he's the one who almost stuck his dirk through your hand, Stoning—has him fooled into thinking it's my fault we grabbed you and his niece."

"So you think the safest place to be is with the people you kidnapped?" I said.

The Scot shrugged. "You seem like a decent chap, and your friends don't seem too bloodthirsty. Could have slaughtered us in that cabin if you'd had a mind to."

Colonel Nobody looked at Chester. "Do you believe him?"

Chester nodded. "I rather like the fellow. He's one of very few chaps that's ever knocked me unconscious."

I didn't quite see the correlation there, but Chester's logic is not always linear.

"Do you have a name?" Nobody asked.

"Most people call me Scot, but you have your fancy 'Nobody' hullabaloo. So, you can call me Somebody."

Colonel Nobody stared at him for a long ten seconds. The Scot seemed as cool as one of my cats at home licking itself clean.

"What are you running from?" the Scot asked. I'll call him the Scot because "outlaw" is generic, and I'm not calling him Somebody. One misused pronoun as a name is more than enough in any single group of people.

"We're not running," Chester said. "We're strategically repositioning ourselves."

"You need a place to hide?"

"A place to defend."

The Scot spit the grass blade away. "I know a place in the mountains. Food, weapons, it has everything you need."

I cleared my throat. "Yes, and no doubt lots of your friends waiting to kill us."

"I don't think anyone is there. It's where we go when the settlers and soldiers get mad enough to come hunting."

"And, why would you help us?"

The Scot cocked an eyebrow. "Maybe your colonel isn't the only man who likes to be mysterious."

Colonel Nobody snapped his fingers. "Chester, get his weapons." He put his arm around my shoulder and turned away from the Scot. "Do you think we can trust him?"

I bit my lip. Logically, the outlaws would create a place of last resort, and if they did, it was the best place for us to be when the Assassins found us. But why was this fellow being so friendly? Maybe his friends really were after him. And maybe he thought there was safety in numbers against Russians in the hills.

"I don't trust him, but I think our best option is to go where he says, keeping both eyes very wide open."

Colonel Nobody nodded. "Agreed. Chester will be responsible for him."

I looked over my shoulder at the two of them. Chester was playing with the man's boomerang. I shook my head.

"There's something very odd about him," I said.

"The bushranger, or your brother?"

"Yes."

Chapter 23
Lawrence

"Has your brohzer asked you yet?" Jacques said.

I pushed my feet into the stirrups and lifted enough to shift my posterior. Days of horseback riding left me feeling like a caterpillar stuck on the bottom side of a drum skin.

"Asked me what?"

"Chemistry. He vas going to ask you how to make somezhing awful-smelling."

"Hush, Jacques." Chester pulled his horse even with Jacques and me. "Forget about that, priorities changed."

"What, you haf fallen in love vihz her now?"

The Scot, riding on my right flank, tipped his hat back from his eyes. "This sounds interesting."

Chester growled and looked over his shoulder. Pacarina and Maria rode about fifteen feet behind us.

"This *gallant*," Jacques said, "has been searching for every vay under zhe sun to keep zhe young noblewoman avay. Not zhat I could be of much aid, as zhe ladies do not exactly stay avay from me—" he preened. "And now, vhat, he no longer cares to keep her avay?"

"Aha," the Scot said. "So all that fuss you made about the two of you not being together, you meant all that?"

"Of course I meant it," Chester said. "Look, she's still not my favorite person in the world, but she grew a bit of a backbone. I think she deserves another chance. I think everybody deserves a second chance."

We were deep into the mountains now, riding through forests of eucalyptus trees which spiced the air with their scent. We came out of the trees to a scar of black rock. A river cut a deep channel on our left and rushed with what must be above average speed, swollen by the rain. The river was about thirty feet wide.

"Tell your Nobody," the Scot said, "this is it."

"Hallelujah," Chester said. He dug his heels into his horse's ribs and raced to Nobody's side.

Chester wasn't supposed to leave the Scot. I watched the outlaw for signs of attack or escape. He selected a new blade of grass from the handful perched on his pommel and pinched it with his lips. He cocked an eyebrow at me as if to say, 'I'm not going anywhere.'

"I don't see it," I said.

The Scot shrugged. "Did you expect a sign saying, 'welcome crazy English refugees?'" He pointed ahead. "This is our River Styx."

"You do know the Styx led to Hades, right?"

The Scot chewed his grass. "Maybe it will for the fellows following you."

The river narrowed into a channel between rock walls, with a ledge on the right side barely wide enough for my horse to walk, and only a foot or so higher than the water.

I reined my horse in next to Nobody's. We stared at the path.

"A single man could turn this into a death trap," Nobody said.

"That's what you asked for," the Scot said.

Colonel Nobody hunched forward, propping his left arm on his pommel, and stared into the Scot's eyes. His fingers brushed the pistol holster on his horse's neck.

"How do I know one of your friends hasn't already done so?" Nobody asked.

"We only use this place when there's nowhere else to go. The rest of the time the only people here are an old man and his wife."

"Both are well equipped to put a bullet in one or more of our brains," Nobody said.

Colonel Nobody's left fingers curled, ready to grab his pistol-butt. His horse's neck was between the holster and the Scot, so I don't think the Scot could see.

The cliffs on each side of the river looked like a knife cut them sheer up and down. They wrapped right and left like a steep bowl with a slice cut through one wall plopped upside down on a plateau.

I tapped Nobody and motioned with my eyes that we should send the Scot first. If a trigger-happy outlaw was sitting around the next bend, we had a better chance of survival if he shot the Scot first or didn't shoot because the Scot was there. Colonel Nobody took my suggestion and we rode in single file. A chill prickled my skin as I entered the deep shadow between the cliffs.

Colonel Nobody rode behind the Scot, then came Chester, me, Pacarina, and Maria. Jacques, O'Malley, and Petr guarded the rear. The passage bent left at about a forty-five-degree angle, enough to hide anyone who might be on the other side. Colonel Nobody kept his horse's nose touching the leading horse's flank as they rounded the bend.

There was no gunshot or death-scream, so I took that as a good sign. When my turn came I found the passage led straight for about twenty feet and then bent again to the right. The narrow passage forced the river down to three times less than its normal width, so the water raced through at—I don't know what speed. Fast. I could calculate the speed by dropping sticks in the water and measuring how quickly they went from point A to point B, then calculating how much the volume of the water below the surface affects the sub-surface velocity.

My horse stopped. I blinked out of my reverie to find that Nobody was also stationary and pointing two fingers at Jacques and O'Malley. The duo swung off their horses and crouched behind the first bend. Anyone to follow us around that bend was a dead man.

The passage was wider at the base than at the top, making the walls almost or actually impossible to climb. The dirty gray stone was too smooth to give many handholds. If anyone was above us, a few well-placed boulders would save the Assassins much work.

This was the perfect trap.

I fixed my eyes on the next bend and lay on my horse's neck. If I were defending this place I would have men waiting at this turn, I would have men above us ready to drop an avalanche, and I would have men waiting to slip behind us and cut off our retreat. The river would whisk our bodies away in seconds.

The Scot rounded the corner first. There was no shot. Of course not, his friends wouldn't shoot him. Colonel Nobody disappeared next. I gripped fistfuls of horse hair between my sweating fingers. Still no shots, and I was at the corner. If I was going to die, I would do it well, as Chester would say. I would grin in the face of death. I clenched my teeth, lifted my lips, and rode around the corner.

No one shot me.

"Lawrence, do you have a toothache?"

I opened my eyes.

The Scot and Nobody stopped in the path, watching me. I snapped my lips shut. Actually, that's the cliché for teeth. I did something actively with my lips to shut them and decided that was the last time I would grin in the face of death.

I looked past the Scot and Nobody, realized where we were, and my lips dropped open again.

The water poured from the passage into a river thirty yards wide. The river cut the plateau in half. Most of the space was covered by semi-tropical trees, but there was a wide strip of meadow on either side of the river. The plateau was maybe a quarter mile from cliff-edge to cliff-edge. The cliffs fell sheer to valleys hundreds of feet below.

A stone house sat halfway up the plateau on the left side of the river. We were to the right of the water, so the only way to reach the house was across the torrent.

The Scot pointed. "That's what you're looking for."

Boats tied together spanned the river across from the house.

"Are you outlaws or engineers?" I said. "That's a pontoon bridge. Remarkable."

"Donovan is a little bloodthirsty for my tastes, but he has a head for planning."

I sensed Pacarina and the others filing out of the passage behind us, but I couldn't tear my eyes away from this hidden world. It was Vallis Deorum, only much smaller and without the Ancient Romans. The bridge was made by anchoring two parallel lines of boats, tying them together, and using their buoyancy to support a five-foot wide plank bridge stretched from bank to bank. The brilliance of a pontoon bridge is that it rises and falls with the water level. As long as the anchors hold, it doesn't go anywhere. Cut the anchors, and the mini castle on the left bank has a rushing, hundred-foot wide moat.

The Scot grinned in his detached way. "Think of this as a peninsula. We came here on a mountain ridge. This is the end of the ridge, and on three sides the mountain drops off. There are two ways out, but only one in."

"Explain," Nobody said.

"Listen." The Scot winked at me.

I frowned. The water next to us made the normal gurgling sounds rivers make. Wind whistled through the passage. A sheep bleated. Birds called to each other. Maria chatted to Chester. The sounds were all normal, except . . .

"You hear that?" the Scot said.

I cupped my ears. Beneath the water sounds next to us there was a different pitch, a faint roaring as from a distance. A roaring I've heard before.

"A waterfall," I said.

"You fall into this river, and in thirty seconds you're dropping off the face of the mountain on the crest of a few hundred tons of water."

Chapter 24
Lawrence

Crack.

I jerked the reins left to put my horse between Pacarina and Otho, and the shooter on the other side of the river.

My pulse surged into my temples and wrists. There was no cover on this side of the bridge or anywhere close enough to ride before another bullet screamed at us.

Chester dug his heels into his horse's flanks. The beast plunged towards the water then stopped at the river's edge, lifting its left foreleg to avoid stepping off the brink. Chester pulled the horse's chin back parallel with its backbone and leveraged its lack of balance to drag it down to the ground. As it lay down he wrapped himself around the horse and landed prone with his rifle resting on the horse's back, aimed at the house on the other side of the river.

The Scot threw his hands in the air. "Samson, you fool, it's me."

"I know it's you and I know you ain't allowed to bring strangers here," called a man's voice from the other side. The way the voice cracked on the 'a' in 'ain't' made me guess he was in his sixties.

"I have a shot," Chester said.

"No," Nobody said.

"They're no threat," the Scot yelled. "They need a safe place. I'll take responsibility for them."

"Donovan will skin your hide."

"Not your problem. They've got assassins hunting them. Take Eliza and get out of here while you can."

Silence.

"I can't see him," Chester said.

Colonel Nobody pointed at me. "Take the women out of here."

"Not wise," the Scot said. "No sudden moves. The longer he talks to his wife the better."

Colonel Nobody's eyes roved the bridge. He was counting how many strides it would take to cross. Far too many to beat a bullet coming the other way.

A grizzled head inched into view at the closest window. "You're lucky Eliza likes you. Get out of here and I won't kill you."

The Scot swung his right leg over the saddle to dismount. Chester swung his rifle to cover him. The Scot held up his hands and dropped to his feet.

"Leave this to me." He waved at Samson. "Don't be daft, man. We'll take care of the animals. That puts you out of a job. I'm serious about the assassins, and you don't want Eliza anywhere near this place when they get here."

A slightly more feminine face rose next to Samson's.

"You milk the cows twice a day, you hear? And no usin' my good towels to clean your guns, understood?"

The Scot tipped his hat. "Yes, ma'am."

Half an hour later, Samson and Eliza were riding out of the passage and not looking too sad, either, at the opportunity to leave.

The boat in the pontoon bridge closest to the house was anchored to a column of mortared rock. Ten seconds of hatchet-work would send the bridge downstream and over the waterfall.

The house was built at right-angles with the bridge, two stories, with small windows enfilading the pontoon. The door was a massive block of eucalyptus banded to four hinges by a lengthwise metal strip.

Inside, the bottom floor was a single room with a cooking area on the far wall. A stone counter jutted from the wall to halfway across the room, separating this area and making a sort of table, or surface for cutting meat, or who knows what else. I was more surprised to see a sofa, sitting atop a rug, among other chairs and tables. Surprisingly comfortable.

Chester plopped onto the sofa.

"Not a bad place to die."

I cocked an eyebrow at him.

He frowned at me, then looked at the women. He raised his hands. "Of old age, I mean, after a long and fulfilling life."

Colonel Nobody turned to the Scot. "Thank you for bringing us here. Now tell me why I should let you stay."

The Scot raised his eyebrows. "Perhaps because I'm hosting you here? And the cows. They need milking, you heard."

Colonel Nobody looked at me. I nodded. There was more to this outlaw than met the eye.

Pacarina nodded at Nobody and clapped. "Come, Maria, let's make some supper."

Maria paused with her hand on the sofa-back near Chester's head. "I'm afraid I won't be much help . . ."

"Nonsense, it's time you learned a few things." She waved Maria toward the kitchen.

Chester leaned back and whispered up at her. "I'll tell you all the details later."

Colonel Nobody turned to the Scot. "All right. Why are you really here?"

The Scot straddled a chair backwards. "You brought me."

"You brought us to your secret hideaway, and now you want to stay. You're betraying somebody. I want to know if it's us, or your outlaw friends."

"Somebody? You're forgetting I'm Somebody." The Scot grinned at me. "Oh, don't pretend you don't like seeing someone dish that pronoun silliness back at him." He looked back at Nobody. "How can I betray you? I don't owe you any loyalty."

"I don't particularly want to be shot in the back while I'm shooting at Russians. You've brought us to this place, you saved us from trigger-happy Samson, and you want to stay where you know there's a good chance you'll be killed. Why?"

"Maybe I'm curious why Russian assassins are trying to kill you."

Colonel Nobody crossed his arms and stared at the Scot. "You're double-crossing somebody. I want to know who."

The Scot held the stare. "I'm not double-crossing myself. But trust me, I seem to be the least of your problems."

Chapter 25

Lawrence

"This does not feel natural."

I held my right thumb and forefinger up for inspection.

"Not like a pistol, Law." Pacarina pried my other three fingertips out of my palm and squeezed my thumb and forefinger together. "Like a clamp. There you go."

I looked back at the cow. She chomped grass, ignoring me and my milking stool. I shook my clamped fingers at Pacarina.

"Remember, not all of us grew up milking cows on the family farm."

"I did," Chester said.

"No, you grew up pestering our tenants into letting you milk their cows while I was learning useful skills."

"Like how to organize appendixes," Chester said.

"The correct pronunciation is appendices, but you're talking about indices, and yes, knowing how to organize an index saves countless hours for posterity."

Chester squirted milk at me. "You're delaying. What, do you want to read a book about how to milk a cow?"

"Yes, do you have one?"

Chester blinked. "That was a joke, Law."

Pacarina guided my fingers to form a clamp at the base of one of the cow's teats.

"Grip it gently and squeeze."

I did. A pathetic dribble of white liquid plinked into the bucket. Pacarina tried to hide a smile and laughed when she saw I saw.

"My brother-in-law had a saying: 'Some skills are birthed. Some are acquired.'"

I grunted. "That was the brother-in-law who tied me up and ran me through the jungle."

Chester squeezed consistent milk-spurts into his bucket. "You're blessed to have a wife who can handle animals. Plenty of Society women wouldn't know the difference between a fetlock and a hock."

I chose that moment to become extremely attentive to my milking. I have no idea what the difference is.

Footsteps crunched towards us from the direction of the house.

"Ah, there you are!" Maria said. "I woke up and I couldn't find Pacarina and I couldn't find anyone and I thought, what if the Assassins came and killed everyone, and missed me, and how would I get home . . . anyway, what are you doing?"

"Pumping breakfast," Chester said.

Maria giggled. "Oh, you're always so witty."

I rolled my eyes at Pacarina. I hadn't spent much time with Maria since her and Chester's little adventure, but ever since they returned, Chester seemed different around her. Being firmly invested in Chester's future—and knowing that I'm stuck with whoever he marries as my sister-in-law—I decided to explore the situation a little further.

I worked my cheek muscles into my best smile and beamed at Maria. "Would you like to join us?"

"Me? Milk cows?" Maria's eyebrows climbed her forehead.

"Oh, silly me," I said, "of course, it's not something you've done before. Don't worry about it. I only thought of it because we were talking about Society, and good qualities in a wife, and Chester mentioned how important it is for women to be good with animals. I say," I said, snapping my fingers as if I had just thought of it, "why don't you help Chester with his cow?"

Chester's head jerked up. His eyes were vacant for a moment, then he realized what I had done and glared paper-thin daggers at me.

"Oh," Maria said. She smoothed her hair. "Well . . . I . . . of course I love animals. I've never had the, er, the, opportunity, to milk a cow, before."

"Then no doubt Chester will be delighted to teach you. Won't you, Chester?"

I expected him to give me his Crooked Eyebrow look, where his left eyebrow slants down at his nose and his right eyebrow slants up towards his temple. I know I got him good if I get Crooked Eyebrow. Instead, he just looked at me.

"We're out of stools," Chester said.

"You're resourceful. I'm sure you'll find something to sit on."

Chester shrugged, vacated his stool with a flourish, and fetched a coil of rope to sit on while Maria made herself comfortable on his stool and removed her hat.

"All right," Chester said, "give me your hands."

He pressed his palms against the backs of her hands and guided her fingers to the cow's udder.

"Remember that bushwhacker rascal with the scraggly beard? Pretend this is his throat and squeeze away."

Maria smiled up at him. "Anything you say."

What was going on? Chester should be grimacing like a clown walking through a field of rotten eggs at the idea of holding hands with Maria. Not offering it.

"You planning to do any work yourself?" Chester said.

I looked down. I'd forgotten to keep milking.

"I declare a race," Chester said. "If Maria gets more milk in her bucket than you get in yours, you have to stand still and let me throw knives around you."

Five milk buckets later—at least half of one was mine—I noticed a sheep near the river. Seeing sheep resurrects the smell of innards I discovered when dressed in a sheep's skin to reach the Pit in Vallis Deorum. It's like rotting spinach mixed with ground beef. That's not among my top two-thousand favorite memories.

This particular sheep was munching something that wasn't grass.

"Maria—is that your hat?" I asked.

Maria screamed. She cleared the fifteen yards between us and the sheep faster than I thought possible.

A throaty grumble made me whip my head back around to make sure the cow wasn't plotting to play cricket with it. I do not trust cows. It may be silly, but I think if there is any animal that plays lazy and dumb to get you off your guard so it can wallop you, it would be a cow.

"That's probably not a good idea," Pacarina said.

I spun around. Maria was playing tug-of-war with the sheep. Her back was to the river, and she stood on the bank.

The sheep decided the snack wasn't worth the work. At least, that's what I assume, as it let go. Newton's third law of motion took over, and Maria fell backward into the river.

Chester scrambled up and charged for the human-sized ripple that showed where Maria fell.

"Chester, don't jump—" the sentence wasn't out of my mouth before Chester dived after her.

Pacarina stared at me, eyes wide.

"Bad," I said.

The river was too strong. Even if Chester caught up with Maria he couldn't fight back to the bank before they reached the waterfall, and the water would move them faster than I could run along the bank.

"Very bad," I said.

I heaved the rope coil over my shoulder and headed for a barebacked horse chewing grass between me and the river.

"Make it go!" I yelled at Pacarina.

I can ride horses, but I'm no showman like Chester. I like my horses quiet and saddled. Oh, well.

I grabbed the horse's neck and kicked my right leg up. I crooked my right boot over the horse's backbone and hung horizontal from the beast. Pacarina did something to the horse's rear that made it jolt forward so fast I nearly bounced onto my back. I didn't, and we raced the river. From what I saw between the horse's chin and chest, we were barely beating the current.

Chester's head burst from the water. His hair was plastered to his scalp. His hands didn't surface, which meant he was holding on to Maria. The next second, he was under water again.

Five . . . four . . . three . . . two . . . one . . . I let go of the horse and dropped onto my left side. I half-plowed, half-tumbled through six feet of grass and landed without doing anything that felt permanently damaging.

As I rolled to the bank, Chester's head appeared again. Thank God, I timed it right. I hurled the end of the rope at his head. His left hand shot from the river and grabbed it. I wrapped my end around my chest, under my armpits, then made a few turns around my wrist, and rolled away from the bank.

A jerk on the rope half tore it from my hands. I dug my boots and nose into the dirt and prayed for the strength to hold. That roaring in my ears wasn't just my blood pressure. The waterfall was close.

The ground trembled under another horse's hooves and then Pacarina was wrapping her arms around me. We strained against the tons of water pulling Chester and Maria towards the drop-off.

The rope slacked. We rolled away from the river and heaved. Slowly, oh so slowly, we pulled farther and farther away, until Chester emerged from the river with his arms and the rope wrapped around Maria.

They collapsed into the grass in a sopping heap.

I relapsed into my own heap with Pacarina.

Pacarina kissed me. "You did well, Law."

I grinned up at Chester as he staggered to us, half-dragging Maria with him.

"Chester, you'd better never forget I saved your life by hanging onto a wild horse."

Chester rubbed a dripping handkerchief over his face. "Thanks, Law. You've got a good brain in that stuffy cranium of yours. But—" he grinned. "That horse wasn't wild."

Chapter 26

Lawrence

The next morning, Pacarina and I clomped downstairs to the smell of roasting mutton.

Chester and Jacques bustled around the kitchen filling bowls with breakfast. Nobody and the Scot sat in the common room. That left O'Malley and Petr guarding the Passage, and Maria still sleeping.

"I'm not joking," Chester was saying. "You snore like an asthmatic sheep."

Jacques made a sound not unlike what an asthmatic sheep's snort might sound like.

"It is a slander," Jacques said. "Frenchmen do not snore. Only *boeufs* like O'Malley snore."

"Oh, O'Malley was doing his fair share too, but I heard plenty of French-accented trumpet blasts last night." Chester waved a knife at me. "Not all of us are pampered enough to have their own room."

I settled onto the sofa. "One of the benefits of marriage, Chester. You should try it."

"You're hopeless, Law."

I winked at Pacarina. "I'm happy. So, Nobody, what are your latest plans for surviving the Assassins?"

Colonel Nobody took a piece of paper from his breast pocket and propped it on the mantle. He'd drawn an excellent outline of our mountaintop. The passage was shaped like a snake's tail enfolding into an enormous mouth, distended to swallow the plateau whole.

"We have decisions to make," Nobody said.

The Scot propped a boot on a side-table next to his chair. "These fellows chasing you . . . any chance they'll give up if they can't find you?"

"Zero."

The Scot shrugged. "It may take them a long time. This place was made to not be found."

"Your friend Donovan's men are scattered all over these mountains. The Assassins will find some, and then learn about this place."

"I grant you they may find some of the boys," the Scot said, "but Donovan would skin any of us alive if we talked about this place. Which tells you a lot about what good graces I'm in with him at the moment."

Colonel Nobody smiled. "Donovan's gang may be on the top of the ladder by Australian standards, but the Assassins will eat them alive. Maybe literally. Trust me, they'll find us again."

"They'd better," Chester said. He slid a tray of steaming bowls across the table. "I'm tired of running from fur-hatted specters."

Colonel Nobody turned back to me. "Our first and best line of defense is the Passage. Two men with rifles at the inner angle can crush an attack. How would you attack the Passage if you were outside?"

I thought for a moment. "By land and sea. Metaphorically, of course. The ledge is the obvious way to attack, but it's also the obvious way to defend. I would have men attack on the ledge and at the same time I would have men drop into the river. The current is ferocious. If they can get a few feet below the surface, at the current's speed and the refraction of light, we probably couldn't shoot them."

"Exactly," Nobody said. "We need a way to stop or kill them in the river before they get through the passage."

We chewed mutton and gruel for a few minutes in silent thought.

Chester was the first to speak. "I could spear-fish them."

I shook my head. "You might get one, but I would send multiple at once. The second and third man would get past you."

"Then let's stick spikes into the bottom of the river. They jump in, come swishing around the curve, and splat, no more Assassins."

"The riverbed is solid rock. We don't have the manpower or tools to embed spikes into it."

The Scot coughed. "Is this normal breakfast talk for you fellows? Spear-fishing and spikes?"

I sighed. "Trust me, it's not my fault." I snapped my fingers. "What if—yes, a single marksman might fail, but a dozen wouldn't. How many rifles do we have?"

"Half a dozen," Nobody said.

"We need more."

The Scot smiled. "I may be able to help you, there. This place was built to hold a slew of people. How about you check beneath your seat."

I didn't know what he meant, but he kept looking at my sofa, so I stood, and Chester slid it and the rug beneath it out of the way. There was a trap door in the floor with an iron ring screwed into the planks. Chester grabbed the ring and lifted. The musty smell made me gag.

Chester jumped into the hole. "Hand me a light," he said, his voice muffled.

Pacarina lit a candle at the fire and passed it down.

"Bless Donovan's blackguardly heart," Chester said. Metal rattled. "And his beady eyes. And his silly mustachio. And his Napoleon swagger. And . . ."

Chester's head popped up. "Scot, if I were French, I would kiss both your cheeks." His eyes were as big as when Father gave him his first horse on his fifth birthday. "There are enough rifles, and swords, and knives, and beautiful things down here to put the 'arm' in 'army.'"

The Scot gave a mock bow from his seat.

"Excellent," I said. "We build a frame and mount a dozen rifles covering the width of the river and, say, six feet long. We tie the triggers to a central pull cord and one man can put a dozen bullets into a swath of the river."

"I like it," Nobody said. "But I don't think it's enough. Three men in the water with a second's time between each will be too far apart. At least one would survive."

"I'm telling you, spikes," Chester said. "Law will think of a way. He just has to exhaust his pessimistic thoughts first."

I frowned. There was no way to embed spikes in the riverbed. Holding a spike at the right angle against that current would be hard enough, let alone pounding it into solid rock at the same time. We could drop a grid of spikes on the bottom and weight it with boulders, but if the spikes reached the water level the Assassins would hit the sides of the spikes and push through without a problem. If they were below the water level the Assassins would swim over them.

Everyone was looking at me.

"Look, I just gave you a perfectly good idea. Spikes naturally come to mind, but there's not a practical way—" I stopped.

"Here it comes," Chester said.

I blinked. "The current will slam a body against each of the two curves. They could cushion themselves with arms and legs to take the blow, but if we had spikes on the rock wall itself . . . that would do it."

"Behold the sage," Chester said. "How do we get them there?"

"We build a wooden grid and drive double-ended spikes into it. Drop it longways up and the very pressure of the current will keep it against the side of the wall."

"Good work," Nobody said. "And in case anyone makes it past those two traps we'll build something at the end of the passage with a lever that can drop two or three boulders into the water and crush anything beneath."

Chapter 27
Chester

I waved at the people on the ground. Pacarina waved back.

Oh, I should mention I hung from two knobs thirty feet up a rock wall. Hanging by my hands, not my neck. Contrary to what Law tells me I don't think I'm going to be hung.

You see, the Scot insisted the cliffs at the entrance to our little paradise were unclimbable. There's no such thing. You can climb anything if you work hard enough.

If our Russian friends figured a way up and we weren't there to meet them, they would use us for target practice. Noble agreed with me, but he can't climb well with his bad arm, so obviously it was my job to find the way up.

The rope coil tied crisscross on my back pulled my vest against my neck. My day's agenda didn't include choking, so I ripped off my neckerchief and tied it pirate-style under my hat. Ha. Law was probably grumbling about me and my headgear.

I've heard you should climb rocks slowly, test each foothold and hand-grab carefully, and all that. Not really my style. I already decided on my way up. Time for action.

I sucked some Australian wind into my insides, flexed my toes, and jumped.

The moment my bare feet touched the cold rock I pushed up and grabbed a ledge, swung off it to another foothold, up again to a ledge, swung left, right, whoa—loose rock—one hand—two—none—

The rock crumbled beneath my feet and hands and I dropped. I clawed the mountain, fingernails and toenails grinding to bloody pulp in seconds. My right knee jammed something and stopped working. No time—I think there was a ledge to the left—I threw myself left, falling left and down, keep fighting the mountain—ouch!

I looked down. I stood on the ledge, a good ten feet left of the way I came up. My left leg was so jarred I'm surprised my hip bone didn't spike into whatever organs are on top of it. My jammed right knee was too weak to hold me up, but it was one of those bone shocks that come and go quickly. It's not as if this was the first time I've been banged up.

People below yelled at me. Probably Law asking if I was okay. I waved at them in general and focused on the way up. Just a minor setback.

The way up from here looked less promising than my first way. That wasn't exactly encouraging since the first way almost turned me into meat jelly. I glared at the mountain. No piece of rock is going to beat me.

In a few minutes my right knee felt more like a joint, and up I went.

Many, many minutes later I pulled myself up between two rocks and beat the cliff.

The wind bullied the mountain ridge. Law could say how scientifically fast it was blowing, but for me it was handkerchief-blowing-off speed. I double-knotted my pirate headgear and held my arms out to the group below. The unclimbable cliff was clumb. Climbed. Clumben. However you spell it.

I held my top of the world pose for a few seconds, letting the wind whip my beard, then limped to the other side. Wouldn't bother me if the limp stayed around for a few days. There's something about limping that makes you feel and look like you just came through a battle.

The green grass at ground level looked awfully long away. Still, a good eye at the end of a good rifle could plump a bullet into a body from up here. My job was to make sure the only eyes and rifles here were mine.

I had another reason to be here. Up here, on the top of the world, with a canvas of mountain peaks around me and a hidden valley below me, with wind at my back and sun on my face, I could think. I have this habit of talking when I'm around people. Like the old saying goes, people have two ears and only one mouth, so they have plenty of listening space to hear what I'm saying. But seriously, I just like talking with people.

And I don't think enough when I talk, and I don't think enough before I do things, and that's what I need to fix. I almost got Otho killed. Killed!

I shivered, thinking about that day in Peru when I killed Pacarina's servant. I try not to think about that. Doesn't do any good, thinking about it. But maybe it does. If I could just remember mistakes like that when I'm under stress, maybe I would think about what I'm doing before I do it.

Law said to grow up. He would know. He's the smart twin, with life all figured out, and an amazing wife, and a child. I think I've always realized that, always envied him. And I do things like riding horses Roman style and sleight of hand because I want to be good at things. Prove myself.

Maybe that's why I wanted to come with Noble to Australia in the first place, before the whole Assassin thing, when it was a simple seek-and-find and see the world while you're at it, mission. Prove to myself that I can be more than a trigger-happy buffoon. Learn from Noble. Talk about a chap I could learn some things from. Here he is traipsing Australia to pull danger away from Liana, when I'm sure the only thing he wants to do is be with her.

I took off my hat and pirate handkerchief and let the wind rake my hair. Getting sentimental in my old age, eh? I looked up at the sky and asked God for strength to grow up and for the wisdom to not put people in danger while doing it.

All right, then. Back to keeping people safe.

The Passage was too wide to jump, but there were some boulders on the other side I was able to lasso and use as leverage to swing over.

That was the last of the fun. I spent the rest of the afternoon hauling ropes and tools up the rock-face and building us a nice little pulley and lift contraption under Law's direction.

The sun was red and low when we finished. The Scot came up to see the view and together we went back to the Passage and watched the sun set. We probably made a nice silhouette if anybody below was looking.

I pulled a boomerang from my vest. "I've been wanting to do this all day."

I flexed my wrist, cocked the wood at just the right angle, and let her fly. I felt good enough to send it all the way back to Sydney. Something a long ways out grabbed my eye. Did I really throw it that far? No, impossible. I squinted in the dying light.

Then I realized.

"Scot," I said. "The Assassins are here."

Chapter 28
Lawrence

I was thinking about the warm embrace of the blanket beneath which I would soon be crawling, when the Scot ran in to tell us the Assassins were here. Forget blankets. Time for full-scale war.

I think I can say without boasting that I have a decent head for planning, and I used it to prepare for this time, but now that battle was upon us, Nobody took command.

"Arm," Nobody said. He tightened the leather ties strapping the metal strips to his forearms and shins. "Jacques and O'Malley are already at the Passage. Lawrence, you take the gun-frame. Scot, man the logs."

Petr gripped a pistol butt. "Me, sir?"

"Guard the women."

Petr's lips twitched. "I should be at the front, sir."

"You know exactly why you shouldn't."

They exchanged a look even Chester would mark as bearing upon some secret they knew and we—or at least, I—didn't.

Petr said no more. One doesn't argue with Nobody when he is in battle mode.

The way I felt standing behind my makeshift gun frame reminded me why I never became a soldier. One pull on the rope in my hand would rip open the flesh of any man in a twenty-square-foot swath of the river. Why is it that man is most ingenious when devising new ways to kill his fellow man?

I admit a certain sense of pride in my contraption. One wooden frame supported twenty rifle barrels. The second frame supported the rifle stocks, while a lattice of poles and rope tied the two frames one yard apart and bound the rifles to the frames. A finely-calculated length of twine led from each trigger to the knotted rope in my hand.

I stood as taut as the ropes holding the framework together. The last twenty percent of the top of the sun dipped below the cliffs and we were in night.

"All's well," O'Malley called.

"All's well," I called back.

It would soon be so dark we couldn't see each other, so calling was the only way to confirm we hadn't been assassinated. We would do this every few minutes. Not that I expected Jacques or O'Malley to be caught with their rifles lowered.

A shout would mean someone was in the water abreast of them, which would start my six-second countdown until pulling the triggers. Darkness was the Assassins' friend, because I couldn't see what was below the river's surface. Based on my calculations, it would take six seconds for a medium-weight body to float from Jacques and O'Malley to the zone covered by my gun-frame.

If I were the Assassins, I would watch the Passage for several hours, and if nothing came out, I would send a single scout through to find what was to be found. He would die, leaving us thirteen left to kill.

Then again, I don't have much practice thinking like a Russian Assassin. The man who did was back in the house. Why Nobody chose Petr to stay away, I did not know.

What were the odds all of us would survive? Fourteen Assassins needed to die before we were safe. Ten of us needed to stay alive. If we posited a one-to-one exchange of life, there needed to be fourteen exchanges during which none of ten people died. Fourteen exchanges times ten, equals one-hundred and forty, out of which there was only a single instance in which all of them died and none of us died, a zero point seven percentage chance . . .

I blinked. If I didn't stay alert, our odds would become even more horrible.

As my eyes adjusted, deeper shadows merged from the night, and I picked out the Scot leaning against the log stack. No doubt he was sucking a blade of grass.

I exchanged the password telling the others I was alive and entered the next few minutes of silence. I was wrong earlier. If I were the Assassins, I would wait several nights before attacking to fray our nerves into raw fibers. I forced myself to release the knot and let it hang perpendicularly from the frame, feeling for it with my hand to make sure I could grasp it immediately. If someone shouted and I was holding the knot, my reflexes might fire the rifles faster than my mind could stop me.

I imagined Pacarina standing here beside me. Not that I wanted her here—far too dangerous—but she would be a comforting, steadying presence. It's strange that people tell me that I'm calm, that I'm a rock to lean on. I usually feel more like an active lava flow.

Password after password went by, each with its agonizing second of silence before the reply came, until it all faded into sweaty-palmed monotony.

Something touched my shoulder. I jerked and strangled a scream. Thank God I wasn't holding the rope.

"Relief," Nobody whispered.

I coughed to clear the scream from my throat. "How long has it been?"

"Four hours."

I shivered. The night had been so slow, and yet so fast.

"You've been here just as long yourself," I said.

Colonel Nobody pushed me aside. "I was pulling night watches when your tutor was teaching you your first Latin conjunctions. Go sleep."

I didn't argue. He didn't know how early in life I learned those conjunctions, but then again, I don't know how old he is.

Chapter 29

Lawrence

"Do you think Chester can take it?" I asked.

Pacarina cocked an eyebrow.

"Being alone, I mean."

She laughed. "I don't think Chester is going to collapse just because he's by himself for a few days up there. He's pretty comfortable with himself."

"It's an act," I said. "He seems all-sufficient, but he really doesn't do well by himself. Did I ever tell you about the time I locked him in Father's study?"

Pacarina snuggled into the sofa-back. "I didn't think that was your style."

"It was strategic. He kept stealing my Latin books, which kept me from studying, so I put him in Father's study. He howled like I dropped him in a pit and pulled up the rope."

"What did you do when you let him out?"

I scratched an itch-prick behind my left ear. The animals around this house must have fleas. "He broke through the window, cut himself, and bled all over my Latin books."

"And you were . . . how old?"

"Four."

Pacarina laughed so hard she nearly sloshed me with her cup of tea. "That's the problem, Law. You were studying Latin at four."

It was the evening following our sighting of the Assassins, and I had a break from watch-duty for the first half of the night. Really, I should be in bed, but it was just too nice to sit here with Pacarina and talk about safe things, things other than dying and killing. I hadn't been able to spend much time with her these last days. Poor girl, cooped up with Petr and Maria. Otho was safely abed upstairs.

"But seriously," I said, "do you think he's maybe thinking about not staying alone?"

"Do you mean . . . getting married?" Pacarina looked around. We were alone. "He's not in love with Maria, if that's what you're asking."

"But he's been different with her. More . . . I'm not sure what. Women do funny things to men's heads."

"I think 'kind' is the word you're looking for. He's being more kind to a girl who was raised in Society and for the first time in her life has been introduced to the real world. Trust me, I'll know when Chester is in love with someone. And what, exactly, do you mean by 'funny things,' hmm?"

Maria barged through the front door, rescuing me from that little pitfall. "He's impossible. He won't say a thing to me."

"Petr?" I said.

"Well, I'm not a brick wall, I have to talk to someone." She removed her hat, which looked a bit more well used than before that sheep munched it.

Petr doesn't even talk to people he respects. I allowed myself a small interior glow for not saying that aloud.

"Is it dark yet?" I asked.

"It's almost as dark as his face, and that's saying something."

Pacarina tilted her head at the kitchen. "Jacques left you some buns."

Maria's face tightened with the struggle between keeping her waist thinner than the nib on a worn-down feather pen, and eating anything Jacques made. She went into the kitchen.

"So," Pacarina whispered, "is that why you're always looking for a wife for Chester? To keep him from being lonely?"

"He needs someone. Of course, he has us, but he needs more than us."

"And . . . if he has someone special, he's less likely to drag you around the world."

I raised my palms. "Every great strategist appreciates positive side effects."

Crash.

Pacarina's cup hit my leg and lukewarm tea soaked my lap.

Bang.

Another gunshot. Higher-pitched, like a poodle's yap compared to the wolfhound roar of the first shot. The first must have been a rifle, the second a pistol. Petr had both.

The front door burst open and Petr stood framed against the night for a moment before he stumbled inside, slammed the door shut, and dropped the bar into place with his left hand. His jacket was black with blood.

Maria took one step from the kitchen, dropped a bun, and fainted. Some calm compartment in my brain made a note to figure out how she never cracked her head open when she fainted. The rest of my brain screamed a hundred things at once.

"I got one," Petr said. His voice was thick. A knife stuck in his chest.

Something flickered at the window next to the door. I grabbed Pacarina's shoulders and wrenched her off the sofa, falling with my body covering hers. A bullet blasted the top quarter of the sofa to bits and flattened against the kitchen wall.

"Upstairs," Petr said.

We scrambled towards the stairs, Pacarina's hand tight within mine. The door was in the far right corner, facing the kitchen-wall. The window was next to the door, also facing the kitchen, and between the door and the stairs. The stairs were safe from someone firing through the window, but if he reached their hand inside, he could shoot up the stairs.

Petr stumbled to the waist-high wall between the kitchen and the open room. It was the perfect defense from which to cover the door, which was no doubt why the outlaws put it there. We reached the landing and I held Pacarina's head below the level of the window. Every window in the place was barred to keep bodies out, but there was plenty of space for a bullet.

That was supposed to be so the people inside could shoot out.

I forced down the urge to panic. I had responsibilities.

"There's a pistol near our bed," I said. "I'm going to get it and load it."

"It's not loaded?"

"Of course not, I don't want to accidentally kill someone."

Pacarina's face tightened that way it does when I say something wrong. "We're in a war, Lawrence."

"I'm sorry, I tried to balance preparedness against not accidentally killing someone."

"Under my pillow—there's a loaded pistol."

"Under your pillow! You're telling me—" I clenched my teeth and dash-crawled for our bedroom. "If we survive this, Dear, I'm checking under your pillow for the rest of my life."

Something pounded the front door. It hit three more times before I was back at the top of the stairs with Pacarina's loaded pistol. Did they have a sledgehammer?

"Stoning," Petr called. "I can't lift her."

He must mean Maria. Of course, she was lying between the half-wall and the door, and with Petr's wound he couldn't lift her to the safe side. She could wake any moment. Pacarina would have the sense to stay where she was until she figured out what was going on, but Maria would pop that vacant head of hers right up into a bullet.

Great. Heroes run around in front of loaded guns. Real people like me are supposed to stay under cover. Oh, well.

"Diversion," Pacarina said. She took the pistol and poised it level with the windowsill.

I sucked a breath. "I love you."

I was halfway down the stairs when she fired. The yell I was hoping for didn't happen, but someone returned the shot. I hoped it was the Assassin at the front window.

I planted my right foot and pivoted my body towards the kitchen. For a sickening second, my back was exposed to the window. The gunpowder fumes made my mouth feel like I'd been sucking bullets. The hammering at the door stopped.

I balanced my hands on the broken sofa top, leaped, and landed next to Maria's body. Her mouth twitched. I grabbed her waist and dragged her to the half-wall. She must have eaten more of Jacques' rolls than I realized.

Petr fired at the window. The blast turned my ears into vacuums shadowed by vague ringing. I couldn't hear my breathing, or the thump that must have happened when I heaved Maria onto the half-wall.

"Down," Petr rasped.

I dropped Maria on the other side of the wall rather less gently than I would usually handle a woman and threw myself over. Another shot burst through the silence in my eardrums and pots and pans cascaded from the wall.

Petr's face was visibly white.

"Has the bleeding stopped?" I asked. My words sounded far away.

Petr shook his head.

The black slick around the knife-hilt spread towards his trousers. I flexed my fingers. My natural reaction was to pull the knife out, but the blade was plugging the hole. Removing it would be like popping the cork on a champagne bottle.

Think, I told myself. I'm good with anatomy. Assess, decide, act.

If the knife moved in the wound it would do more damage. The first thing to do was to stabilize the knife.

The bleeding must stop. I squinted through the smoke, my eyes smarting, looking for something I could use. There was a lumpy bundle on the floor next to Petr's leg. I grabbed it, shook out a few pounds of potatoes, and folded the sack into a square.

I pressed the square around the knife-hilt and looked round for something to tie it there.

In the novels Chester reads, they're always cutting strips from the bottom of the girl's dress, but there's nothing fast about that. Ah, her scarf. I jerked the scarf from Maria's neck and wrapped it over the pad on one side of the knife, around Petr's abdomen, and back over the pad on the other side of the knife.

I crossed the scarf ends and pulled as hard as I could. Petr's breath hitched, but that was the only sound. These Russians are hardy.

There was a problem. Any knot I tied here would loosen, releasing the pressure against the sack. Pressure was the only way to immobilize the knife. The fabric, too, was flimsy. It was already stretching.

There was no rope at hand, nothing else I could use to tie. There was a foot-long wooden spoon.

I brought the scarf-ends back around Petr's chest and wrapped them around the spoon.

"Twist this to tighten it," I said.

Petr growled. "This is not my first stab."

"No, and let's hope it's not your last. I mean, I hope it is your last, but not because you're dead."

"Ahhh!" Maria jolted back to this world.

I released Petr and grabbed the girl before her head topped the half-wall.

"Two things," I said. "Don't talk. Don't move."

Whether she was capable of not doing either was another question, but not one I had the luxury to answer right then.

All was quiet outside. My hearing seeped back, and with it the realization that my body was trembling.

How did the Assassins come here? The only way in was through the Passage. Or was it? If they'd come through the Passage, that meant our friends were dead. No, it couldn't be. I never believe these stories about impregnable fortresses. But if they got through somewhere else, where was it, how many got through, and were they attacking our friends from the rear?

As if to answer my thought, there were gunshots in the distance. It sounded about as far away as I would expect the Passage to be. The good news was our friends hadn't been dead. The bad news: they might now be.

"Lawrence," Pacarina called. "They're at the bedroom window. Otho is in there!"

"Wait!" I yelled.

"Can you give them a target?" I asked Petr.

"Give me a target."

Great.

He loaded his pistol faster with one hand than I loaded on a calm day with both. He jerked his head.

I chest-vaulted the wall and landed on all fours. Petr's pistol barked above me. Something thudded outside the window.

Pacarina was at our bedroom door, her hand on the doorknob. I grabbed her shoulders, made her move aside, and pushed into the room.

Someone was messing with the window bars. They shouldn't be able to do that with a second-story window, but at this point I was almost willing to believe the Assassins had wings.

Down below they had the advantage because it was light inside and dark outside. Up here there were no lights, so I was in shadow while anyone at the window would be framed against the sky.

There was a shadow against the window, darker than the star-studded night beyond. I ran pictures of the room in daylight through my brain, trying to remember something to use as a weapon. Ah, yes. Chester had strewn weapons all over the house 'just in case.' There was a sword leaning against the dresser.

I leaped up and ran for the sword. Faster than it takes to tell, I heard the tinkle of glass and something whooshed towards me. I dodged right but a terrific blow struck my left shoulder and spun me into the dresser. My left arm hung limp. The absence of pain must be shock. I tossed those thoughts into the recesses of my brain, groped for the sword-hilt with my right hand, and plunged it through the window-bars.

A dying man's scream is a sound no mortal should ever hear. I've heard more than a few, but this in particular is seared into my memory. Perhaps it was the shock of hearing these omniscient stalkers vulnerable. At any rate, it's not a sound I like to think about.

The man had been balanced on a pole leaning against the side of the house. His body and the pole both now lay on the ground. I didn't see anyone else, but I staggered away from the window before an avenging friend could put a bullet in me.

"Law! Are you all right?" Pacarina peered through the door.

"I'm all right," I said. "That wasn't my death-rattle. I expect I'll give some kind of weak gurgle when I die."

She flung her arms around me and held me against her beating heart. That reminded me of my left arm, which I should feel. It was beginning to tingle, like a dead fish out of water giving a final twitch or two.

I ran my right hand's fingers across the floor, feeling for the thing that hit me. I found a round metal ball with cord threaded through the top. Like an apple, if the apple was steel, and the stem was sticky rope.

Someone outside the front door yelled in Russian.

Petr answered, also in Russian.

I didn't think Petr would answer an enemy's taunts, but the sound of his voice in reply made me catch my breath. I had never heard that tone. Pain? Fear? Whatever it was, the Russian or Russians outside did not answer.

"Vive la France!"

"A Stoning!"

The war-cries outside were punctuated by clashing steel. I dropped the metal ball and stumbled back to the window. A rope of sparks shot skyward from the friction of two swords meeting. The man fighting Jacques and Chester stepped backwards with measured paces, his sword flicking from blade to blade with a speed I could never hope to attain.

"What?" Chester yelled. "Is that the best a Frenchman can do?"

The smaller shadow, which must be Jacques, caterwauled. He dove for the Assassin's legs as Chester whacked at his head. The Russian dropped and Jacques rose, wiping his blade with a handkerchief.

I was so glad to see him that I could have kissed both his cheeks.

Chapter 30
Lawrence

Pacarina and I rushed down the stairs to welcome our rescuers. Chester and Jacques pushed warily through the front door.

"Everyone all right?" Chester asked.

"Petr is shot," I said. "The rest of us are all right." My left shoulder didn't feel all right. Whatever hit it—it felt like a rock—left quite the impression, but I don't think it was injured beyond bruising.

"Chester!" someone yelped.

I sensed something running so quickly behind me that for a moment I thought an Assassin snuck inside and was about to kill me. Then I realized an Assassin wouldn't be screaming Chester's name in a girly, hysterical voice.

Maria rushed into Chester's arms—or rather, threw her arms around Chester's unyielding body—and released the floodgates of her tears.

"They shot me, Chester, oh, they shot me, I can feel it, I can feel the pain in my head."

Chester looked at me over her head, which was smooshed into his chest.

I shook my head. She wasn't shot in the head. Although, this might explain that bang I heard when I dropped her over the kitchen half-wall.

Chester gingerly parted her hair to look for the supposed wound.

"There's a bump," Chester said. "A little bump the size of a midget egg. Bullets don't make bumps, they make holes. You'll be fine." He patted the bump.

"How is Petr?" Chester called to Jacques, who was already in the kitchen.

"Zhe Silent One vill live," Jacques said. He was on the floor checking

Petr's bandage. "You did vell, Stoning Number One. I vill get this knife out and make a real bandage, but you did vell."

Praise from Jacques, while not as meaningful as praise from Nobody, is even rarer, so I accepted it.

"Two of the fellows got away," Chester said. "How many did you get?"

Petr grunted. "I shot one."

"That was probably why the chap Jacques and I fought had blood dripping from his side. These fellows are tough."

"I got one," I said.

Chester whistled. "You'll make a soldier yet, Law."

"I'll make a dead man if we don't figure out how they got here. This place is supposed to be impregnable."

Chester and I went outside to check the bodies. We did it by moonlight, no torches, as the other two Assassins might be waiting in the trees to shoot us. The man by the front door had a bullet hole in his left side and the death-wound from Jacques' blade.

I forced myself to touch him to search for a wallet or bag that might contain information. His clothes were made of scratchy wool. I shuddered at the invisible blood soaking my fingers. But wait, there was no way his clothes were completely soaked by blood. He must have been in the water.

The other body's clothes were also saturated, and his hair was plastered onto his skull. The sword stuck from his chest. I knelt next to the man, forced myself to look at his face. It was Egor. This man almost killed my son—anger jolted through me so unexpectedly that I almost fell over. All I wanted to do was kill this man over and over again at the thought of the danger he put my son in. I shook myself, tried to clear my mind, to remember I should not hate my enemies. But oh, how hard it is to be a father and not hate the man who tried to kill Otho.

There was nothing identifiable on either body. Just coarse clothing, heavy boots, leather belts, and a couple of pistols and knives Chester confiscated.

Only when we were back in the protection of the house did I let my shoulders relax. I rinsed my hands in a pot of water in the kitchen and wiped them on the discarded potato sacking.

"Did these Assassins get through the Passage?" I asked.

"Impossible," Chester said. "We were watching it as closely as I watched your sweetmeats when we were children. We heard shots here before they attacked us. They rushed the path. Probably hoped we were distracted by the shots. They stopped when we gave a good volley."

"Praise the Lord," I said.

Two more Assassins down without any of us dead yet. Our mathematical chances of survival were improving, but the odds that not a single one of us would die still had more zeros than I cared to count.

"Now," Chester said, "we have to hunt down the fellows who made it in here. I don't like thinking some chap may take a potshot at me any minute."

"And," I said, "we have to warn the others. If any of them come to check on us they'll be ambushed."

Chester hooked his thumbs behind his bandoliers. "We'll get ambushed if we try to get through to warn them."

I kneaded my left shoulder. It was probably turning a royal shade of purple. How could we warn our friends at the Passage to wait until we found the Assassins, assuming we could even do that?

"Ah," Chester said. "Carrier pigeons."

"Do you have carrier pigeons?"

Chester frowned. "Message in a bottle?"

"Yes, if you want to warn somebody at the bottom of the waterfall."

Chester snapped his fingers. "Smoke signals!"

"Do you know smoke signals?"

"You know smoke signals," Chester said.

I shook my head. "No, I don't."

Chester snorted. "You're the language fellow, Law. I'm sure you know smoke signals."

"Smoke signals are not a language, Chester."

Jacques rapped his fingers on the kitchen half-wall. "I know smoke signals."

Chester spun on him. "You're telling me the French know smoke signals?"

"No, you *boeuf*, we use smoke signals in zhe 42ⁿᵈ. Zhe Colonel vill understand my message."

"Ah, right." Chester turned back to me. "You should know more about the Squad we're honorary members of."

"You knew we had smoke signals?"

Chester shrugged. "That's beside the point. So, we smoke the heavens at first light and then go Russian-hunting. Anything else?"

"Yes," I said. "We have to find out how they got in so we can stop any more from getting in."

"Obviously they must have found a way up the cliff. I'm telling you, there is no such thing as an unclimbable mountain."

I shook my head. "That's just an assumption. What bothers me is how wet their bodies are." I turned to Petr, who was now lying on the bullet-blasted couch. "Where did you first see them?"

"They came from the river on this side of the bridge."

That was odd. Something didn't add up.

"Seems obvious to me," Chester said. They climbed the cliff on the other side, swam the river, and pushed their steel into Petr."

"Petr, did you see them swimming the river?" I asked.

"No," Petr said. "I kept good watch."

"So they swam quietly," Chester said. "What's so surprising about that?"

"You don't just quietly swim that river," I said. "The current is strong. If they got in the river on the other side, it would carry them far downriver before they got across. Which means if they came up close to the bridge, they would have had to start practically at the Passage, under your nose. You of all people should know how fast the current is."

"Hmm," Chester said. "It was a beast. It sucked me towards the waterfall like a hound playing one-dog tug-of-war with a bone. It even felt like it was pushing my legs out from under me." He cocked his head at me. "Much as I hate saying you're right, I would have been over that waterfall long before I swam to the other side."

"Wait—what do you mean it pushed your legs?"

"Well . . ." Chester stooped and pushed my legs. I staggered against the wall. "Rather like that."

"It did this the whole time you were in the water?"

"No . . . it was more of a one-time push a few seconds after I was in the water."

"Underwater current," I said. "If I placed wagers, I would wager there are one or more underwater channels feeding from outside into our river. And I think the Assassins swam them."

Chapter 31
Lawrence

Magpies warbled me to consciousness the next dawn. Their songs were throaty at the base, punctured by squeaky trills. Deceptively pretty, given there were people waiting outside to kill us.

Chester was chomping mutton at the table when I came down.

"There you are," he said, through a mouthful of meat. "Ready to send some smoke signals?"

I pressed myself next to the window and scooted left until I saw the yard outside and the river. Several hundred yards away, the trees undulated in a light breeze.

"Petr? How do you feel?" I asked.

The Russian lay on the couch behind me, his hands folded above the foot-wide bandage Jacques wrapped round his wound.

"I live," Petr said.

"You know how these Assassins think. If they really used an underwater passage, my guess is they only sent a few men, as no one would be able to swim back against the current to say if they actually made it. Do you agree?"

"Yes."

"How many would they send?"

"I do not know. The Assassins work alone. For all sixteen to have the same mission—they must have great respect for Colonel Nobody."

"Do you think they would send more than four? We killed two, and Chester saw two more leave."

"It is unlikely," Petr said.

Chester joined me at the window. He was armed, with swords on his back, bandoliers across his chest, and all the rest of his paraphernalia.

"Well, Law, do you think they're squatting in the trees out there waiting to pick us off when we come out?"

"If they came underwater I doubt they brought rifles."

"Then a fire it is." Chester lifted the plank off the brackets on either side of the door, propped it in the corner, and strode outside.

"Chester!" I ran to the door. "I don't know for sure that they came underwater."

"If they shoot me I suppose we'll know they didn't."

He grabbed wood from the pile beside the door and arranged it into a fire circle. He dug deep in the pile to find green logs that would smoke.

No one shot him, praise the Lord, so I left the house and Jacques followed to direct the smoke signaling.

They sent up a short puff, followed by three long puffs. They repeated this three times.

"Zhey know to stay," Jacques said, folding the blanket he used to create the puffs.

"Ouch!" Chester exclaimed. He looked at his leg. "Something bit me. Ouch!" He jumped back from the fire.

"Snake?" I said.

"No, it's—ouch!" He leaped back again. "They're jumping!"

A horde of giant ants swarmed out of the ground next to the fire.

"You built your fire on top of a bull ant colony," I said.

"They're jumping! Law, they're—ouch!" Chester hopped and swatted his legs.

"It's postulated that bull ants are one of very few ant species that can see well."

"They can see me?" Chester dashed for the river, trailing pistols and swords as he ran. A line of hopping ants chased him.

I meandered inside before the ants blamed me for Chester's fire-building location. I watched from the window as Chester held on to the side of one of the pontoon bridge boats and submerged his clothed body, boots and all, in the river. His face alternated between relief at the water's soothing coldness and screwed up pain as stowaways in his pants buried their stingers in his legs.

He came out of the river hobbling like an arthritic lobster.

"Don't say a word," he growled. "Let's go hunting."

In the house, I reviewed the medley of weapons Chester arranged on the table. To Chester, more weapons means better prepared. Personally, I prefer not collapsing under the weight of the weapons I carry. Not looking like a weaponized porcupine is also nice.

I selected a rifle with a shoulder strap, two pistols, and a short sword. I wanted only one pistol, but knowing my aim, the likelihood of hitting someone on the first try is low, and given how long it takes me to load a pistol, having a second loaded one ready makes sense. Chester also forced me to strap a knife below each hip.

"This is like fox hunting," Chester said. His cheerfulness seeped back as the ant stings lessened.

"Yes," I said, "except that they're humans, not foxes, we're not riding horses, we have to walk through a semi-tropical forest, and the humans are trying to kill us."

"Exactly. Petr, where would these fellows be waiting for us?"

"I would separate but stay close. I would look for high ground and find none. So I would stay on this side of the river. I would find a place with rocks and trees and wait for someone to come. Then I would kill them."

"Wey-ho," Chester said. "That's quite enough, thank you. Don't need Law going and getting nervous."

I pressed my elbows against my sides to trap the sweat dribbling from my armpits. Yes, keep Law from getting nervous, indeed.

"Who is staying with the girls?" Chester asked.

Petr grunted. "I will take care of them."

"Are you sure, what with your sliced innards and all?"

Petr glared at him.

"Right, you can," Chester said. He turned to Pacarina. "And you can take care of yourself. I would hate to be the Russian at the end of your rifle."

Pacarina smiled and wiped a cloth down the barrel of her rifle.

"And . . ." Chester winced. "Maria?"

Maria looked up from her last bite of Jacques' scrambled eggs. "What did you say, Chester?"

"Can you fire a rifle?"

I doubt Maria has ever held anything in her life more hostile than a fan.

"Oh, I . . ." she trailed off. "Can you show me how?"

Chester looked at me. "Law, how about you—"

I raised my hands, palms facing him. "I'm the last person who should teach someone how to shoot."

Chester looked at Jacques. The Frenchman glared at him and muttered something about risking no more dinners. Chester sighed.

"It's simple," Chester said. He lifted a rifle from the table and motioned Maria towards him. "You brace it against your shoulder, point, and pull the trigger."

He handed the rifle to her. She looked up at him. "How do I hold it?"

Chester pressed her hands into the right grips and raised the rifle to her shoulder.

"Press the stock against your shoulder so it absorbs the kick. Point the gun at the Russian trying to kill you. Pull the trigger. Bang."

Bang.

I blinked through the smoke and deafening ringing that filled the room.

As sound faded back, like noise to the ears of a swimmer surfacing, I heard Maria whimper.

She lay on the floor nursing her right shoulder. The rifle lay next to her, smoke curling from its barrel.

Chester smacked his head. "You pulled the trigger. You pulled the—"
he spun around. "Is anyone dead?"

"Yes," Petr said.

Chester scowled. "Fine time to discover a sense of humor." He smacked
his ears. Must have the same ringing as tortured mine. "Better idea. Maria,
don't touch the guns."

Chester poked at a dent in the wall next to the window. "Where did
the bullet go?"

I leaned over next to Jacques and fingered a flat piece of metal. "Here."

Jacques' eyes boggled. He patted his face, then his skull. The bullet's
second ricochet mark was in the wall six inches above his head.

"Good thing you're a dwarf, not O'Malley," Chester said.

"If I vere O'Malley I vould velcome zhe release from life by a bullet."

"All right," Chester said, "we're agreed. Don't let Maria near the guns.
Let's go hunting."

An hour later we were blocking the two underwater passages we iden-
tified by the current, and an hour after that, we were deep in the forest.

The forest was semi-tropical, meaning there were many leafy green
plants, ferns growing on rocks, and a general lush greenness, but it wasn't
as thick as the Amazon rainforest. The trees—mostly eucalyptus trees with
straight trunks and few lower branches—spread far enough apart that I
could see quite a distance through the forest. This made it harder for the
Assassins to ambush us, but there were still plenty of hiding places.

We paused by a ten-foot rock to swig our water flasks and wipe the
sweat from our faces. The weather was cool, but not enough to counteract
traipsing through the forest lugging all of our weapons.

"You're quiet," Chester said to Jacques. "I don't often see you without
O'Malley."

"Oi. Zhe *bouef* does not give me peace."

"You two put on a good act, but you know you're the best of friends."
Chester signaled to move out again. "How did you chaps meet?"

"Ve vere soldiers," Jacques said.

"Oh, come on. There's got to be a story there. Did you mistake him for a fire-headed giant, or something? I'm bored, I want to hear."

Bored? Only Chester could be bored while walking through a semi-tropical forest in Australia waiting for a Russian Assassin to shoot him.

"He vas Irish," Jacques said. "It is not easy to be Irish in zhe English army. It is also not easy to be French, so I helped him survive zhe ohzer soldiers."

"So you became fast friends immediately?" Chester asked.

Jacques skirted a tree in our way and appeared on the other side. "My sister helped."

"Hmm?"

"O'Malley became betrohzed to my sister," Jacques said.

"O'Malley married your sister?"

"I did not say zhat." Jacques tugged at the right half of his mustache. "My sister vas out late at night vihz O'Malley. They became cold, and wet, and it attacked her lungs. She died of what zhey call pneumonia."

"Oh," Chester said. "I'm so sorry. For both of you."

That story seemed to quiet Chester, as we walked for several minutes with no more sounds than the crunching of sticks and leaves beneath our legs. Things like corn cobs grew from many of the tree branches. Must be the Australian version of pinecones. I made a mental note to take samples home with me to England for analysis. Yet another reason to survive this place.

"So," Chester said, "you got past blaming O'Malley for having your sister out late?"

I considered kicking the back of his knee. Surely, he could have asked that question better—by not asking it, for example.

"He vas proposing. It vas night, in beautiful, romantic, *Paris*. The rain—it could have been a storybook. But it vas not meant to be."

"I'm sorry. Just . . . forget what I said."

"I alvays do zhat," Jacques said.

I laughed. It's such a pleasure to see Chester's medicine returned to him.

Chester held up his hand to halt us.

"I don't think this scheme of ours is the brightest. We can traipse these woods until Law learns how to shoot straight, and still not find these chaps. We need to make them come to us."

"I like the concept of a trap," I said. "What would we use as bait?"

"You."

"I beg your pardon?"

"Well obviously it should be you since you're the only one of us who can't shoot straight," Chester said. "When they pop you, Jacques and I pop them."

"*When?*"

"I mean, when they *try* to pop you."

"Well, what if they succeed?"

Chester frowned, "No, we get them first."

"But what if you don't?"

Chester shrugged. "Then you're popped."

That was how I found myself feeding branches to a fire in a clearing in the forest. My rifle rested on my knee—not that it gave me much security. Theoretically, Chester and Jacques were hidden in the trees around me, waiting to shoot whoever came to shoot me.

It was simple enough, as plans go. I sit here by the fire and make sure there is plenty of smoke so the Assassins can see it from wherever they're hiding. Not having to slog through the forest was appealing, and now that I wasn't moving, the fire was not an unwelcome heat source. My biggest fear was that they would instead attack the house again. It wasn't likely, as the house was not a good place to attack in daylight. But possible.

I wondered what Pacarina was doing right then. Petr was probably lying on the couch holding a rifle and not saying anything. Maria was probably saying everything, and no doubt seventy-five percent was about

Chester. And Pacarina—she was probably keeping watch at the window, keeping Maria occupied, and keeping Petr comfortable.

I always pictured myself marrying some sober English woman who would have quiet tête-à-têtes with her friends and not bother me in my study. She would be plain—maybe on the verge of being an old maid and willing to marry me for security. I didn't think anybody younger and prettier would be interested in me, and anyway, I wasn't interested in them.

I cracked a branch and tossed the two halves into the fire. The green needles exploded in tiny flame-bursts and smoke-trails.

The thought that Pacarina married me still makes me a little giddy. A gorgeous Spanish girl with a personality more sparkling than shaken champagne and a heart kinder than anyone I ever met. She even plays practical jokes! Not quite my vision of married life, and yet immeasurably better.

Not that we never have bad days, and we don't agree on everything. But on the whole, an amazing experience.

I tended the fire for at least three hours. The sun was over the clearing and making its westward journey home. I wondered if Chester ever mastered how to tell direction by the position of the sun.

"Hello."

My limbs jerked, my rifle bounced from my knee, my chest contracted on my heart, and I fell onto the ring of stones around the fire.

I spun around, clasping my burned hands.

Bogdan sat on a stump. A fur-hatted body stained with blood lay at his feet.

"Ho!" Chester yelled.

Chester and Jacques burst from the undergrowth on opposite sides of the fire and pointed their rifles at Bogdan.

Bogdan raised his hands. "I just saved your life," he said to me, his voice not one note higher than usual. "Could you ask your friends not to kill me?"

I blinked. "How are you here?"

Bogdan shrugged and made it look nonchalant even with his hands in the air.

"Your friends didn't see me. Or the Assassin into whose head I just threw a knife." He lowered his left arm and lifted a knife from the ground. "Perhaps you would like the knife he was going to throw into your head as a souvenir?"

Jacques and Chester were by my side. I looked at my brother.

"Chester. Why are there two people with knives ten feet from me?"

"I've been watching my side closer than the Hunchback of Notre Dame watched Esmeralda. I've barely blinked."

"You ate an apple," Bogdan said.

"You ate an apple?" I said.

Chester definitely blinked now. "I don't have to blink while I'm eating an apple." He turned to Bogdan. "And how do you know I ate an apple?"

"I watched while I snuck past you."

My heart began to pump blood at the appropriate rate again.

"How did you get *here?*" I said. "Not, here at my fire, but here on this plateau?"

Bogdan placed the knife on the stump and crossed his arms.

"I have been following you, and the Assassins. I saw them find the underwater passage and followed them here."

"Hold," I said, "were you an Assassin too?"

"No. I have fought the government my whole life. I know a few things about not being seen."

I sucked a deep breath through my nose and exhaled from my chest.

"I'll be honest, I didn't trust you, Bogdan, but you saved my life. I am very grateful."

"You can show your gratitude by convincing your friend of his duty to Russia."

So, he hadn't given up at getting Nobody to be Tsar. That must be why he was still following us.

Chapter 32
Lawrence

"Were you at the attack on the house last night?" I asked Bogdan. He shook his head.

"Then, there's another Assassin in the woods?"

Bogdan nodded.

"All right. No more setting traps with bait." I speared Chester with my eyes. "Let's split up into two search parties."

"Right-o," Chester said. "Since you're such good friends with Bogdan now, you go with him. Jacques and I are going to go kill an Assassin."

"Very well," I said. "Do you have any more apples?"

He glared at me before stalking away with Jacques.

Ten minutes later, Bogdan and I were skulking through the forest. We were at the edge of the plateau, and blue sky blinked through the trees. The tree-covered mountain slopes in the distance were blanketed by the blue haze that gave these Blue Mountains their name. My theory is that evaporating droplets of the eucalyptus oil from the trees refract sunlight to create the blue mist.

"Will you?" Bogdan said.

"What?"

"Will you convince your friend to do his duty for Mother Russia?"

I tore my gaze away from the blue haze. "If my friend truly had a duty, he would be the first to fulfill it."

"He is the rightful heir to the throne. The people need him."

I looked at him. "Why are you doing this, Bogdan? Why come so far, work so hard, risk so much for this?"

Bogdan made a fist and pressed it over his heart. "They are my people. Our Tsar is cruel. My people suffer. It is in my power to bring to the throne a man who will lead my people justly."

I shook my head. "The Tsar isn't going to accept a replacement. If you tried to put Nobody on the throne you would start a civil war, and if you know anything about history you know war is the worst possible catastrophe for an innocent people."

"Russians sacrifice. We are willing to sacrifice for Mother Russia."

"Well then I'm sorry, because Colonel Nobody is not."

Bogdan was silent for a moment. "You won't convince him?"

I laughed. "You don't just *convince* Colonel Nobody of things. When he makes up his mind, it's like this." I tapped a boulder.

"I do not believe it," Bogdan said. "He will change his mind."

I shrugged. There wasn't much more to say.

I felt twenty-five percent safer here near the edge, since the Assassin could only conceivably be on three sides of us, not four.

Something moved in the trees ahead. I grabbed Bogdan's shoulder and crouched behind a boulder.

"Do you see that?" I whispered.

He made a hand signal. If I were Russian I might know what it meant, but I'm not, and didn't. I eased my head around the boulder until I could see.

"I see eyes," I whispered. "Someone's watching us. The eyes are— strange—they're not—they're not human." I blinked. "It's one of those Koala bears!"

The tension lifted from my shoulders and I leaned on the boulder to take a better look. The Koala hugged the lowest branch of a eucalyptus tree, maybe ten yards from where we stood. It was around two feet long, though it looked longer because its furry legs hung from its rear. It had a thick, black nose that reminded me of a soft beak. Its ears stuck straight out as if it had just woken from a long nap, which, if what I've read about Koalas is true, is what just happened.

"Look at that, Bogdan. It's the first one of these I've seen. It's so—adorable! I think it's the most adorable thing I've ever seen. It's like a big, fur-covered baby, after it's been fed, and burped, and everything, and it's happy and lovable. Pacarina would love this. I can't believe I'm saying this sentence, but, after we kill the Assassin, let's come back to get this."

"I am not here to look at pretty bears."

And I thought *I* was focused. This fellow didn't think about anything other than Nobody.

"In a very small way, seeing something that adorable almost makes coming to this place worth it."

"Let's keep walking," Bogdan said.

The Koala turned his head to watch us as we walked past. I had to shake myself to remind me why we were here. Hunting a man may be the worst feeling in the world. Well, no, being hunted is worse. Running through a cave in South America from natives and crazy Spaniards is an experience I will never forget.

My right leg hit something and stopped moving. My upper body kept moving. Half my brain said to grab something, and half said to hold onto the rifle and not accidentally pull the trigger. Before either side could win I was on the ground with my nose planted in the dirt. My cheek rested on the rifle barrel, but I was hazily grateful I had not pulled the trigger.

"A rope," Bogdan said.

I scrambled to my feet. Rope meant humans, and humans meant Assassins.

One end of a rope was tied around a thick stump here a few yards from the edge of the cliff. It led over the cliff.

"These cliffs are supposed to be unclimbable," I said.

"Someone is going down," Bogdan said.

I dropped to the ground again and crawled towards the edge. The rope was taut.

A man clung to the rope twenty feet below. He was using it to hold his weight as he shifted his feet from one foothold to another. I eased my rifle over a rock's lip and aimed it at him. He continued to descend, oblivious. My mouth became bone-dry. How could I just pull the trigger and shoot a man at unawares? He wasn't attacking me, he was leaving. But he would be back, no doubt.

I wiped sweat from my eyebrows and poised my finger over the trigger. *No.*

"Stop!" I yelled.

The man lost his footing and hung, swinging, from the rope. He looked up.

"Scot?"

It was the Scot, our outlaw companion, trying to leave the plateau.

"What are you doing?" I called.

He looked around him. "Oh, just going for a hang. How about you?"

I blinked. Sometimes he reminded me scarily of Chester.

"Where are you going?" I called.

"Down."

The rascal was even chewing grass.

"You're going back to your outlaw friends?"

"Maybe." He looked back up at me. "It's been nice visiting, but I have a mountain to unclimb. Give my love to the others."

I aimed my rifle again.

"You're not leaving."

The Scot smiled. "Sorry, Stoning, but you're not going to shoot me."

My index-finger twitched. Of course he was right, I couldn't shoot the Scot.

Bogdan grabbed the rifle from me and leaned over the cliff-edge.

"I will shoot you."

The Scot blinked. "Hello, random coat-wearing stranger. I don't know where you came from, but I believe you." He looked down. If he dropped, he would bounce off the mountainside and land skewered on a eucalyptus tree far below.

For a long moment I thought he was considering it. Then he reached a hand up to grab the rope above his head and ascended, hand over hand. I helped him over the edge while Bogdan covered him with the rifle. It took five minutes to raise the rope, coil it, and hide it in a bush.

The Scot watched, arms crossed, frowning. "You should have let me go."

"Quiet," I said. "We'll handle you later."

As I coiled the rope I was excruciatingly aware the other Assassin could be hiding behind a rock with a pistol aimed at my skull. We made enough noise to alert anyone in the area.

Crack.

Someone fired a pistol in the distance. A rifle followed it.

I spun to Bogdan. "I guessed they didn't bring rifles with them through the water. Was I right?"

Bogdan nodded.

"Then that should have been Chester or Jacques."

Chapter 33
Chester

After Jacques and I left Law and that crazy Russian, we plowed into the forest. Isn't that what they always say in the books? Not that anybody would want to drive a plow into a forest. We did kick up some dirt and leaves on the way, though.

"I should be court-martialed," I said. "Letting a Russian sneak right past me! I might as well have been snoozing with my head in a down pillow."

"Do not feel too bad," Jacques said. "Zhese are Russian Assassins. Zhey are zhe best in zhe vorld."

"Who cares? I let him waltz right on by to go stick a knife in Law. If it hadn't been for that crazy Russian, Law would be dead, and I don't trust that crazy Russian, and certainly not enough to stake Law's life on him."

"Remember, ve are talking about zhe kind of man who can infiltrate Squad One of zhe English Army and earn zhe trust of Colonel Whiting and Colonel Nobody. It is not such a terrible zhing zhat such a man can sneak by you in a forest."

"Mmm. Did you know Petr was an Assassin before he told us?"

"Of course. I have known for years. Zhe men of Squad One keep few secrets from each ohzer."

I glared at the trees, hoping the Assassin would pop his head around one. It was getting towards late afternoon and the ridiculously early sunset would be here soon.

"What was your sister's name?" I asked.

Jacques growled. "I knew I should not have told you zhat story."

"Oh, come on. Hunting is lonely work, and mad as I am at this Assassin, I'm not the silently angry type."

"I had two sisters."

"Ah. Did O'Malley love them both?"

Jacques glared at me. "*No.*"

"I didn't mean at the same time, I meant subsequently."

"O'Malley loved Adelaide. Susette is my baby sister. She is probably your age."

"My age?" I held up my hand. "Come now, Jack Frog, you're not *that* much older than me."

"You do not get to call me Jack Frog. The Irishman, the *bouef,* may call me Jack Frog. You may call me Jacques."

"All right, crazy Frenchman."

We came to a boulder. I signaled Jacques to take left and I took right. We circled the rock without meeting any Assassins.

"So," I said, "is your 'baby' sister still alive?"

"Of course. But I have not seen her since she vas young. She is gorgeous."

"How do you know, if you haven't seen her since she was young?"

"Zhe Lefevre family has been known for its beauty for centuries."

"Ah. Then how do they explain you?"

Jacques tugged his mustache and glared at me.

I spotted something strange ahead of us. I pulled Jacques behind a tree with me.

"See that?" I pointed around the tree trunk at a fur hat stuck on a bush.

"Be careful," Jacques whispered. "It may be a trap."

I kept as much of my head behind the tree as I could while I watched the hat. If there was a pistol connected to that hat, I didn't want it spitting at my head.

"Let's go," I said.

We stepped from behind the tree, rifles pointed. Nothing happened.

We stepped towards the hat, rifles aimed at the clump of rocks and bushes where it was, and my eyes roving for any place an Assassin might hide to put a bullet in us.

A pistol blasted and Jacques dropped like a block tower that's had its base yanked away.

A blur moved in the leaves at our feet. I jumped. A hand and sword sliced the air under my boots. I landed on Jacques and tumbled backwards.

"Get the cursed Russian!" Jacques yelled.

The Assassin burst from a layer of leaves covering a hollow in the ground. If I stayed on my back one second longer I was dead. I threw my legs up and pivoted on my right shoulder to do a pretty nice little flip. I came up with my rifle pointing at the Assassin and fired.

The fellow pushed the barrel away before I pulled the trigger. The bullet went blasting off somewhere into the unhelpful distance, but the barrel-metal burned the Assassin's sword-hand. He growled and dropped his sword.

I opened my mouth to say something clever about even Russians being able to feel pain, but before I could he already somehow had a knife in his right hand and slashed at my face.

I jumped back too slowly and the tip of his blade cut my eyebrow. Blood squirted over my eyes. The thrill of battle pulsed into my veins. This is life!

I threw my rifle at his head to buy a second to get into fighting stance. The Assassin blocked it and picked up his sword in his left hand. Must be left-handed. The burn left a red welt across his left knuckles. Jacques rolled in the leaves.

I pulled both swords from the X scabbard on my back. Time to put free-fighting to the test on an Assassin.

I ran at a middling-sized eucalyptus tree to the right, jumped, kicked off the smooth bark, and sailed at the Assassin, swiping with both swords at him like a child swiping a sharpened butterfly net at a deadly butterfly.

He blocked the cut, but my momentum pummeled him into the

ground. I blocked a knife-stab and we rolled apart. Since when do other people do flips to get up from the ground! That's supposed to be mine and Nobody's trick.

He lunged at my stomach. I crossed my blades under his sword and forced it up. We both kicked at the same time, but my boot-toe hit his shin and did more damage. We hopped apart.

He tossed his knife into the air, caught the tip and flung it at me. I barely blocked it with my crossed swords before he was at me again with his sword. We fought too fast to remember the steps, him slashing and stabbing and me barely a step ahead. At first when I pulled both swords against his one I felt bad because it's always the villains who get to have two swords against one, but now I wished I had three.

I wasn't winning. Have to change the rules. I blocked a cut as hard as I could, dropped my swords, and leaped. I hugged his sword-arm to his side before he could cut me and wrapped my right arm around his neck.

He dropped his sword and grabbed me. I wrapped my legs around his body and tried to power myself around to his back so I could choke him with my forearm. His hair smelled like weeks'-old sweat and looking inside that fellow's ears was scarier than delivering kittens.

The Assassin slammed my back into a tree.

"I—don't—break—that—easy," I said, fighting to get my arm under his chin.

His head slammed up into my chin. I got a good look at the solar system under my eyelids, but held on. There was no way I was letting this fellow kill me so he could go kill Law.

The muscles under that coat made me feel like Law. Instead of me choking the Assassin, the Assassin was steadily peeling my arms away and he would have me down in a minute. Time for another rule-change.

I let go and dug into his side with both elbows as hard as I could. Ribs cracked. I did it again and the Assassin rolled away, coughing.

Crack.

The Assassin stopped moving.

I wobbled my head towards Jacques. Jacques dropped his smoking pistol and grabbed his bleeding leg again.

"You took your time," I said.

His mustache bloomed black against his pale face. "I had a bullet in my leg."

"And I was hugging an Assassin." I sucked a lungful of air and slowly the smile came back to my face. Life is amazing.

"Jacques, we did it! We beat another Assassin! We survived!"

"You survived, I am on zhe ground bleeding to deahz. Vill you tie up my leg or vere you too busy learning flips to find out how to tie a tourniquet?"

I grinned and slipped off my leather belt. "You'll be right as rain. And I must say, I'm awfully glad it's you and not O'Malley who I have to carry back home."

Chapter 34
Lawrence

Bogdan, the Scot, and I were within thirty yards of the house when a rifle poked through the window beside the door.

"Stop!" Pacarina called.

I stopped. "Pacarina? It's me."

"Put the rifle down," Pacarina said.

I blinked. Why was she telling me to put my rifle down? Wait—I looked at my hands. I didn't have a rifle. Bogdan was covering the Scot with it. Oh . . .

"It's all right," I called, "Bogdan is a friend. He saved my life. And the Scot isn't a friend . . . long story, but please let us inside."

Another rifle protruded from the upper-story window.

"Pacarina—does Maria have a rifle?"

"No, of course—Maria!"

I raised my hands and backed away. "Maria, don't touch that trigger, pull the gun in slowly, don't touch that trigger, do not dare shoot me!"

Pacarina's rifle disappeared and a moment later, so did Maria's.

I wiped my forehead. "At least she was aiming at us. Statistically, she couldn't have hit us."

Pacarina wrapped her arms around me the moment I was through the door. I hugged her to me, breathing in the eucalyptus and tea tree that perfumed her hair. It was good to be alive, a state of being we both knew might not last much longer.

"You can put the rifle down," the Scot said to Bogdan. "I promise I'm not going to run. Nor will I single-handedly kill you all." His words had his usual bravado, but there was something different about his tone. Almost—defeated?

Pacarina's face twisted in confusion. She pointed to Bogdan. "Where did he come from?"

"Short story," I said, "he saved my life. And as for the Scot—we have to assume he was planning to betray us to the Assassins until proven otherwise."

The Scot shook his head. "That's not it." He sat at the table and propped his chin on his hands. "I'll explain, but Colonel Nobody needs to be here."

"Why?" I asked.

"Because it involves him."

Maria pushed forward. "Where is Chester? Is he all right? Did anything happen to him? Why isn't he with you?"

I held up my hand. "He was fine when we split up." I turned to the Scot. "You're not in a position to bargain about who is or isn't here when you explain what is going on."

"Why not?"

I thought about that. He had a point. I had no way to make him talk.

"I see someone." Pacarina pointed out the window.

Someone came from the trees and for a moment, I wasn't sure what to make of him. Then I realized it was Chester, bent double with rope or something around his shoulders. He was dragging a sort of sled, on which Jacques lay.

Ten minutes later we were through the initial greetings, incredulous questions, answers, and Maria's effusive delight that Chester was alive.

"We need Nobody back here," I told Chester. "Send a smoke signal."

Chester snorted. "I'm not going anywhere near that ant hive."

"Technically it's not a hive, but—just build another fire somewhere else."

Colonel Nobody came.

"What are you doing?" Nobody said to the Scot. "You promise to help us, you fight by our side, and then you desert your post? I gave you a chance to leave. Now you know how our defenses are set up. Why should I believe you weren't leaving so you could sell your information to the Russians?"

The Scot stared at Nobody. "Look, I . . ." his hands clenched. "I wanted to see what it was like."

"What *what* was like?"

"Why he followed you. He was always braver than me. I guess I thought I could be closer to him if I did what he did."

The Scot's usual smug expression was gone. His lips compressed, and his eyes shifted from person to person in the room with quick, darting glances that reminded me of a deer startled in a forest. Not that I had seen any deer since coming to this foreign land.

"Who are you talking about?" Colonel Nobody said.

"Edmund." The Scot stood, slowly, and extended his right hand to Nobody. "Hello, Colonel Nobody. My name is Jamie Burke."

I needed to sit.

Colonel Nobody blinked. He thrust his fingers through his hair. He tried to say something, but his voice caught. He cleared his throat.

"You're—Edmund's brother?"

"By blood. And you're his other brother—by bloodshed, I suppose."

How on earth could the Scot be Edmund's brother? I wracked my brain for something to discredit it. Jamie was in Australia—so was the Scot. The governor said Jamie was an outlaw—so was the Scot. Jamie was Edmund's older brother—the Scot was older than Edmund would be if he were alive now. The Scot was Scottish—but wasn't Edmund Scottish? And an older brother would have been more likely to retain the Scotch accent.

I think all of us were taking the same thought journey as me, perhaps with the exception of Maria, who cocked her head like a confused cat.

"But," Chester blurted, "you said you'd never heard the name."

"I lied."

Colonel Nobody cleared his throat. "If you're Jamie Burke, why didn't you say so before?"

The Scot—even if his name is Jamie, I still think of him as 'the Scot'—lowered himself back into his chair.

"Do you think I'm proud of being an outlaw, stuck on this forsaken continent? My brother was a war hero and I'm, what, a horse-thief?

I never said goodbye to Ed. How could I? One day we were together, the next I was on a prison-ship. Ed was all I had, so of course I thought about him every day while I learned to survive in this place. Then one day when I'm breaking my back plowing rock a soldier drops a newspaper in the mud, and I grab it, and hide it, and read it that night. It has a story about a strange officer in Siberia, a soldier without a name."

The Scot nodded at Nobody.

"But there was a name in the story. Edmund Burke. How strange, I thought, the same name as my brother's. And then I saw the sketch in the paper, of the colonel, and of his lieutenant-colonel. And, thousands of miles away from him, I found myself staring into my brother's face. Reading about his friendship, brother-like, with this odd Nobody."

"So you know . . ."

"Yes, I know he's dead. And I know it's because you were too late to save him." The Scot's lips twitched. "So, are you surprised that when I suddenly find myself with you, I should want to watch you, and learn who you are, and what you really thought of Ed, before I tell you who I am?"

"He was my best friend," Nobody said.

"I know." The Scot looked at his boots. "You became the brother I failed to be." He looked up. "Why did you want to find me?"

Colonel Nobody sucked his bottom lip between his teeth. His neck muscles twitched. "To meet you," he said. "To tell you about Ed."

"And you kept looking for me even after you found out I was an outlaw. Why?"

"The same reason."

Chester raised his hand. "Sorry to disturb the touching moment and all, but why are you an outlaw?"

"Because I'm not an animal. The soldiers treat us like animals, worse than I treat any animal. I stole some food in London. That gives them the right to make me a slave? I escaped because I couldn't take it any longer. So, an outlaw is the only thing I can be."

"I still don't understand," I said. "Why were you running away?"

"Because I'm a coward!" The Scot slammed his fist onto the table. "I thought I would be all noble like Edmund and fight for your freak of a colonel. I guess I wanted to respect myself. And then I heard the shooting here, and I'm staring into black night out of which some kind of mythical warrior is going to emerge and cut my throat, and I couldn't take it. So I sneaked away, and went to the secret way out, and tried to leave. Because I'm not like you crazy people."

Colonel Nobody wiped his sleeve across his forehead. "Let's go outside. We have a lot to talk about."

Chapter 35
Lawrence

I pressed my thumbs into the knots in Pacarina's shoulders, diffusing the little pockets of lactic acid into her bloodstream to relax her tension. Having us back at the house was a burden from her shoulders, and more because it meant we were alive than because it relieved the pressure from her of organizing the defense of the house if the Assassins came.

Our numbers were dropping. With Petr and Jacques wounded, and the Scot in whatever state of mind he was in, our number of able-bodied defenders was woefully small. True, Bogdan was with us, but that mystified me. And I was not the only one.

"All right, Bogdan." Colonel Nobody finally returned from his conference outside with the Scot. "What are you doing here?"

The Russian bowed to Nobody. "You know why I am here. To remind you of your duty."

"I know my duty, and I'm doing it. Here."

"Here?" Bogdan swept his hands over the room. "I am sorry, Colonel Nobody, but your men are dying. You say your duty is to save your friends? You are not going to save your friends by facing some of the best fighters this dark world has ever seen. You are all going to die."

"We'll do our best. The rest is up to God."

"God sent a messenger. Me. I am offering you life."

Chester snorted. "What, you can wave a magic wand to make these Assassins go away?"

Bogdan pointed to the Scot. "That man knows a way out. We can leave now. Beat the Assassins to the coast and sail for Mother Russia. Our people will flock to your standard and you will become Tsar. The Assassins are only loyal to Nicholas because he is Tsar. If you are Tsar, they will be loyal to you. Those you love will be safe."

Colonel Nobody looked at the ground. I know he thought of Liana, back in London. Hopefully, safe. Truth be told, she was the only one who mattered in this disastrous situation of ours. Yes, Nobody was our friend and leader and all those important things, but at the core of life, Liana was the one who mattered to him. As a husband, I understand in a way I couldn't fathom before I met Pacarina.

"If you don't come," Bogdan said, "I will have to find another. You know Ivan?"

Colonel Nobody's head shot up. "Ivan is an imposter."

Bogdan shrugged. "He says he has a claim to the throne. And he is willing to sacrifice for Russia."

"You're not a fool, Bogdan. All Ivan cares about is himself. You try to put him on the throne and you'll create the bloodiest revolution in centuries."

"Then give me another choice. Come to Russia."

Chester raised his hand. "Not to be the dolt in the room, but, who is Ivan?"

"He's called Ivan the Ugly."

"That's a great name," Chester said.

"I had—dealings, shall we say, with him when I was in Siberia. He is a barbarian. He'll murder and torture anything in his way."

"Mother Russia is bleeding," Bogdan said. "Hot steel pains the body, but it stops the bleeding. I will heal Russia, and if I cannot use a physician—" he pointed at Nobody, "I will use hot steel."

Colonel Nobody raked his right hand through his hair. "Russia is not my duty, Bogdan. That's not the life I've promised Liana. No."

Bogdan's face was expressionless. He bowed again, wrapped his coat closer about him, and retreated to the corner.

One of those uncomfortable silences happened where you know everyone is thinking how uncomfortable it is and everybody knows somebody is going to have to break it, but no one wants to break it because they know everybody else knows the only reason they're talking is to break it.

"I know what we need," Maria said.

Chester grunted. "A regiment of soldiers."

"Nothing so horrible, no, what we need is tea."

Chester stroked his chin. "That's a surprisingly good idea. Pacarina, would you do the honors?"

"I'll make it," Maria said.

Chester blinked. "Er . . . you make tea?"

Maria flounced into the kitchen. "It can't be any challenge at all. Why, anybody can make tea, my maids could make tea blindfolded."

Chester shot me a look that said he wanted to say her maids also knew how to dress themselves by themselves. Oh, no. I knew what Chester wanted to say by just looking at his eyes. At this rate I might start thinking like him soon.

Chester coughed. "I really think that a little help—"

"Don't patronize me," Maria said. "I can make a cup of tea by myself."

Chester cocked an eye. Maria talked back to him about as often as Jacques complimented O'Malley.

"I'm going back to the Passage," Colonel Nobody said.

"Not without a cup of tea," Maria said.

"I don't like tea."

"Nonsense, everyone likes tea."

Colonel Nobody opened his mouth to protest but Pacarina signed for him to agree. I suppose none of us wanted to deal with another fit from Maria. We should have.

I won't detail the tea-making process other than to say it took a long time, with a high number of alarming exclamations from Maria, and a steady stream of people in and out of the kitchen to monitor the progress in silence.

At last an enormous pot of black liquid was finished and Maria poured a cup for every single person in the house. She handed them out with such pride at having done something useful that to refuse a cup would have made me feel like a monster.

"Drink up!" Maria said. "If you don't drink it I'll know you think I'm a terrible tea-maker and can't do anything."

Chester sat at the table holding the cup between his hands and staring at the curling steam as if it might poison him. I sat beside him and clapped his shoulder.

"The faster you drink it the faster it will be over," I said.

Chester eyed Maria, who faced away from us as she handed cups to Petr and Jacques. He screwed his face, closed his eyes, and gulped through the cup. His eyes shot open and he plopped the empty cup down.

"My mouth," he croaked. "I hoped it would burn off my taste buds. It's horrible." He covered his mouth and bent away from the table.

I tilted the lip of my cup against his and the liquid in my cup happened to flow into and fill his cup.

"Chester!" Maria called. "Aren't you going to drink my tea?"

Chester unbent himself and stared at his cup. He looked at me. "You despicable—" he coughed. "Yes, Maria, of course I'm going to drink your tea." He shivered a little bit, lifted the cup, and drank through it.

"It's quite something," I said to Maria.

She smiled.

"Mr. Burke," Maria said, "you haven't drunk your tea."

"I tasted it," the Scot said. "Frankly, it's not very good."

Maria gasped. "Why—Chester thought it was wonderful. Didn't you, Chester?"

Chester opened his mouth. I coughed warningly. Pacarina glared at him. He blinked back at them. "It—the tea I drank—it was—unlike any other cup of tea I have tasted."

"There, you see?" Maria said. "I don't mean to offend you, Mr. Burke, but I'm afraid your time away from England has warped your taste for real tea."

The Scot shrugged.

Chester squirmed in his chair and glared at me. I smiled back, thinking of the day years before when Chester and I sat in a Peruvian rainforest and I encouraged him to take a second helping of *masato*. I didn't yet realize this drinking would have different consequences.

Chapter 36

Lawrence

"I feel like a nap," Chester said.

That was the first sign something was off.

Maria was collecting the tea-cups from everyone and stacking them in the kitchen.

Colonel Nobody stood. "Get some rest, Chester. You have night-duty tonight." He yawned. "I won't mind a bit of sleep myself tonight."

The Scot also stood. "Goodbye, everyone."

"What are you talking about?" I asked.

Colonel Nobody spoke. "Jamie and I understand each other. I've made my peace with him for—for what happened to Edmund. He's leaving."

Chester raised his hand. "This is the absolute worst time to lose a fighting man."

"That's our problem, not Jamie's."

"I'm going to get help," the Scot said. "I will come back."

"No, you won't," Nobody said. "This isn't your fight. I've been the death of one Burke, I'm not going to let that become two." He stifled a yawn. "Come along, I need to get back to O'Malley and you need to get down your secret path."

They left.

I expected more talk but no one else seemed interested in saying any-thing. Jacques and Petr were both sleeping. Chester waved goodbye and climbed the stairs.

I turned to Pacarina. "Dear, I don't—" I stopped. Her eyelashes fluttered.

"I don't feel very well, Law." She put a hand to her forehead. "I think I'm going to lie down."

That did it. Something was wrong here. Something hit the floor upstairs. It sounded like a body. Was Chester tired enough to fall on the floor? I looked back to Pacarina to see if she heard it. Her head touched the table and drool dribbled from the left corner of her lips.

The cups in the kitchen stopped clinking and Maria gave a little sigh. "I'm so tired." She looked at me as if I was far in the distance, and then sat on a stack of potato bags. Her head faded from view behind the ledge.

Something was majorly wrong if Maria was going to sleep on potato bags. I blinked. What did she put in that tea? I hadn't had any . . . something rustled in the corner. I made up my mind. Everyone except Chester thought I drank that tea, so I should be falling asleep as well. I forced a yawn, slumped back in my chair, and closed my eyes. I drew my line at drooling, though.

A chair shifted. Someone was moving. I cracked my eyelids and watched Bogdan emerge from his corner and step from person to person, watching their breathing.

I closed my eyes and forced my breathing to be slower than the pounding of my heart. If he went upstairs toward my sleeping son, I would take him down. I felt his eyes boring into my face. It felt like ten minutes—then the door latch lifted and the door thudded closed.

I forced myself to stay silent for another minute, in case it was a trap. Then I opened my eyes. I was alone in a room full of sleeping people. Bogdan was gone.

"Pacarina?" I whispered. I lifted her head from the table. It was as limp as the ragdolls Chester used to practice firing squad upon.

I laid my index and middle fingers on her neck. There was a pulse. I bent close and heard the slow intake and exhale of air. She was alive, thank God, but drugged.

Jacques snored in his sleep.

I ran my hands through my hair, trying to wrap my mind around the timeline. Who drugged Maria's tea? Had Bogdan been able to slip something in? We all were in the kitchen at different times—he must have. The blood movement from walking might delay the onset for Nobody, but if he had the same dose as everyone in this room he would be collapsing soon as well. But wait, why would Chester fall asleep even before the wounded men or the women? I slapped my head. Thanks to me he'd had a double dose of tea.

Did Bogdan drug us so he could escape? That wouldn't make sense. He wasn't technically a prisoner, and even if he felt he was, this was far too complicated and risky a plan. He was after Nobody.

I took the stairs two steps at a time. Chester lay on the floor by my bedroom door. I rolled him over and slapped his cheeks.

"Come on, Chester, wake up. You're the one who dragged me out here, you can't go to sleep now." I slapped until there were red finger marks on both sides of his face, but he didn't even grunt.

I exhaled. All right, Lawrence. It's up to you.

The window at the top of the stairs covered the path Nobody and the Scot would have taken. I sidled to the left jamb and peeked out. The flapping tails of Bogdan's coat disappeared into the trees.

I ran down the stairs. I had my sword, not that I could do much with it. I had my pistol—same concern. A pair of rifles leaned against the wall. I grabbed one. Rifles are easier to point and shoot than pistols and more likely to sink a bullet in the target.

I waited another thirty seconds, to let Bogdan get beyond the initial tree fringe, and then I slipped out the door and set off after him.

A stiff wind blew over the plateau and cumulonimbus clouds scudded above me. The weather was going to turn ugly soon. I glanced at the river to see if the level had risen, which would point to rain upstream. What? At least one yard of riverbank that was covered by water earlier today was bare. The pontoon boats, usually at a level with the bank, were now bouncing against each other.

I shook my head and refocused on my goal. One problem at a time.

At first, I ran with my rifle pointed ahead, but if someone with Bogdan's skills knew I was following him, I would die, rifle at the ready or not. I slung it over my shoulder and focused on minimizing the sound of my footfalls.

The birds were raucous because of the brewing storm. At least three spiders, each as large as my hand, scurried up the eucalyptus trunks. The sound of the rushing water on my left faded as I ran deeper into the forest.

Wait. The water on my left—I couldn't reach the Passage from this side of the river. This is the way the Scot would come to get to his secret path, but Nobody would have crossed the pontoon bridge to go to the Passage. So was Bogdan going to escape the plateau using the Scot's path? Perhaps he wasn't after Nobody at all. Or . . .

I threw myself against a tree. Bogdan knew the Scot was the only one of us who didn't drink the tea, so Bogdan must be following him to make sure he left the plateau. Then he would come back for Nobody, who was probably asleep on the other side of the river. And Bogdan would come back straight through me.

I searched for a place to hide. There was little undergrowth—just bare trunks, fat and skinny, that didn't blossom into leaves until five or ten yards above my head. Even if I could climb one of them the branches weren't thick enough to hide me. The twittering birds mocked me. They could hide their chirpy little bodies and laugh at me as much as they wanted.

What would Chester do?

I remembered the ground became rockier closer to the edge of the plateau. I could find some rocks to hide in, but it meant continuing to follow this path, and Bogdan might return by it any minute. I growled. It was my only choice.

Three hundred yards and a pint of fear-sweat later, I found a cluster of boulders to hide within. I slithered into the gap on my stomach, poked my rifle out in the direction of the plateau edge, and pushed the rifle-butt into my shoulder. I felt like a snake waiting to spit fire upon its unsuspecting victim. Grr. Why did I have to think of snakes?

There is an unwritten rule in life that I plan to prove through scientific experiment. As soon as you start thinking that something might be, it will begin to feel that way. I've heard a friend was sick and immediately began feeling as if I'd drunk days' old cream. I can think about an itchy nose and my treacherous proboscis immediately begins twitching. So when I think about snakes while lying face-first scrunched between two rocks on the cold ground—yes.

Please, Lord, let there be no snakes here. Or spiders. I remembered the gray arachnids I saw scurrying up the tree-trunks. Snakes are a thousand times worse than spiders, but the prospect of either scurrying up my trousers was enough to make me jump to my feet. I tried to access the part in my brain that would tell the rest of me that these fears were irrational and overstated. That part was playing an excellent game of hide-and-seek with me, but I managed to find enough of it to keep me there on my stomach.

I counted time to occupy my mind. Each time I reached sixty seconds I pressed another of my fingers into the dirt and restarted.

One minute. No sounds but birds.

Three minutes. The same.

Five minutes. I tried calculating how far we were from the spot we found the Scot leaving the plateau, divided by the average man's walking pace, plus a little extra speed to account for the Scot's determined stride, and ended up losing my minute count.

Somewhere around ten minutes, I reran my mental calculations about Bogdan's reason for coming this way. Maybe he meant to kill the Scot and I was hiding when I could be saving a life. No, Bogdan was smart. Smarter than the rest of us, with his twisted scheming. If the Scot was removing himself from the situation, trying to kill him would increase the likelihood of something going wrong and Bogdan's plan failing.

I was eighty-five percent sure Bogdan was returning my way.

Maybe eighty percent.

I was down to forty-two percent when I heard crunching.

My right hand involuntary clenched and I blessed Chester for teaching me to never keep my finger on a trigger.

Bogdan's coat and beard came into view through my little window between the rocks. He was walking three feet to a stride, like a man who wants to run but knows he can't keep running for as long as he needs to.

My rifle barrel pointed at Bogdan's stomach. If I pulled the trigger now I might not miss him. I touched the chilly metal band that would release the bullet and my shoulder automatically tensed for the recoil.

I swallowed. I have killed before—and the memory of each visits me in my dreams—but always in the rage of battle. To shoot a man in cold blood is another matter. A thousand reasons why I should not shoot him flashed to mind, and they were good.

There was a chance I was misunderstanding Bogdan. The man saved my life, and he hadn't killed me when he thought I was drugged in the house. Maybe there were even more wrinkles in this unironed mess of a situation than I knew. My moment of opportunity passed before I decided, and he walked right past my rocks.

I closed my eyes. Yes, I know it's like an ostrich burying its head in the sand and thinking it can't be seen, but I did it. Regardless of the state of my eyes, Bogdan must not have noticed me as his steps continued right past me without a break. I could risk moving for the chance to shoot him from behind, but I would probably make too much noise, and besides, I wasn't sure I should shoot him.

Bogdan's steps faded back towards the house. I relaxed my chest muscles and exhaled a lungful of stale air. I shivered my shoulders to ease the ache where the back of my neck met my spine.

Now, I had a choice. Follow Bogdan, or count on my prediction he would come back this way again being true.

He was not interested in hurting the people in the house, at least not this moment, or he would have done so earlier. Colonel Nobody was the person I could count on him not hurting as his whole purpose for being in this ridiculous situation was to return Nobody to Russia alive. So, my best plan was to wait where I was. Although, I should turn around.

Chapter 37
Lawrence

The spider stared at me.

An hour of lying in this grimy cranny made me grumpy enough to not care that the eight-legged creature seemed to contemplate climbing my head. He chose the rock next to me instead and scurried from sight. The brewing storm explained why the animal population would be on the move, but did not explain why they would be going up. Creatures hide from storms. These seemed to have Chester's attitude of running towards the danger.

An hour of second-guessing my decision to ambush Bogdan had me at the point of banging my head on a stone just to distract my brain. Bogdan could be doing anything he wanted to anyone. The Assassins could be attacking our undermanned Passage. I could be sealing our death-warrant by lying here, doing nothing.

Something more guttural than the birds' screams interrupted my thoughts.

I gripped the rifle and squinted.

Someone said something in Russian. It wasn't one of the few words I learned after finding out Russians were trying to kill me, but judging by tone, it was a curse. It came from the path to the house.

Something came into view from between the trees. I blinked. It had—I blinked again. Four arms and a shapeless lump where the head should be. For a moment I thought we had entered the land of monsters.

Then I realized it was a man carrying another man draped over his shoulder with his head and arms hanging down. The man carrying the body wore Bogdan's coat. A steel strip peeked past the right sleeve of the man being carrying. Bogdan was carrying Nobody. I was right.

I couldn't shoot Bogdan without hitting Nobody unless I aimed at Bogdan's legs. Colonel Nobody's hands dangled against Bogdan's knees. No, I would not risk that. I thanked God the choice was made for me. I was brain-tired of death and killing.

I gathered my legs, pressed my boot-toes into the dirt, and leveraged myself into a standing position. My joints tightened in protest so that I had to lean against the rock to keep my balance. I gritted my teeth against the stiffness and leveled the rifle at Bogdan.

"Set him down," I said.

Chester would have spent the last hour thinking of the perfect quip to say now—assuming they don't just come to him as naturally as swimming to fishes. Me, I was tired, hungry, stiff, and done with being lied to, so I skipped the funny lines.

Bogdan looked up and cursed again in Russian.

"You should be asleep."

"I would be if I drank my tea. Set him down."

Bogdan growled. He hesitated a moment, then lowered Nobody to the ground, looking more like he was glad to rest from the burden than that he feared for his life.

"Are you going to shoot me?"

"Not if you leave right now and promise never to return."

Bogdan stroked his fingers through his beard. "I don't want to hurt any of you. Let me go and I will make your friend the Tsar of Russia. Is that such a bad thing to do?"

"There are only seven words I want to hear from you," I said. "'I promise to not come back here.' Say that and I will let you go."

"You're not a killer," Bogdan said.

"I am what I need to be. I've seen enough death for a lifetime, but I'll do what needs to be done. Even if that means more of it."

Bogdan's right hand hovered beneath his beard-tip. In a moment it could be within the folds of his unbuttoned coat to grab whatever weapon might be hidden there.

I curled my index finger around the trigger.

"You're thinking," Bogdan said, "that I could grab a knife from within my coat and skewer you."

"You could try," I said.

"You're not a killer," Bogdan repeated. "But I believe you have killed. And you would try to kill me if I tried to kill you." His hand moved back to his beard. "What is it that you want?"

"I want you to promise to leave us alone."

"And you will shoot me if I don't?"

"I will shoot you for trying to kidnap Colonel Nobody." I laughed. Not quite the cool, sarcastic laugh Chester would have managed, but I was proud of it. "You honestly think that when Colonel Nobody wakes up he will magically do what you want?"

"I will do whatever I need to do to get him to see the light. If I have to keep him drugged until we get to Russia, I will do so. When he sees the power he can have, he will join us."

I shook my head. "You're talking about a man who sailed to the ends of the earth to protect those who depended on him and then let his best friend die because he found another, greater duty. You aren't going to tempt him with power and riches."

"He's a human. Every human wants something, and I will find what it is."

"Right now what he wants is for all of us to survive this place. And currently you're an obstacle to that."

Bogdan's eyes flickered. "Perhaps all of you are the chains holding him back. Perhaps all of you need to be eliminated."

"As if the Assassins are just going to kill all of us and let you walk away with the one person who is the reason the rest of us need to die. They'll kill you, too, when they find you."

Bogdan smiled. "You know little of the ways of the world. You think they don't know about me? You think I could have followed you here and come through the underwater passage behind them without them knowing?"

I paused. It was amazing to think that the best assassins in the world could be so outwitted and used. But if they knew about Bogdan, what possible reason could they have for not killing him? Preventing Nobody from joining Bogdan's people was the reason they were trying to kill Nobody.

Bogdan folded his arms. "You think that in the world there is black and there is white. Men are friends, or men are enemies. That is not how the world works. The Assassins are of use to me, and I am of use to them, and as long as both are true, we tolerate each other."

"How are the Assassins useful to you? They're trying to kill Nobody."

"Exactly. That danger to him and all of you was my best way to convince him to do his duty. Coming with me to Russia is his best way to survive and keep you all alive. That danger of death—as long as he does not actually die—is my best tool."

"But how are you useful to them?"

Bogdan smiled. "How do you think they knew so quickly where you sailed to? Or where you went after you came to Sydney?"

I blinked.

"Assassins are good, but they are not magicians."

"You treacherous little pig," I said.

Bogdan shrugged. "I get things done."

The depth of this man's plans boggled my mind. Things that seemed random made sense.

"You have two choices," I said. "You can promise to leave right now, go back to Russia, and never bother us again."

"Or you shoot me?"

"You grasp options quickly."

Bogdan's arms remained crossed. He looked down at Nobody's body. I willed my hands to hold the rifle level. The strain of holding the heavy gun pointed at Bogdan's stomach was making my muscles quiver.

"Very well," Bogdan said. "I promise."

I blinked twice. I didn't expect this to be so painless. And I didn't trust this man. For all I knew I was working right into his grand scheme.

"How can I know you won't break your word?" I asked.

Bogdan shrugged. "Maybe I will. Maybe I'm a liar. You could still shoot me—but can you justify killing a man who has promised to leave you alone?" He smiled.

I raised the rifle six inches to point at his chest bone and steadied myself for the recoil.

He contemplated me from beneath those bushy eyebrows, measuring whether I would do it. I'm not sure what I would have done, but he must have had enough doubt to decide not to risk it.

"I swear on my dead father," Bogdan said, "I will leave this place and return to Russia and never bother you again."

I exhaled. "Good choice. March."

I marched him to the edge of the cliff and watched as he picked his way down the path the Scot showed us. Just before he disappeared into a clump of stunted undergrowth that bristled off the mountainside in the middle of the path, he looked up at me, smiled, and gave a mocking wave. Then he was gone.

I pulled the rope up, stepped back from the edge, and sat in the dirt. Cold wind ripped past and through me, chilling the sweat that soaked my body. I rubbed the cold-bumps on my arms. I should be in my study with a fire blazing on the hearth and a cup of steaming tea sitting next to my open book.

Chapter 38
Chester

"Chester."

The fists kept coming. Slam, slam, slam into my face. I swung at it as hard as I could, but nothing happened.

"Chester."

The voice was louder, somebody calling my name, behind the fists. I couldn't see anything. As hard as I looked, I couldn't see anything. Wait. My eyes were closed.

I opened my eyes. *Whack.* My cheek tingled from the blow. I blinked. There was something familiar about the voice.

Wetness sloshed over my face and up my nose. I snorted and slapped at my face to protect it. This time my arms actually moved, and I caught the hand that was hitting me.

"Chester."

I knew that voice.

"Pacarina?"

"Wake up, Chester."

I shook my head and blinked up at the light shining into my eyes.

"Why are you hitting me?"

"You call those 'hits?' Get up, Chester."

I groaned and forced myself to sit up. Pain skewered my skull's innards. Pacarina knelt beside me, her hand cocked back to slap me again.

I shook my head. "I'm awake, I'm awake. What's going on?"

"He drugged us."

I shook my head again to make my thoughts stop stumbling around like a cripple playing Blindman's Bluff.

There was a wall next to me and a wooden floor beneath me. A very uncomfortable floor, at that. The aches in my bones shouted at me more loudly than the tingling in my cheeks from Pacarina slapping me. I brushed my dripping hair out of my eyes.

"Who drugged us?"

"Bogdan. He's gone, and so is Law."

I remembered sitting downstairs and drinking that ridiculously horrible tea and then that despicable Lawrence giving me his cup. I went upstairs . . . ah, I must have laid on the hall floor. My elbow smarted. A lovely purple splotch covered it. I guess I didn't exactly *lie* on the floor.

I scrambled to my feet.

"Are you all right?" I asked Pacarina.

"I'm fine, but Law is gone."

I frowned. "Was it the tea? That rascal gave me his. He didn't drink any, so he wasn't drugged."

"Then where is he?" Worry lines wrinkled Pacarina's face.

"Is there any blood?"

Pacarina shook her head.

"Well there's going to be when I get my hands on Bogdan." I growled at the dizziness and tramped downstairs.

Maria sat at the table with her head in her hands. Jacques and Petr sat on their beds looking like they were waking up from drinking a bottle of whiskey each.

I checked for broken chairs, scuffs on the floor, anything that showed a struggle. Nothing.

Pacarina followed me downstairs. "Law wouldn't just leave us here."

"Not unless he thought there was a greater danger out there."

I looked around for weapons. "I'm going after him. When I find that

Bogdan . . ." I let their imaginations figure it out.

I stuck two pistols in my sash and strapped my sword-belt around my waist. The straps on these rifles were fantastic. I slung one over each shoulder and stuck a handy axe in my belt. I grabbed my bag and headed for the stairs, slipping knives from the bag into my clothes as I went.

Downstairs I emptied the bag on the table and grabbed my Death Gauntlets. The tension wasn't quite where I wanted it, but who cares. I slipped them one after the other onto my wrists and tied off the leather straps with a good tourniquet knot. It was about time these things did real service.

I plopped my hat on my head and headed for the door. Pacarina beat me there. She held a rifle.

"Where do you think you're going?" I asked.

"With you."

"Dear Sister Heart, you're not stepping outside of this place. I don't know what's out there."

Pacarina didn't budge. "I do. My husband is out there, and I'm going to find him with you."

She propped her rifle against the wall and lifted Otho onto her hip, then bent and shifted him around so he lay face-down on her back. She wrapped a shawl around his back and tied off the ends under her chest and stomach. She picked up the gun.

"Let's go."

I grunted and turned to the others. "You lot think you can survive without us?"

Jacques waved me away with one of those disdainful French sniffs. "Go get zhe coward who dared desecrate tea, however poorly prepared, vihz his ungodly herbs."

Maria gasped. I got out of there before she could start calling on me to defend her tea, drugged or not.

I got about two steps outside before I stopped in shock and Pacarina slammed into me. At least she knows not to carry her rifle pointing forward. That's why I avoid walking in front of Law when he's armed.

I pointed at the river—or rather, where the river should have been.

"Did that drug make me hallucinate, or is that a waterless river?"

Pacarina gasped. "What happened?"

There was a deep, empty gash in the ground where the river should be. The pontoon boats lay grounded on the slimy river-bottom.

Gray clouds plugged the sky. Farther up, lightning flashed within the clouds. The thunder roll that followed was low, but there.

I scratched my head. "I know Law is the scientist in the family, but—I thought storms added water, not sucked it up."

"They've dammed the river," Pacarina said.

"Then that means they've got a beautiful paved road leading right to us. We have to get to the Passage now."

My lungs felt as sucked free of air as the river was free of water by the time we reached the Passage. Pacarina didn't say a word. We don't talk about my asthma.

O'Malley crouched at his post. He swiveled to see who was coming and glared at us.

"Ye took yer sweet time. What, did ye all decide tae take naps while I sweat it out here alone?"

"Yes," I said. "Long story. Have you seen Colonel Nobody or Lawrence?"

O'Malley frowned. "They're with ye."

"No, they're not. They haven't come this way?"

"No, and thankfully the dirty Assassins haven't either, yet." He nodded at the river. "Ye may not 'ave noticed but there doesn't happen to be any water in this river."

"We've got to find the Colonel and Law," I said.

"We have tae guard this." O'Malley stood and stretched. "I'm scarce enough tae guard a river Passage, let alone a dry-shod Passage. We need ye here."

"They're in danger," Pacarina said.

O'Malley nodded at the Passage. It was a deep shadow scar in the dimming light. "And we're not? If those Russians get through this place we're all dead."

Chapter 39
Chester

Sitting on a wet rock in a riverbed pointing my rifle at the dark space between two rocks is not my idea of fun.

Pointing my rifle at a spot where bad blokes might pop out is fun, but not when the blokes take hours to pop.

O'Malley convinced Pacarina and I—or is it Pacarina and me? Who cares, he spun his dastardly arguments about logic and best things to do and dusty things like that, and we ended up sitting by the Passage waiting for the Assassins to walk down the beautiful little road they drained themselves.

The sky spat at us and did an awful lot of growling. The lightning was like jagged teeth. He must find it terribly painful to chomp birds and things with those grinders.

"What are you looking at?" Pacarina asked.

Ahem. I was still looking at the sky. "Just watching the storm," I said.

"Now probably isn't the best time to daydream."

That girl, she could always tell what I was thinking.

"Trust me, I'll not miss the first Russian who tromps his way through that Passage. And you'd best not miss the next couple." I nodded to the rifle-rack for which she was holding the trigger string. "It's the ones after that who worry me."

Another thunder-roll let loose. The sky must be gargling. I dismissed it and was about to explain how I would deal with the fourth and fifth Assassins when something strange about the noise flicked me on the brain. I cocked my ear.

"Have you ever heard thunder that long?" I asked Pacarina.

The whites of her eyes stared at me.

"I don't think that's thunder."

Thunder is supposed to taper off after it has its laugh, but this noise kept getting louder and my seat rumbled.

"Water!" O'Malley bolted from the Passage. "Run!"

I kept my rifle trained on the Passage. What was so frightening about water that—*crash*.

The sound was like thunder with a wet cough on top of cracking rocks.

A black wall of water spurted through the Passage.

For a second my legs planted roots while my brain caught up with the rest of me and then I dashed helter skelter behind Pacarina for the left bank, swords and rifles and things banging against my back and hips and shins as I ran. I cupped my hands under Pacarina's boot and threw her up the bank.

She swung her arm down and helped hoist me up beside her. The water sucked the bank underneath me and I crawl-rolled away from it as fast as I could. The dirty water followed me for twenty feet, totally obliterating the riverbed because there was just so much pent-up water forcing its way through. I thought the river was fast before, but this was like comparing a wet tortoise to a wet hare. All right, it's a weak comparison, but if I've got to pick one to chase me for twenty feet I'd rather have the tortoise.

We collapsed next to O'Malley. Pacarina swung Otho to her hip and cradled him, bouncing him up and down and hushing him to stop crying.

O'Malley spat. "There go our guns and spikes."

I couldn't see anything in the water rushing past us other than the whitecaps in the eddies, but I knew our spikes, and the rifle-rack, were all on their way to the waterfall. Worse yet, we couldn't get anywhere close to the Passage because of the water.

"Do you think their dam burst?" I asked.

O'Malley shook his head. "I think the rats burst it themselves. They couldn't have thought up a better way tae get us out o' that place."

"But they can't get through either," Pacarina said.

"Trust me, this is no accident. They've got themselves some kind of a black plan."

The water was leveling. Not getting calmer, more like a race horse figuring out what track to run and putting its nose down. Space appeared between the water surface and the bottom of the Passage. Then something filled it up.

"What's that?" I pointed at dark masses coming through on top of the water.

They answered me with a flash of light and a gunshot. The bullet whistled by.

Boats! I swung my rifle off my shoulder and squeezed a shot at them, but I doubt I got anywhere close. You try hitting a man on a boat that's going downstream and sideways at seventy yards. The fact that somebody on such a boat got a bullet near me with his first shot sent some unpleasant thrills through my arms.

The two boats shot downstream towards the house.

"So much for being impregnable," I said. "We've got to get back to the house before they do."

"How do ye propose we do that?" O'Malley said. "In case ye haven't noticed, we're on the wrong side of the bank. And also in case ye haven't noticed, there's a lovely raging river goin' right past us ready to sweep ye off the edge of the world if ye jump in."

"And people say I exaggerate," I said. "Fine, let's go get any that land on our side."

I handed Pacarina one of my rifles. She set hers down when she stationed herself at the rifle-rack, so it was gone off the edge of the world by now.

"Stay close to me, Sister."

We set off through the trees. All our plans to keep these Assassins out of this place failed, as I thought they eventually would, so now it was time for the real thing. Kill or be killed. And being killed was part of no plan of mine.

Chapter 40
Lawrence

"Lawrence," Colonel Nobody said.

I wiped sweat from my forehead on my right sleeve.

"Lawrence. Why are you dragging me?"

I dropped his upper body in the grass. "You're much heavier than you look," I said.

Colonel Nobody struggled to sit up and swiveled his head at the peaceful forest scene around us.

"What happened?"

I told him.

"I see." Colonel Nobody rubbed his temples. "I should have known even Maria couldn't make tea taste that bad. It's been so long since I had tea, I thought my memories of it were better than the reality."

He seemed to be taking my summary of events rather well. If I woke up with somebody telling me what I told him, I would be as confused as a scholar translating an Ancient Roman manuscript and finding it was an ode to Queen Victoria. Then again, I suppose Nobody is inured to life being strange. Then again, again, I was getting plenty of that kind of inoculating myself.

Colonel Nobody gripped my hand and staggered to his feet. "Is anyone hurt?"

"I don't think so."

"Thank you." Colonel Nobody brushed leaves from his trousers. "Did

Bogdan think he could keep me drugged until he got me to Russia?"

I shrugged. "He's a persistent fellow."

Colonel Nobody sniffed the air. "Storm."

"The atmosphere is doing strange things. The animals are taking to the trees, and the river level is dropping."

"Dropping?" The dullness from the drugs faded from Nobody's eyes. "We have to get to the Passage. Where are we?"

"On the other side of the river."

"Come on, we have to get to the bridge."

He set off in the direction of the house and I followed, rubbing the soreness from my arms and back. I had new respect for Bogdan, if he could carry Nobody from all the way across the river.

"It sounds like you did well," Colonel Nobody said over his shoulder.

"I don't know about that. I'm not exactly at my best in the face of—all that's going on here."

"Do you know what I love about you, Lawrence?"

I had to quicken my pace just to keep up. "What's that?"

"Your innocence. I know that sounds strange, and I don't mean you don't know how the world works or that you haven't seen more than your fair share of the worst parts of it. But you're not used to it. And that's good."

"What do you mean?"

"Me, I'm a soldier. I was born for war." Colonel Nobody shook his head. "I was practically born *into* war. I literally can't remember a time in my life without it. Blood, and killing, and all that, I'm used to it. I don't enjoy it, but it's natural to me. It's not natural for you, and I pray it never will be."

Lights from the house's windows blinked through the night when we emerged from the forest. That meant people were alive.

"Who goes there?" Jacques called.

"It's me," Colonel Nobody said. "Is everyone all right?"

I hurried past Jacques to find Pacarina. The only woman downstairs was Maria, which is about as opposite from Pacarina as one can be. There was something else that bothered me, something that was missing, but I couldn't tell what.

"Where's my wife?"

Jacques hobbled from the window, lowering his rifle and leaning most of his weight on his good leg.

"She is gone vihz your fool of a brohzer to find you." Jacques sniffed. "I am not surprised to see zhat he failed."

"He must have gone towards the Passage. We'll cross the river and find them."

"River? You must not have seen in zhe dark. Zhe river has gone zhe vay of my mohzer's crêpes. Zhat is, zhey—and it—are no more."

"What do you mean the river is gone?"

"Zhe vater in zhe river is gone."

I paused. That was what was missing. There was no rushing water. There was thunder, and the patter of rain on the roof, but no river-sound.

Colonel Nobody grabbed a rifle. "Come on, Lawrence, that can only mean one thing. We have to get to the Passage before the Assassins attack."

At that moment a different sound joined the thunder.

We stared at each other.

"Petr," Colonel Nobody said. "What are they doing?"

Petr sat on his bed with his arms folded above the white swath of bandage around his abdomen.

"Flood," Petr said.

Flood? I blinked. How could we have a flood if all the water was gone?

Colonel Nobody growled. "They've learned some new tricks since you hunted with them," he said to Petr. "Lawrence. Will the water reach us here?"

The water? Ah. They must have dammed the river and then burst the dam—oh, that's bad.

I tore through the calculations in my mind. Take the hours the river was kept from flowing, and the average rate of flow, subtracting the runoff that must have happened—they couldn't have dug or built a dam fast enough to dry up the river without using some type of runoff channel—take into account the likely distance between the dam and the Passage, far enough to be hidden from our guards, then increase the velocity when the narrow Passage limited the volume capacity of the water . . .

Numbers and guesses and variables swirled in my brain.

"I think we're far enough away," I said. "But if any of our people stay in the Passage . . ." I bit my lip.

"Let's pray they aren't. And that they have not gone too far." Colonel Nobody's face was tight. "The Assassins will be behind the water."

I pressed my face against the window-glass. A wave of water, darker and yet lighter at the same time than the surrounding shadow, rushed towards us. It spread far beyond the riverbanks, sucking the soil away in one massive act of erosion.

The water reached the pontoon boats and I expected to hear the chains holding them in place snap, but the water sucked away the posts to which the chains were tied, and everything disappeared downstream towards the waterfall.

I started breathing again when the water's horizontal spread slowed before it reached our house's walls. Even so, it was closer to us than I calculated.

I bent my head in prayer. My wife and baby were out there in the middle of this storm and flood and whatever else was coming next. *Lord, protect them.*

A gun fired, followed seconds later by another. The Assassins were here.

"Boat!" Colonel Nobody said. "Down!" He slammed the door and threw himself on the ground.

I caught a glimpse of a dark shape flying on the water-crest towards us. Sparks erupted from the shape and the window-glass I was leaning into with my face gave way. Shards sliced my right cheek before I could even think to lean back. There was that terrible moment of suspended reality where you know you're about to be in great pain, but the shock temporarily dulls it. Then the pain came.

I spun away from the window and grabbed my cheek. It was wet, and the pressure from my hand made the blood well up to the tips of my fingers.

Colonel Nobody grabbed me and pulled me away from the window.

"Are you hit?"

"I've—no idea."

"It vas only zhe glass," Jacques said. He pointed to a bullet hole in the wall opposite the window.

"Lights out," Colonel Nobody said.

Petr grabbed water we stored for washing and doused the fire in the fireplace. Jacques and Nobody blew out lamps and candles until we stood in complete darkness, with dying candle-smoke smell hanging in the air.

Men shouted outside in Russian.

"Here we go," Colonel Nobody said.

I sensed, rather than saw, him taking his position at a window.

"Here," Maria whispered.

Her hands brushed my face and she slid soft fabric beneath my hand against my cheek.

As the initial throb of pain dulled a little, I had some mental room to grab at my scattered wits. Someone fired at me from the boat outside. The bullet missed me, but it must have spidered the glass I was leaning into like the fool I am. Yet again Death had been inches from me.

Maria looped strings around the back of my head and pulled, tightening the cloth against my cheek in a smooth movement that hurt and felt good at the same time.

"Thank you." I jumped up. This wasn't the time to be distracted by cuts and bruises.

"Jacques," Colonel Nobody whispered, "take the high ground. Take Maria with you."

Jacques stumped towards the stairs. I wouldn't have sent him up them with just his single good leg, but I'm sure Nobody had a good reason.

Someone outside shouted in Russian. It sounded like he was shouting at us. He waited, as if expecting an answer, then shouted again. I berated myself for the seventy-fourth time for not knowing Russian.

Petr called back in Russian.

I crawled to Nobody's side. "What's going on?" I whispered.

Colonel Nobody put a finger to his lips.

I don't know what Petr said, but the fellow outside did. He was talking loudly—not shouting, it was too dignified for that—but whatever he was saying sounded serious. Either that or anyone speaking Russian sounds serious. Petr and Nobody always did when they talked Russian. Thunder punctuated the Assassin's sentences.

"He's distracting us," I whispered.

Colonel Nobody shook his head. "It's more complicated than that."

"Is he giving us the option to leave?"

Colonel Nobody said nothing.

The man stopped speaking. The thunder and rain and rushing torrent filled the silence. Then another voice spoke. It sounded older, and somehow, I don't know how to describe it, it sounded powerful. He was in charge.

He repeated one word at least five times. It sounded like he was saying "sin," but it was unlikely an Assassin was accusing us of being sinners.

As soon as he started speaking, Petr started like a man touched with a red-hot poker. Colonel Nobody drew a sharp breath.

The voice ended with what sounded like a question.

No one in our house said a word. I looked from Nobody to Petr, and back. It was too dark to see much of their faces, but the room was tense.

"What did he say?" I asked.

Colonel Nobody was silent.

"He said," Petr said, "if I do not fight them, they will not kill me."

It was my turn to be silent. "I suppose," I said at last, "that's fair from their point of view."

The older voice spoke again. He repeated that word, "sin."

"What does that word mean?" I asked. "'Sin.' He keeps saying that word. Does it mean 'die?'"

No one said anything.

"Look," I said, "we're all about to die here. I deserve to know what is going on. Consider it my last act of curiosity, if you want."

"It's Petr's to say," Colonel Nobody said.

Lightning flashed the room white for a moment.

"Son," Petr said. "It means son."

"Why is he saying 'son?'"

"Because he is my father."

Chapter 41
Lawrence

"Your *father* has been chasing us around the world trying to kill us?"

Petr nodded.

I turned to Nobody. "You knew?"

"It's Petr's secret, to do with as he wishes."

"But why would your own father want to kill you?"

"He doesn't," Petr said. "I would have been killed for betraying the brotherhood long ago were it not for him."

"He convinced the others not to kill you?"

"He ordered them not to."

"Oh. So your father is in charge of the men who—" I stopped. "Your father was Vlad? The man who almost killed my son?"

Petr bowed his head. "I am sorry."

The man outside called again.

For a long moment, Petr fingered his rifle. He exhaled. "Nyet."

"What did you say 'no' to?" I asked.

"I said I would not leave the fight."

"Then—they'll kill you?"

"They will try."

"And—you will fight your father?"

Petr's rifle barrel clunked against the windowsill. "I will do what must be done."

I crouched below the level of the windows just before bullets thudded into the walls and shattered glass.

"Flashes," Colonel Nobody said.

He and Petr each stood next to a window. They spun into the killing zones and fired before spinning away and grabbing fresh rifles. Gunpowder fumes attacked my nostrils. The sound was deafening.

Ah, they were shooting at the muzzle-flashes outside. Even Assassins can't mask the spout of sparks that accompanies each bullet. And they must be firing at our flashes. I didn't stand up and shoot, not because I was afraid, although I was terrified, but because I knew I didn't have the skill to hit them or not be hit by them.

I wouldn't be useless, either.

I lifted my rifle so the barrel pointed out the window, towards the sky, and fired. Every muzzle flash I gave them to shoot at without a person behind it was a shot I saved Petr or Nobody from receiving.

Something knocked the rifle from my hands. I groped for it and burned my hands on hot, twisted metal. They shot the rifle.

Jacques screamed things in French upstairs and kept up a steady fire.

"By the door," Petr said.

Colonel Nobody spun to the window by the door. As he fired, something flew through the door and rolled on the floor towards me. It trailed sparks.

"Grenade!" Colonel Nobody said.

I'd never seen a grenade. They weren't known to be reliable and they made no sense in modern warfare with weapons that would mow a man down before he could reach throwing distance, but I've read of them being used in close combat in ship fights and in siege warfare. We were under siege.

The black ball rolled against my leg. Sparks spat from the fuse in a line of fire eating towards the inside of the ball. I grabbed the ball and threw it out the closest window, my mind registering surprise at how cold it felt. I suppose the sparks made me think it would be hot.

The explosion rocked the house and blew a cloud of noxious gunpowder fumes through the window.

I was gasping for breath from the first explosion when a second ripped through the upstairs and showered us in dust.

A third grenade flew through the window above my head and thudded into the far wall. The fuse flared in that last bright glow before it reaches the gunpowder.

That grenade brought with it such a clarity that I was almost grateful amid the chaos of gunfire and smoke and dust and the ringing in my ears to know exactly what to do. I could reach it before it exploded but I wouldn't have enough time to grab it, aim for a window, and throw it outside before that dull black ball became an orb of fire. There was only one thing I could do.

I scrambled across the room—I can't remember if I was on two feet or all fours—and pounced on the grenade like I've read about the footballers in Rugby jumping on the ball in their strange version of the game. I pressed the grenade into my stomach so hard it felt like it was inside my ribcage. I willed my body to cushion the explosion enough to save Nobody and Petr.

My last thought was of Pacarina's eyes.

I kept thinking of her eyes. And thinking. And thinking. This was a long last thought.

The grenade pressing into my innards forced a gag reaction and I coughed.

"Lawrence?" Colonel Nobody said.

I rolled off the grenade, an inch at a time, until I saw the fuse. The fuse had burned away, leaving a charred mark on my waistcoat where it pressed against the fuse.

"It must be a dud," Colonel Nobody said.

I confess that the shudders grabbed me and gave me a long shake. Truly accepting you are about to die, and then not dying, is an experience I strongly recommend against.

"Thank you, Lawrence," Colonel Nobody said.

"No man," Petr said, "will ever again call you a coward in my presence."

I forced a shaky laugh. "Nice to know people have been in the habit of doing so."

A fresh round of shots reminded me my preparation for death might still come in handy.

"I don't think we can stay here," I said.

"You're right." Colonel Nobody lifted the grenade between his thumb and forefinger and tossed it out a window.

Jacques stumbled down the first few stairs, coughing. His teeth were a white gash in his powder-blackened face.

"Zhe blackguards have blown a hole in zhe wall," Jacques said.

"Is anyone hurt?" Colonel Nobody asked.

"No, it vas in zhe room next to us."

"All right," Nobody said. He scanned the room. "We're going out that hole. Everyone upstairs."

"Colonel," Jacques said, "I vill not be much use to you vihz zhis traitor leg of mine."

Colonel Nobody paused. "All right. Trojan Horse."

He kicked the sofa toward the half-wall and pulled the trap door open. Jacques stepped down and Petr and Nobody replaced the sofa, hiding the trap door.

"They'll kill him," I said.

"Only if they find him." Colonel Nobody shouldered a rifle. "Let's go."

I followed him up the stairs. Petr brought up the rear. Everything was eerily quiet. Yes, there was the thunder and rain, but that sounded like crickets chirping compared to the explosions. I massaged the soft flesh beneath my right earlobe, hoping my eardrums were not permanently damaged.

Another explosion shook the house and threw us to the floor. I narrowly missed breaking my nose on the back of Maria's head and ended up tangled on the floor with her.

"I want Chester," Maria said.

"That makes two of us," I said.

Petr grabbed my hand and hauled me to my feet. If we had been below, we would all be dead right now. And the Assassins might think we were. This must be what Nobody called 'using the enemy's tactics against them.'

We ran towards a ragged hole at the end of the hallway through which moonlight beamed. Colonel Nobody reached it first, but he didn't stop. He leaped, throwing the rifle away from him as he fell, landed with a roll that started with his palms, then left shoulder, then back, until he was on his feet without stopping. This was the "free-fighting" he and Chester developed.

I stopped at the hole, looking for a less dangerous way for myself and Maria to descend, but Nobody wasn't finished. He came out of his roll running and charged a man loading a rifle.

The Assassin dropped the rifle and pulled a pistol from his belt, but Nobody reached him before he could pull the trigger. Colonel Nobody lifted off from the ground, kicked the hand holding the pistol with his left leg, and kicked the man's chest with his right.

The pistol flew into the air and the Assassin exploded backwards and landed on his back. Colonel Nobody also landed on his back, but he somehow levered himself up onto his feet. The Assassin sprang up. Moonlight glinted off steel in his hand.

I covered Maria's eyes.

The knife struck Nobody's left forearm and clanged against the steel beneath Nobody's sleeve. The Assassin swung up with his left arm, but Nobody deflected it with his steel-plated shin and closed with the Assassin, his forearms crossed in front of the man's head. He brought them together like a pair of scissors on the man's neck and the Assassin dropped his knives and staggered back, grasping his throat.

Colonel Nobody released a flurry and kicks and left arm strikes, each blow landing with a sickening crunch. The Assassin stepped backwards, trying to block the blows, until a final kick to the head leveled him. He didn't move.

Colonel Nobody stepped away from the body and waved for us to come.

Chapter 42
Lawrence

When I woke, I stared up at eucalyptus trees and gray sky peeking between the sparse branches. My stomach was as empty as an inkpot in the desert. I reached to touch Pacarina's hand and felt cold steel. I sat up with the sudden memory of where I was and what happened last night.

Maria lay a yard from me, snuggled into a pile of our jackets. Colonel Nobody sat on a log, his rifle leaned against his shoulder, and his eyes on the forest. Petr sat against a tree on the other side of Maria. His eyes were closed, but I think he would know if something moved in the forest before I saw or heard it.

Colonel Nobody looked away from the forest and nodded at me. I scooted to his log, rubbing my arms to chase some of the cold from my bones.

"Do you ever sleep?" I asked, keeping my voice quiet enough to not wake Maria.

"I'll sleep when this is over." The wrinkle lines on his forehead were deep, and there were dark sacs beneath his eyes, but his eyes were not dull.

"How do you think it will end?" I asked.

Colonel Nobody shook his head. "I don't know. God has been good to us so far."

I clasped my arms around my knees. "Do you think we'll survive?"

"If we kill all the Assassins. Which hasn't been done since . . . ever."

I rubbed my hands. "That's a little less cheerful than I'm accustomed to hearing from you."

"I don't have to paint the world bright for you. You see it for what it is."

There is something special about being complimented by Nobody. I suppose it's because I have so much respect for him, or perhaps because some part of me envies him.

"How many of them are left?" I asked.

"We killed two at the church, and the four who came underwater. I shot one by the door last night, and then the man behind the house. Eight down, eight left."

"I have a confession," I said. "Last night, when you killed that man, I didn't feel very innocent. I wanted it. I didn't want to want it, but I wanted it."

"Why, do you think?"

"They came so close to killing Otho." I shivered. "You can't know what it means to almost lose a child until you have one of your own."

Colonel Nobody nodded. "Revenge is human. It's not right, but it's certainly not a weakness unique to you. I've had my own demons to slay. I have not always been clean of heart during the slaying."

I gazed at my trouser knees and counted the number of fray marks between the grass stains. It looked like a decaying game of noughts and crosses.

"Noble," I said. "How do you forgive?"

He sighed. "When men wrong me, when they kill those I am close to, I think about myself. I think about how terrible I am. The things I would do if Christ had not redeemed me. I realize the men who hurt me are no more monsters than I am, and I thank God for saving me, and pray he will do the same for them."

"And you find peace?" I asked.

"Eventually."

I sat back against the log and watched the sunlight seep in to brighten our little space between the trees. Brighten is too strong of a word, as the storm's gray and chill hung over and through us. I couldn't decide whether the water driblets falling were only from the dripping trees, or if they were mixed with rain. Colonel Nobody drew a handkerchief from his shirt sleeve and draped it over Maria's face to protect her from the drops.

"How is he at peace?" I asked, nodding at Petr. "My own history with my father is a little checkered, but I cannot begin to imagine him trying to kill me."

"He finds peace in doing what is right," Colonel Nobody said.

"And you trust him?"

"With my life. With Liana's life."

"How long have you been waiting to marry her?" I asked.

Colonel Nobody shook his head. "At this rate I'll be an old man before we tie the knot."

"And approximately how long will it take until you're an old man?"

He smiled. "You and your age questions." He rose. "I'm going scouting."

I settled back to my watching. We were close enough to the waterfall to hear the rushing river terminate into a dull roar as the water cascaded off the mountain.

Maria stirred, pulling the jackets around her as if she could suck warmth from them into her bones. Her face lightened for a moment when she saw me, then blanked.

"Sorry, I'm not Chester," I said. "Hungry, cold, and sore?"

She nodded, although it was more of an upwards shiver.

"You did well last night."

She looked at me as if I was making fun of her. "What do you mean?"

"Well, you didn't faint."

Red spots pricked her cheeks. "You think I'm a coward."

"You're in a different world. I know how it feels, that first time you're pulled into what feels like a completely different planet. For me, it was Peru."

She looked up. "Pacarina has told me about Peru. You and Chester don't really talk about it."

That was because we avoided talking with her about anything as much as possible, but that wasn't the best thing to say. And I suppose it wasn't really true of Chester anymore. Besides, she looked fragile, in a way. Not that she ever looked strong, but that layer of feminine bluster was thin.

"I wasn't brave in Peru," I said. "Frankly, I was what Chester would call a 'wet blanket.' I complained my way across that country."

"Pacarina saw something different."

I shrugged. "They say love is blind. The point I'm trying to make is that I understand what you're going through. It's scary, and hard. It can measure a man's, or a woman's, character, but it can also grow character."

"What you mean is that my character has been wanting up to this point, and I should use everything we're going through to grow my character." She laughed at my face. "I'm not always as dense as I seem." She sobered. "And I've learned a lot from all of you these months. I know I'm not like you all, but, if I can see that now when I couldn't before, doesn't that mean I've grown?"

"I think it does," I said.

"I hope I get a husband as good as Pacarina's, Lawrence."

I thought it was another unsubtle hint that she wanted to marry Chester, but her eyes were too serious to be scheming.

"I hope you get one much better," I said.

Colonel Nobody returned. "I don't think they're nearby."

"Then I apologize for the extreme practicality of the thought, but what are we going to eat?"

"I think that's exactly what the Assassins are asking themselves about us. The truth is, there isn't much in these woods to eat, and they may wait a day or two to let hunger sap our strength before they attack again."

Petr nodded his agreement, and I noticed for the first time that there was a blood splotch on the bandage around his abdomen. His wound must have reopened. He looked sapped of strength already.

Chapter 43

Chester

"Tell me they're alive, Chester," Pacarina said to me.

"Oh, they're alive. They have to be, our people don't die that easy. Although bringing throwing bomb thingies into the war is a bit unsportsmanlike. I would despise them for it if I didn't think it was an amazing idea. I have to make some of those things for myself."

"You would blow yourself up."

I rolled my eyes at her. "Fine, I'll badger Law into making them for me."

She smiled with her mouth but not much made it to her eyes.

"Seriously, Sister, I don't think he's dead. If he was, the rascals would be in their boats coming over here to finish us off."

"Aye," O'Malley said, "ye're right there. They'll stay on their side until they mop up the rest of them, and then come over here fer us."

I frowned at him. "Put it more negatively, why don't you?"

He frowned back. "Do ye think I like what's going on here? And that fool of a Frinchman with a bullet in his leg? How they ivir managed to hit Jack Frog in the leg is more than I can say. They must have been crawling like sarpents to reach something as is that low tae the ground."

"As I see it," I said, "we have two options. Stay here and moon about what's going on over there, or figure out a way to get over there, and change what's happening."

"Ye think we can get across that river?" O'Malley said. "Ye're crazy if ye think we can even get tae the river."

"What are you talking about?"

O'Malley stuck his cap on the end of his rifle and raised it above the bush we were hiding behind at the edge of the forest. Two seconds later a bullet ripped through the cap. We scrambled away from that bush faster than cats running from a screaming child dressed as a mouse. Don't ask how I know how fast that is.

I glared at O'Malley. "I'm supposed to be the one who does crazy things like that."

O'Malley shrugged. "It was a might safer than counting on ye listening to me."

"What about bending the trees down like trebuchets and launching ourselves over the river?"

Pacarina looked at me.

I held up my hands. "It's just an idea. We're getting over there somehow. What about the plateau edge? Maybe there's a way around the river."

"Ye mean across where the waterfall jumps off the edge?"

I grunted. "Never say never until you've seen the never. Let's go explore it."

The waterfall was absolutely amazing. It was great before the flood, but throw all that extra water into it, and it was amazing. Law would have all sorts of fancy words for it. Majestic. Royal. Sovereign. I guess those are all synonyms for being a king. Anyway, it was amazing.

One of my favorite books is *Last of the Mohicans*. Cooper is the best, even if he is American. Well, not the best, because you have Scott and Austen, but he's up there. The battle at Glenn's Falls with the cavern behind the waterfall and Heyward and the savage fighting on the edge of the precipice—that's a story. And it got me to thinking. What if our own waterfall had its own cavern?

"I know what you're thinking," Pacarina said.

"What am I thinking?"

"*Mohicans*."

"It could be there!"

She smiled. "I'm not saying it's not. Let's find out!"

I turned to O'Malley. "Help me tie the rope around this tree."

I took the rope coil from O'Malley's shoulder and we tied it around the tree closest to the river. It was at a right angle to the river and the edge of the plateau, maybe twenty feet each side. I wrapped a few turns of the rope's free end around my right arm and walked towards the river.

"Are ye crazy?" O'Malley said. "Ye can't just walk intae the river and go over the edge."

I gave him a good eyebrow-raise. "Says the man who just asked the Assassins to shoot at his hat. Two pulls means come on down. Three pulls means haul me back up, and if you see the rope flapping around, it means I fell off. Wey-ho!"

I dove into the river. Talk about fast-moving. I was barely chilled to my marrow before I was over the edge and falling in the middle of an ocean. I tried to open my eyes, but the water pressure forced my eyelids down. I meant to have my face pushed into my arms to protect it when the rope pulled me into the side of the mountain, but I was so stretched out hanging on to the rope that I swung in face-first.

I tensed my face as if that would protect it from smashing into stone, but instead of that happening, I kept swinging in until I was out of the worst of the water. I blinked through the water in my eyes at a dark space and scrabbled with my feet for a toe-hold. I found one. My momentum tried to swing me back into the water, but I dug my heels into the rock and wound some slack from the rope and managed to not go swimming again.

I wiped my sopping sleeve over my eyes to try to clear some of the water out of my vision. I knew it! There was a cave, or at least, a glorified ledge, tall enough to crouch in and deep enough to not be too at risk for falling off. I'm sure there's some geographical reason why caves happen behind waterfalls—or maybe the word is geological—who cares, if I ended up being interested I could ask Law about it.

I gave the rope two tugs and waited.

Only a little bit of light made it through the waterfall, just enough to show me a foot or two of ledge on either side. Sure, I could explore the ledge to see if it actually went all the way, but then I would have to leave the rope dangling without the two pulls and they would think I was dead. Probably should have come up with a better plan before I jumped off the waterfall. Oh well.

Pacarina came swinging through the water into my arms and her soaking hair whipped my face. I spat it out and set her down beside me. She grinned at me. Otho crowed from her back.

O'Malley joined the party and we all sat-stood in our crouch positions behind the water-wall. O'Malley gave his obligatory grumbles about me being a hare-brained reckless fool, but nothing I haven't heard a million times from Law before.

The waterfall was far too loud to talk, so I waved them to follow me and crouch-crawled towards the other end of the ledge. We could be in quite a pickle if this ledge didn't go all the way or there wasn't a ropeless way up the other side.

I kept my eyes on the shadows in case there were any treasure-chests laying around. You never know about these waterfall caves.

The one thing there was plenty of was moss. My boots tore great chunks of dripping moss off the bottom of the ledge and crunched the beetles living there. Better beetles than spiders. I bent away from the ceiling at that thought.

Chapter 44
Lawrence

Colonel Nobody tapped my leg and pointed into the trees in the direction of the waterfall. That wasn't the direction I expected the Assassins to come from—but then again, wherever you least expected them was where you should most expect them. A paradox.

Someone was coming through the woods.

Colonel Nobody motioned Maria to the other side of the log. He and I lay with the log between us and our attackers. I rested my rifle on the wood and ran my tongue around my mouth to try to coax out a little moisture.

Petr remained sitting with his back to the tree, facing us. He was watching the trees at our back, which reminded me that if the Assassins were smart, which they were, they would come at us from both sides at once and place a bullet in my back while I wasn't looking. I resisted the urge to look behind me and instead focused on not pointing my rifle at Petr.

Something red waved.

"O'Malley!" Colonel Nobody exclaimed.

"Colonel! Thank God ye're alive." O'Malley stepped into sight, followed by Chester and—my wife.

Rarely has it felt so wonderful to hold my wife to my heart and know she is safe. I only say rarely because this is not the first time for us to be reunited after not knowing what happened to each other.

"All right, Brother," Chester said. "Next time you two take a break from kissing, would you mind explaining why you're wearing that bandage on your face?"

I gave Pacarina one last kiss and shifted Otho to my hip.

"It's just a scratch," I said.

"No." Chester held up his hand. "You said that terribly wrong."

I cocked an eyebrow at him.

"You said, 'it's just a scratch.'" He repeated me dismissively. "You make it sound like it's just a scratch. You have to say, 'it's just a scratch.'" He repeated the phrase as only Chester can. "There, you see? That makes it sound like it's almost a deadly wound but you're treating it like it's just a scratch because you have more important things to do."

I untied the strings keeping the bandage on my face and pointed at the cut. "There, you see? It's just a scratch."

Chester shook his head. "You're hopeless, Law."

Pacarina stroked the raw flesh. Her fingertips were cool against the heat of the localized inflammation. Strange, her hair was dripping wet.

"If you treat it just right," Chester said, "you can get a nice scar out of that."

"Why would I want a scar?" I asked.

Chester blinked at me. "Hello? Do you know what I would give to have a scar on my face? Every main character worth his salt has scars and creases on his weather-beaten face. Women love scars."

"Yes, well, I already found the best woman in the world, and she didn't marry me for my scars."

Pacarina patted my arm. "No, I married him for his love of adventure."

Even Colonel Nobody laughed.

"How did you get here?" Colonel Nobody asked.

"Cave beneath the waterfall," Chester said.

"Can we get to the other side using it?" I asked.

"We could, sure."

I looked at Colonel Nobody. "We could cross and leave by the Passage."

"You mean keep running?" Chester said.

"Technically, yes."

Chester hooked his thumbs on his rifle straps. "Colonel Nobody, I have a proposal. All we've done since your wedding is run. We ran from church, we ran from your burning house, we ran across the ocean, we ran from Sydney, and so on. Miraculously none of us is dead yet—wait, where's Jacques?"

"He's playing Trojan Horse in the cellar."

Chester turned to O'Malley. "Does that mean he's all right?"

"As long as the Frog doesn't start chattering tae himself, he's probably alive."

"Hmm. Good." Chester turned back towards us. "Anyway, let's stop running. I'm tired of looking over my shoulder. Let's go finish this thing now. Let's take the fight back to them."

Colonel Nobody nodded. "I think you're right."

Chester blinked. "I am?"

I coughed. "He is?"

"We came here to finish this fight without involving innocents. If we run back to civilization, we defeat that purpose. And if we stay in the wild, where else is a better place to fight than here? Let's end this."

The other men nodded. I looked at Pacarina. She nodded.

"All right," I said. "Your logic is sound. Let's go attack Assassins."

Maria raised her hand. "What about me, and Pacarina, and Otho?"

"No place is safer than any other place," Nobody said. "We may as well stick together."

There were no supplies to pack or fire to put out. We shouldered our weapons and moved into the forest. We fanned out until we were a long horizontal line sweeping through the trees, one deep. I kept Pacarina close beside me on my right, and Petr tramped his path about three yards from me on my left. He was in no fit state to be marching to a fight, but one look at his face convinced me he was still worth two of me in battle.

Maria's eyes were serious. She has never looked that serious. I've seen her terrified, and she looked scared now, but she also looked—I don't know how to describe it. Matured, almost. And she didn't fawn or faint when Chester appeared. Maybe she really was growing up.

The way we formed this line seemed symbolic. We were each equally in danger of death, and we were each equally going to do everything in his or her power to prevent that death.

I circled a eucalyptus and walked into a rifle's sights.

A group of men in loose shirts and trousers stood in a glade with rifles and pistols leveled.

"Kill them!" someone shouted.

"Wait!" said a familiar voice.

The Scot jumped between Noble and a small man pointing a pistol at Noble.

"These aren't the Russians," the Scot said.

"I don't care. They're on my land."

I remembered the rifle slung over my shoulder. There was no way I could get it down, pointed, and fired at any of these people before they hit me.

"Move, Scot," the small man said. He was the height of the half-book-case next to my desk at home.

"They'll help us," the Scot said.

"Hello, Donovan," Chester said. "Looking for some mustache wax?"

Donovan swung his pistol to cover Chester. "Gallah, you should be dead."

Colonel Nobody stepped forward. "Truce, Donovan. Help us and we'll leave. Fight us and you'll regret it."

Donovan swung his pistol back to Nobody. I tried to gather my wits from the corners of my skull. These must be the outlaws who kidnapped Chester. They came through the Passage—or perhaps they came up the path the Scot knew about. They wanted to kill Russians. But they also wanted to kill us.

"We don't need you," Donovan said. "Scot, get out of the way or I swear

I'll blow that haggis-eating head off your body."

The Scot shrugged and stepped aside. He lifted a pistol to Donovan's head and pulled the trigger. A red haze blasted from where the outlaw's head used to be, and his body crumpled.

I blinked.

The Scot snapped his fingers.

"I'm in charge now. Anybody have a problem with that?"

A man with a scraggly half-beard stepped towards the Scot, but his comrades murmured something and he stepped back without saying anything.

"Right." The Scot winked at Noble. "Colonel, consider these reinforcements. Those Russians butchered some of our boys to find out about this place, and they chose the wrong ant mound to kick. What's your plan?"

"You came up the path? Did you see any Assassins?"

"Aye, and nay."

They huddled heads long enough for the world to stop spinning for me. The Scot raised his hand and the outlaws trooped after him through the woods back the way they came.

We forged ahead and reached the edge of the forest without dying.

There was the wide swath of open space extending to the river bank and house. A clump of horses grazed at the edge of the forest. At first I thought that meant the Assassins brought their horses through the Passage, but these beasts were bare-backed and native. I recognized the one I rode just a few days ago when I pulled Chester out of the river.

The hole in the house's second story glared at us like an empty eye-socket. The chimney was crooked, probably cracked by the grenade-blasts last night, but there was smoke coming from the top. Wind whipped the gray tendrils away as quickly as they topped the chimney crown. The same wind chilled me as we stepped through the last few trees and into its full brunt.

Chester stared at the sky.

"Law," he said. "What is that?"

The sun was hidden again by clouds, but not the way it usually is. Usually when clouds hide the sun, everything looks gray. These clouds sparkled, as if the sun was reflecting off thousands of shiny surfaces in the clouds. But that's not how water vapor works.

Chester growled. "If this is another Assassin trick . . ."

Something touched my bare arm. I looked down to find a small spider clinging to me. A silk thread trailed across my birthmark. I flicked it away. Something tickled the back of my neck. I slapped it and smeared squashed spider innards on my fingers.

I looked up to find the tree they were dropping from, but we weren't under any trees. We were under the sky. And in that sky, falling in undulating waves, were sheets of spiders.

Chester screamed. "Law, it's spiders! They're falling from the sky! They're falling from the sky!"

I side-stepped another floating spider as I tried to collect my wits. Yes, sometimes when it rains, spiders mobilize by jumping off tall things like plants and trees and letting the wind grab their silk and take them elsewhere. I've seen it happen when I was studying botany with my tutor. But this was thousands of spiders, maybe millions, doing it together.

"I'm sorry!" Chester yelled. "We should never have come to Australia. They're—*spiders* falling from the sky!"

He swung at the air with his sword and danced like a maniac.

Silk fell on patches of earth around us and sparkled like snow in sunlight.

Shouts from the house tore my attention away. Assassins stood outside, also staring up at the sky.

Chester jumped away from a square foot of spider silk descending on his head.

"That's it! I'm ending this!" He wrapped his arms around one of the horses' necks and swung himself onto the beast's bare back. "A Stoning!"

Colonel Nobody looked at me and swiped a spider away from his head. "Now I've seen it all."

He jumped onto another of the horses and dug his heels into its flanks. O'Malley followed suit and raced after them. The last horse—the one I rode a few days ago—stared at me.

So did Pacarina. "Let's go, Law." Her eyes burned with the fire of her Incan and Conquistador ancestors. "Let's end this."

I sucked a deep breath, spit out a spider, and reached for the horse. Pacarina cupped her hands and boosted me onto the bare back. I reached down and managed to swing her up without swinging myself off. Otho clung to the sling on her back. The horse whinnied beneath its double burden.

"For life!" I yelled.

Chapter 45
Lawrence

I wrapped my legs as far beneath the horse's belly as I could and willed my boots to be glue. Pacarina wrapped her arms around my chest and pounded her boots into the horse's flanks.

We shot forward faster than a bibliophile who just caught sight of a first edition in a bookshop, but the other riders had a head start and the distance between us increased as we rode because of our horse's double burden.

When I realized what the others were doing, I can't say I was sorry we were in the rear.

Chester did it first. He threw himself down the side of his horse until he hung with his left arm wrapped around the base of his horse's neck, and the crook of his left foot gripping the ridge of his horse's backbone. At first, I thought he was avoiding the spiders, but he was removing himself as a target for the Assassins' rifles. He looked like a frog caught mid-leap and plastered onto the side of a horse.

Colonel Nobody and O'Malley did the same, although it looked more natural for them. It must have been one of the tricks they did as the 42nd.

That left Pacarina and me being the only people riding like normal human beings. I would like to say I didn't frog-splat because it's impossible to do with two people on a horse, but if those two people were Chester and Pacarina, it wouldn't surprise me if they figured out a way.

So we rode through clouds of raining spiders towards Assassins.

The Assassins moved away from the house towards the far trees. They dropped to their knees and fired at Chester and the others, who were closing the distance. If there was something to hit I believe they would have hit it, but a man hanging from a galloping horse is a hard target even for an Assassin.

Chester's horse jerked upward, in what was almost a jump, but wasn't quite premeditated enough to call a jump, and then stumbled to its knees and skidded on its side across the web-slicked ground.

I thought Chester was crushed beneath the horse, but he was already on his feet running towards the Assassins. I think he landed running.

The Assassins slung their rifles behind their backs. Chester twirled two swords above his head. I think they were more for the spiders than the Assassins, but he looked like what a child might create if asked to draw a mentally unbalanced English assassin with too many weapons.

One of the Assassins drew his sword. Sword-battle was about to ensue. Then they faltered—I think one of them gave the others an order—and they retreated towards the far woods.

Colonel Nobody and O'Malley passed Chester and kept riding at the Assassins. The Assassins reloaded as they ran. They turned again, forming a tight knot with rifles pointing out, and waited. With Chester on foot, it would just be two riders against seven Assassins, and this time the Assassins were waiting to shoot until the riders were upon them. Our men wouldn't survive that volley.

Colonel Nobody must have seen it the same way, because he turned his horse to the left and dashed back towards the house, waving for the rest of us to do the same. I did my best to point our horse's head in that direction. We almost foundered into a fresh-dug pit, but the horse jumped to the right side at the last moment and we survived. We rode to the house and slipped off the horse.

Petr and Maria were running across the open space.

I threw my back against the house wall and raised my rifle, ready to shoot at the Assassins if they attacked Petr and Maria, but they didn't. Instead, they retreated back into the forest.

Colonel Nobody wiped sweat and spider-web from his forehead. "There's one missing. Careful."

That's right, there were eight Assassins alive, but we only saw seven. If they left their own Trojan Horse inside, he could kill one or more of us before we got him. Were they the type to sacrifice a man in that fashion? I motioned for Pacarina to stay outside until we cleared the house, then realized the Assassins we did know about could move towards us at any moment. I motioned her to stay behind me and ran for the door.

Colonel Nobody was the first to enter, followed by Chester. I slipped through the doorway behind them and swiveled my rifle in a sweep of the room. There were no Assassins.

Colonel Nobody jumped the stone ledge between the main room and the kitchen. Nothing.

Chester looked at the ceiling. "Praise God for roofs."

Bits of spider-web dotted his shoulders and the back of his coat, but I let him enjoy his respite without mentioning them or the black arachnids scurrying upon them.

Chester still looked at the ceiling. "All right you foozler, if you're up there you'd better make your peace with the souls you've sent to heaven, because I'm coming up."

Up he went.

I held my breath. There were no shots. No clash of steel. Things bumped on the floor, but it sounded like furniture Chester was kicking. He came downstairs scowling.

"None of the rascals up there."

Colonel Nobody was at the window. "They're splitting up. Circling us."

Petr and Maria came panting through the door. Rather, Maria was panting. Petr should be panting, or maybe groaning, but he didn't make a sound.

"Sir," O'Malley said, "permission tae get the Frinchman?"

"Permission granted," Colonel Nobody said.

O'Malley stepped to the sofa.

"Ye hear that, Jack Frog? I'm opening yer hidey-hole." He raised his boot and kick-shoved the sofa off the hatch-door. "Ye hear that? Ye down there?"

No answer.

"Jack Frog?"

Nothing.

O'Malley pointed his rifle at the hatch. "Jack Frog, for once in yer life someone wants tae hear ye say a word. Helloo? I'm opening this here hatch, and if ye dare shoot me I'll break both yer legs and then make ye run the Ascot twice."

Silence.

Worry-lines creased O'Malley's face. Was this where the last Assassin was hiding? Was Jacques the first casualty on our side of this war? Was O'Malley about to follow him?

O'Malley knelt to grip the hatch handle, waited one agonizing second, and threw it back. He jumped to his feet and pointed his rifle into the darkness.

"It is you," said a French voice. Jacques' head rose above the floor.

"It is me?" O'Malley repeated with rage. "It is me? Who did ye think was yelling yer name, ye wool-headed Frog?"

Jacques blinked in the light. "It could have been a trap."

"What, ye think one of them Assassins was curling his tongue round the English language exactly like meself?"

Jacques sniffed. "Of course I knew it vas you. I refuse to believe zhere is anohzer person upon zhe face of zhis earhz cursed, or vihz zhe desire to replicate, such a voice."

O'Malley's face-skin matched the red of his hair. "Ye knew it was me and ye lay down there in yer safe little hidey-hole munching cheese and wine and not deigning tae speak tae yer old companions, eh? Is that it?"

"It could have been a trap." Jacques lifted himself out of the hole—O'Malley certainly wasn't giving him a hand—and patted dust from his shoulders. "Zhe Russians could have caught you and made you talk to see if anyone was hiding here."

O'Malley thudded his rifle-butt on the floor. "Ye think as I would betray ye in a million years, Jack Frog? Ye think the torture has been invented as could make me betray me comrade?"

Jacques smoothed his mustache. "You know very vell it has. Petr has told us about zhings the Assassins vould do to you zhat made you tremble at zhe very telling of zhem."

"Do ye see me trembling right now, Frog?"

"Not vihz me here to protect you."

Colonel Nobody raised his hand. "Remember, O'Malley, the men we need to kill are outside."

O'Malley saluted, but kept glaring at Jacques. "Well, did ye do anything useful from yer little palace beneath the floor? What are the rascal's plans?"

Jacques shrugged. "You know very vell zhat I do not sully my tongue vihz zhat barbaric tongue. I suffer enough beneahz zhe stench of zhe English so-called language. Petr, my friend, I except you from zhe universal condemnation of your language, of course."

Petr grunted.

"I can tell you one zhing, however. Zhey did a great deal of moving of zhings."

"Setting traps?" Colonel Nobody asked.

"I do not zhink so." Jacques looked around the room. "Ah, yes." He pointed at the kitchen. "No food."

O'Malley growled. "Leave it tae a Frinchman tae talk about food at a time like this."

Jacques sniffed. "Zhey have removed all of zhe food from zhis house. You see?" He stepped into the kitchen and waved at the emptiness. "Not a scrap of sustenance."

Colonel Nobody turned from the window. "They wanted us in here."

I raised my eyebrows in a question.

"This was their plan," Colonel Nobody said. "They've surrounded us. There's a fellow in a pit they dug out there, just within range. There are another three on the other side. They've trapped us all together and they mean to pick us off if we leave for food, or perhaps blow us to bits with more of their grenades. They want us in here."

Chapter 46
Lawrence

"How long can a man survive without eating?" Chester asked.

"Well," I said, "it really depends upon whether you are talking about just starvation, or dehydration as well. Current theories suggest people can survive starvation for weeks or potentially months, but lack of water is probably only withstandable for up to a week."

Chester shook his head. "Of course you would know that, Law."

I must confess that the thought of food and water made me hungry and thirsty. I had trouble remembering my last meal, and my stomach growled at me in protest. Pacarina patted my shoulder. Wonderful, so everybody could hear my stomach.

"I want to see these grenades you're talking about," Chester said. "Do you think they still have any?" He sounded eager.

"Some, probably." Colonel Nobody said. "I doubt they have a large quantity left. Grenades are not safe things to carry around, and they don't have the ability to put them together on the battlefield."

"But you do think they have some left?" Chester asked.

"Probably."

"Chester," I said, "stop grinning. That's a bad thing."

"Oh, I don't want them to blow us up. But if one of the fellows happens to run at us with one in his hand and we bowl him over before he reaches us, and the thing happens to go off out in the field—that would be worth seeing."

Chester reacts to new weapons like I react to new books. Or rather, the way I react to old books, as old is best.

The creases on Colonel Nobody's face were deep. He posted himself by the window beside the door.

"We can keep them out of throwing range in daylight," Colonel Nobody said. "Night will be different."

Chester paced the main room, his hands on the pistols in his bandolier. "This wasn't what I had in mind when I said to take the fight to them. And these spiders—" he paused halfway across the room. He slapped his neck. Spider guts dotted his skin when he withdrew his hand.

Chester gave a muffled shriek and ripped the coat off his back. He struggled through the web of bandoliers and straps and weapons and fabric—and real web—and shuddered the coat and accessories onto the floor.

He stalked away from the pile. "Spiders," he muttered. "Unnatural."

We dispersed, the men to posts from which they could watch our watchers, and the women to hunt for any food remnants the Assassins missed. I stayed in the main room with Colonel Nobody.

"Noble," I said, "I don't fully understand their tactics. I see the wisdom in trapping us in one place, but they probably could have done some damage to us out in the open when they had the chance. They seemed to care more about getting us in here than knocking off one or two while we were outside stone walls."

"They're not soldiers," Colonel Nobody said. "Soldiers seek confrontation. They fight face to face. Assassins work alone, in the dark, with a man's back for a target. I'm not saying they're not devilishly good fighters, but given the choice, they change the fight to their terms."

"And we're back on their terms?"

He smiled. "I think you're forgetting our new friends."

Shots cracked outside.

I ducked, expecting bullets to fly through the windows, but there was no clink of lead pounding into stone, or even worse, the wet punch of lead ripping through flesh.

I raised my head above the windowsill.

The three Assassins on our side weren't looking at us. They were facing the trees. And above the trees, distinct from the patches of falling spiders, were curls of smoke. Someone was shooting. Shooting at the Assassins.

Men streamed from the trees and charged the Assassins.

Chester called out from the second story on the other side of the house. "My rascals are running back to mother," he yelled.

I squinted. One of the first men out of the trees wore a full-length cloak.

The outlaws kept coming from the forest until there were between one and two dozen running at the Assassins.

The Assassins ran towards us.

A body fell from the sky through a clump of spiders, landed on the web-covered ground, and rolled to its feet. It was Chester, in his shirtsleeves, with a sword in each hand and those gauntlet things on his wrists. He must have climbed from the hole on his side of the house onto the roof, ran across, and jumped from above us.

"A Stoning!" Chester roared.

Colonel Nobody spun from the door. "Squad One!"

Petr and Jacques snapped to attention. O'Malley rattled down the stairs and joined them. My fingers tingled. Colonel Nobody's battle speeches are legend.

"Let's go," Colonel Nobody said.

That wasn't quite the speech I expected, but given the circumstances, it was practical. They went.

I kissed Pacarina and ran after the others. The wind sliced me as I stepped through the door, though I don't think I can just blame the wind for the shivers shaking my body. I wrenched my sword from my scabbard and pounded over the silk-white ground.

The three Assassins between us and the outlaws ran at a forty-five-degree angle towards the other four Assassins who were watching the other sides of the house. This battle would be on our terms—face-to-face.

The Assassins emptied their weapons on the outlaws, and the bodies lying in the webs showed it was not in vain. The outlaws howled like banshees with a toothache.

We were going to reach the Assassins before they joined forces.

"Leapfrog!" Colonel Nobody yelled.

Chester stopped running while Nobody ran past him. The closest Assassin stiffened into a fighting stance to receive the onslaught. Colonel Nobody dropped to fists and knees in front of him. Chester, running again, half-walked and half-jumped onto his back. In a single fluid motion Nobody pushed off the ground and Chester jumped.

I've never seen anything like it. Chester flew up, above the Assassin's head, lying horizontal, his arms pointing down towards the Assassin, and squeezed his gauntlets. The Assassin crumpled into a heap and Chester landed and rolled to his feet.

"Well done!" Someone shouted from the group of outlaws. The Scot burst through the front rank and grinned at me. Bogdan ran next to him, not grinning.

We converged upon the Assassins and entered the horror that is battle.

The battle-lines mingled in seconds as groups of outlaws and Squad One singled out Assassins.

I found myself facing a familiar man. Gray tinged his beard and the hair on his temples. His eyes were as cold as the day we locked eyes in front of the altar in St. James' Church. Vlad. His eyes flickered to something he saw over my left shoulder. Pain and anger flashed into those cold eyes.

Petr stepped to my side.

The Assassin opened his mouth. "You would kill me for these people, son?"

"I am sorry, Father," Petr said.

The Assassin's eyes flicked back to ice. He slashed at Petr. Petr parried the stroke and returned it. The bandage around his abdomen, which covered the wound that should be healing, was black with his blood.

Vlad jumped backwards and cut down an outlaw who was flanking him. Petr followed and stumbled. He was in no condition to be in a fight. More importantly, I could not let him kill his father. His father had to die, but to kill one's own father is a cross no man should be forced to bear.

There was no time to call for help. Everyone needed help, as, outnumbered though the Assassins were, they were still the most dangerous men I have ever seen fight.

I ran to Petr's side and swung at the Assassin. I felt like a five-year-old poking his father.

The Assassin retreated, foot by foot, not because we were overpowering him, but to separate us from the melee. He thought he was stronger than the two of us combined, and with Petr's weakened state, I feared he was right.

I tried to remember the many lessons Chester has given me. Lunge, parry, riposte, feint—the names blended and mashed in my mind. Use your body, use your opponent's body, use the ground around you—I leaped away from the Assassin's blade at my chest.

The ground around you. Web whitened the ground, but we were crossing traces of our ride from the woods to the house that had not been covered. That meant we were near the pit. There it was—covered by web.

Now I understand why men yell battle-cries. It tricks the mind into thinking the insanity of running at a person trying to kill you is slightly less insane. That's why I screamed a wordless gurgle—and ran at the Assassin.

I swung left as I ran, gripping my sword-hilt with both hands. The clash of my steel against his jarred my wrists but the force was enough to deflect his sword to my left, his right, and let me within the circle of his sword-guard. I jammed my right shoulder into his chest.

On any other ground, the Assassin would have stepped back and killed me. On this ground, Vlad did step back, but his boot poked through the web and the force of my rush pushed him backwards into the pit. I landed upon him. For a moment we both lay there, crumpled against the side of the pit.

My tingling fingers laid across something hard. I curled them into a fist, wrenched a knife from Vlad's belt, and struck without seeing where I hit. I kept striking until the movement stopped.

Chapter 47
Lawrence

Petr looked down upon me in the pit.

I let go of the knife and tried not to look at the body.

"I'm sorry, Petr."

Petr bowed his head. "You did what had to be done."

I backed away from the body. Blood slicked my shaking hands. I shuddered and wiped them on the Assassin's coat.

Petr reached down to help me out of the pit, but I waved him away. He looked like he needed a hand himself just to stay on his feet.

"Take care of yourself," I said.

The battle was over when I came up, and there were many more bodies than Assassins.

Colonel Nobody stood by himself, arms folded, surveying the bat-tle-field. O'Malley stood three feet away, staring down at Jacques. My heart lurched. Jacques was on the ground—but he was sitting up and holding his already-wounded leg. O'Malley was pointing his finger at him the way he does when he delivers lectures, and that meant Jacques couldn't be hurt too badly.

Where was Chester?

I tore into the crowd, pushing outlaws out of the way. I could not lose my brother. I could not.

"Look who I found!" someone called.

I spun. Chester stepped out of a knot of outlaws with his left arm draped around the Scot's neck.

"Someone decided to come back and bring a little help," Chester said.

The Scot grinned at me and wiggled the blade of grass between his teeth.

I stepped close enough to not be overheard by any of the other outlaws.

"I thought this wasn't your fight," I whispered.

The Scot nodded at the men around us. "I ran into the boys. They were hunting your Assassins when I found them." The smile faded from the Scot's lips. "If you had seen what the Assassins did to the men they caught to make them tell about this place—well, the boys saw it. I told them the Assassins were here, and we high-tailed it for the passage up the cliff."

"So you came back to avenge your friends?"

"I came back because—" he bit through the grass-blade and the outside half floated to earth. "I came back because I couldn't live with myself if I ran away from the only chance I've had in my life to do something really decent." He laughed. "Don't misunderstand me, I'm not going back to be a slave in the colony. But you're getting the royal outlaw escort back to civilization."

I wiped my forehead. The thought that we could head back to Sydney, and then back to England, and life, washed over me like soothing bath-water. We were free. The excitement and terror of the fight seeped from me, and I almost staggered with exhaustion. Chester threw his free arm around my shoulders and held me up.

"Your hand is bleeding," I said.

Chester grimaced. "I need to make a few more tweaks to the Death Gauntlets or they're going to be the permanent death of my knuckles."

"I see only seven," said a deep voice.

I spun. "Bogdan. You swore on your dead father you wouldn't come back."

Bogdan looked at me with something close to a smile. "I never much liked my dead father." The smile disappeared. "But I only see seven Assassins.

Where is the eighth? You," Bogdan said to Chester. "Did you kill any on the other side of the river?"

Chester shook his head. "They all landed on this side."

"You saw eight on this side?"

"Well no, I can't say I ever saw eight on this side, but their boats landed here."

"I don't believe it." Bogdan scanned the other riverbank. "There!"

I tried to follow his pointing arm to see what he found, but before I could locate it, Bogdan leaped towards Colonel Nobody.

A rifle cracked.

Bogdan and Colonel Nobody crashed to the ground.

A man rose across from us on the other riverbank. He dropped a smoking rifle and lifted a second. I looked for anyone with a loaded rifle, but no one was aiming at the Assassin. All the weapons had been fired in the fight.

Chester jerked his arm from around the Scot's neck and grabbed something from his belt. The Assassin leveled his rifle. Chester flung back his hand and whipped it towards the riverbank. The boomerang arced high to the right, flying over and behind the Assassin. He didn't turn to watch it. His rifle pointed at Colonel Nobody's and Bogdan's bodies.

The boomerang returned like a hawk swooping for its prey. Even at this distance, over the sound of the rushing water, I heard the crack of wood on skull and the Assassin pitched into the river. The rifle fired into the air as he fell, and man and rifle whisked away in the river's current.

"Noble!" I yelled.

The pile of bodies moved. A hand stuck out, and Nobody pulled himself from under Bogdan's bulk.

I ran to his side.

Blood spurted from a hole in Bogdan's coat. Colonel Nobody knelt by the Russian and gripped his hand.

"I did—my duty," Bogdan gasped.

"You did."

Bogdan coughed blood. "You must—save—Mother Russia." He closed his eyes, gurgled, and passed from this earth.

Colonel Nobody placed the Russian's hands, one after the other, on the corpse's chest. He rose.

"He gave his life for mine," Colonel Nobody said. "Let us always remember him as a brave man who did what he felt was his duty."

"Amen," I said. "Is—is it over?"

"It's done," Colonel Nobody said. He looked at me. "The Assassins are dead. Let's go home."

Chapter 48
Lawrence

"I see you're wearing a sword," Chester whispered.

I tried to speak between my teeth without disturbing my smile. "Be quiet, Chester."

"So you admit you were wrong last wedding?"

I eyed the crowd. We were back at the front of St. James' Church, standing beside Nobody and Liana as the rector read their marriage vows. I could blink and pretend that all the past months, the two voyages and the bloody whirl between, never happened. And in the beauty of this moment, it almost felt true.

The rector continued reading. "Which holy estate Christ adorned and beautified with his presence . . ."

I looked across at Pacarina. She smiled.

"Therefore," the rector said, "if any man can shew any just cause, why they may not lawfully be joined together, let him now speak, or else hereafter forever hold his peace."

Chester hooked his fingers in the bandoliers across his chest. "If anybody so much as opens his mouth, I'm going to send him to eternal peace."

While I can't exactly endorse the theology behind the statement, I empathized with the sentiment.

A few minutes later, Colonel Nobody and Liana, Viscountess of Bayrshire, were man and wife.

We decanted through the swarm of children Chester hired to throw rice at the happy pair and landed in the house hired for the wedding breakfast, where Jacques directed a small army of cooks. Just as with the wedding, the guest list had more to do with Liana having been a ward of the Crown than with the friends Noble and Liana would actually have invited.

"Congratulations," I said, pressing Nobody's shoulder. He grinned at me and I can say that I have never seen him so happy. He didn't even seem to mind the Society matrons and misses and dandies milling throughout the room. Pure joy, if I've ever seen it.

O'Malley stood by the wall, his shock of red hair floating over the crowd like a pennant on a castle-wall. Chester signaled me and threaded the crowd to him. I followed, not entirely sure what we were doing. Story of my life, I suppose.

"What do you think, you Irish giant?" Chester slapped O'Malley on the shoulder. "Did you ever think you'd marry your colonel off?"

O'Malley grinned. "There was a day I'd have wagered a pretty pound the colonel would niver tie the knot. But the minute I met the Lady Liana, I knew the stars had shifted."

Chester sobered. "I'm sorry that—well, you know—I'm sure you dreamed of having this kind of a day for yourself."

"What's that?"

"Jacques told me about Adelaide. His sister."

O'Malley blinked. "The Frog talks too much."

"Couldn't agree with you more. But . . . since we're Squad One and all, I just thought I would say . . . if you ever feel the need to talk bachelor to bachelor, I'm here for you."

O'Malley opened his mouth, stopped, and wet his lips. He cleared his throat. "That's very kind of you, Stoning Number Two. Chester." He coughed.

"Don't mention it. And don't worry, I won't pretend like I have the history you and Jacques have. I know he was there for you when the Irish-haters were giving you a hard time."

O'Malley frowned. "What do ye mean?"

"He said he helped you survive when you joined the English army."

"*He* helped *me* survive?" A vein popped out of O'Malley's forehead. "He was a Frog. Do ye know how long as the English have been fighting the Frinch? Do ye know how many times I saved that midget rascal's hide from the other boys? He said he saved me—"

O'Malley stormed off towards the kitchen.

I put my arm around Chester's shoulder. "I'm proud of you, brother."

"Eh?" Chester cocked an eyebrow.

"Offering to be there for him. That may have been a bit—awkward, shall we say, but it was very thoughtful. I may need to report back to Father that you're finally growing up."

Chester grinned. If it weren't Chester, I would almost say there was a hint of bashfulness in that smile. He winked.

"You'll get there too, one of these days."

Maria wandered by, looking a little lost. Chester waved her over.

"You all right?" he asked.

"Yes, I'm very happy for Colonel Nobody and Liana. I suppose I'm just a little—" she looked at the corner where the Society girls gathered to gossip. "If you had told me before Australia that I could miss months of the latest news and not care, I would not have believed you. But it seems all—very silly, I suppose, compared to what we've gone through."

Chester winked at me. "Sounds like we're not the only ones growing up."

Maria blushed.

"Well . . ." said a nasally voice behind me.

My body stiffened. Lord Banastre Bronner is one of my least favorite people on the planet.

"Please accept my profoundest congratulations upon returning to civilization." Bronner bent over Maria's hand, ignoring Chester and me but speaking loudly so we could not fail to hear. "It must have been a horrid experience. Practically kidnapped, I hear."

Maria looked up at the fellow. "On the contrary, Lord Bronner, it was a wonderful experience. London can be so stifling to the exercise of the mental and physical capacities that really matter in life, don't you think? There are just so many fops whose sense of adventure does not extend beyond sampling the latest gambling den. It was delightful to see an example of what courage in the real world looks like."

Bronner stepped back and stiffened straighter than the stem of one of Pacarina's paint-brushes. He mumbled something vaguely affirmative, gave the slightest of bows, and retreated without acknowledging Chester or me.

Chester looked ready to hug Maria. "That was absolutely gorgeous."

She grinned.

"That's it," Chester said, "I am officially striking you from my blacklist of Society girls. I will find you a decent chap for a husband if I have to fight every dandy in the Peerage just to find one with more backbone than a chicken's. And speaking of chicken bones, I'd better go chaperone those two international roosters before they start pecking each other and spoil our breakfast. Adios, as the French say." He wandered away towards the back kitchen, from which raised French and Irish voices were already floating.

I found myself beside Pacarina, staring through the front windows at London town.

Pacarina leaned her head on my shoulder. "Do you know what I'm thinking about, Law?"

"Do tell."

"The best decision of my life."

"And what was that?"

She looked up at me. "To marry you."

I kissed her. "Do you know the best decision of my life?"

"When you decided to put ladders on the bookshelves in the library?"

I pinched her cheek. "When I decided to spend the rest of my life with the most amazing woman in the world."

"I think Colonel Nobody would disagree with you about who that is."

"And for once in his life, he would be wrong."

Pacarina wrapped her arms around me. "Thank you for being you, Law."

I rested my cheek on her forehead. "Thank you for making this crazy adventure of a life we live worth living."

The End